Born Free

Born Free is Laura Hird's first novel. A previous collection of short stories, *Nail and other stories*, was also published by Rebel Inc. Two other novellas appeared in the anthologies *Children of Albion Rovers* and *Rovers Return*. Her short stories have appeared in publications such as *The Face*, *Blvd.* (Netherlands), *Barcelona Review* (Spain), *Bang* (Sweden), *Grand Street* (USA), and *Story* (USA). She lives in west Edinburgh.

Praise for *Born Free*

'It's the portrait of a dysfunctional family, sharply observed and told with a mixture of humour and honesty . . . Hird's ear for dialogue is excellent.' *Independent on Sunday*

'The end result is a multi-layered, darkly funny, quietly despairing snapshot of a family falling apart at the seams.' *Uncut*

'Laura Hird's debut approaches adolescence with shocking frankness; yet from its unabashed honesty and sympathy for its vigorously dysfunctional central family, it gathers a positive energy that leaves the shock tactics of many of Hird's contemporaries standing.' *The List*

'There's an adrenaline kick in the words that carries you through the grubbiness and seediness of the subject matter . . . *Born Free* is not a pleasant read, but it is very readable.' *Sunday Herald*

'. . . what differentiates Hird's writing from the pack is the strength of her fictional characters . . . Hird manages to be just as convincing as Joni — a fifteen-year-old itching to lose her virginity — as her nerdy younger brother Jake . . . *Born Free* is shot through with misery-defying humour . . . Her observational skills are shrewd and unflinchingly accurate.' *The Face*

'superb . . . a warm current of humour runs through this saga . . . *Born Free* is peppered with pop culture references which give it a deliciously fresh, contemporary flavour . . . Hird's observational humour is laser-guided.' *Esquire*

'*Born Free* exhibits a maturity that suggests Hird has emerged from the coat-tails of her peers and has ceased to play the literary wee sister . . . Hird's portrayal of a woman in alcoholic free-fall is uncomfortably accurate . . . shifts with ease from the screamingly funny to the gut-wrenching . . . thought provoking and entertaining.' *The Scotsman*

'The dialogue is sharp . . . A tremendous energy carries the reader on, and despite the grimness of the subject matter it is leavened with a kind of black humour that some people simply won't get, and sharp little moments of poignancy . . . Laura Hird thinks for herself and toes no lines.' *The Guardian*

'*Born Free* is warm, funny and empathetic.' *Scene*

Born Free

Laura Hird

REBEL
inc.

First published in Great Britain in 1999 by
Rebel Inc, an imprint of
Canongate Books Ltd, 14 High Street,
Edinburgh EH1 1TE

This edition published in 2000

10 9 8 7 6 5 4 3 2 1

The publishers gratefully acknowledge subsidy from the Scottish
Arts Council towards the publication of this volume

Rebel Inc series editor: Kevin Williamson
www.rebelinc.net

British Library Cataloguing-in-Publication Data
A catalogue record for this book is available on
request from the British Library

ISBN 1 84195 048 3

Typeset by Palimpsest Book Production Limited,
Polmont, Stirlingshire
Printed and bound by Omnia Books Limited, Glasgow

ACKNOWLEDGMENTS

Thanks to SAC for giving me funding to complete this book. KW, JB, MS, JM and everyone at CB, ID and PS at BL and JB at UEA for their encouragement. JH, EL, A&GD, AW, DW, KW, AB, RS, PR and PL for putting up with my shit. RH, JH, J&MG, AH, DP, R&H, AC, AD, CB, PH (all RIP) and JO, AG, JC, ML, AB, HD, GO, WA, IW, BG, JM, BB, DM, DN, CA, ABBA, CRASS and SA for inspiring me. MF for bringing RI to my attention in the first place. GA and JK for research. Everyone at the TA for being so gentle with JP and any other FB that might have slipped my mind.

To
Everyone who buys this
and
everyone who bought the last one
Cheers!

When love becomes a command,
hatred can become a pleasure.

Written by Charles Bukowski from
Notes of a Dirty Old Man

. . . I used to do the I-Ching, but then I had to feed the meter.
Now I can't see into the future, but at least I can use
the heater.

Lyrics by Jarvis Cocker from
'Glory Days' (*This is Hardcore*)

Chapter One

JONI

'CHRIST, WHAT'S SHE doing there? Why's she no at work?'

Crouching on my seat, I keek out the window as a mysterious silver Astra disappears up Lothian Road with my mother.

'Looked like a guy she was with. D'you think he's her lurver?' purrs Rosie.

'Fuck off! Blind men cannae drive.'

Joy-riding – maybe. Affair – no danger. Why am I wasting my time thinking about that old cow anyway? A wee lassie in a tartan dress falls flat on her face as a fat wifie in leggings yanks her across Princes Street. Rosie sees it too. We laugh so much I end up peeing myself a wee bit. By the time I've got it under control, and feel safe to stand up, it's time to get off. Relieving myself in Pizzaland's bogs, we go to work.

My target today is British Home Stores. They sell really shitey, old-fashioned clothes, but I get a buzz dodging the security cameras. Besides, it's not bad for plain tops and t-shirts. As Rosie can't bear the thought of anyone seeing her somewhere so crap, we arrange to meet outside Bookworld in ten minutes.

Pouting at the greasy-faced slob of a security guard, I make a beeline for the back of the shop and grab two lime-green long-sleeved v-necks. Sticking one inside the other, I deposit the extra hanger on the nearest rail. Then I spot these fab leather waistcoats but the bastards've chained them together like black slaves. Too bulky anyway, I suppose. Making do with three skimpy Lycra tops, I stick them under the v-necks then hit the changing rooms. Only declaring one item, I pull the security tags off the hidden ones, layer them under my jumper and hand back the one on the hanger. The chip-pan-pussed guard flashes me a gappy smile as I saunter back out to meet Rosie. The deep pockets of her jacket are stuffed with horoscope books she's going to sell for 50 pence each at school. Rosie's more organised than me, see. She steals to order.

As we cross over to the benches, I lift up my jumper and show off my booty, layer by layer.

'You're no seriously gonna wear stuff from there, are you? Go to Gap or Next. You never get anything decent.'

'Communal changing rooms,' I remind her. 'Anyway, the stuff's easier to get over there. Nobody wants it anyway.'

Bored by my reasoning, she goes to stand at the bus stop.

'D'you want to just come back to mines? Mum's working. There's loadsa Kit-Kats.'

I'm sold on the idea by that fact alone, then she adds,

'. . . John left a video the other night. It's absolutely gross.'

You beauty! I practically leap onto the next bus. John, Rosie's uncle, is a major spunk bucket. They're always watching porn together. He's quite old, maybe thirtyish, but flirts like mad with me, y'know, says really filthy stuff, then looks all innocent. I never get to go round when they're watching videos, but I'd really love to. Not with Rosie, though, just me and him. Even thinking about it gives me hot bum flushes.

When we get along to Shandwick Place it's complete chaos. Loads of sirens, ambulance and police lights flashing all over the place. Everyone on the bus is straining to see what's going on. Rosie and me run down the front for a better look. There's so many people crowding round whatever's happened, though, I can't make anything out. Rosie's doing contortions against the window.

'She's dead. She's fuckin dead,' she squeals, vacating her prime viewing spot for me and some other nosy folk who are now queuing up for a look. There's a woman lying face-down on the road. The ambulance men seem too scared to touch her. As our bus slowly moves past the scene, I see a car about 15 feet up the road with the windscreen smashed out.

'How'd she get that far? She's gone miles,' I shout, as the nebby passengers rush up the back for a final look. Sick bastards.

'She was definitely dead, eh? See her brains on the road?'

She's winding me up.

'You're joking. I saw a wee bit blood. Where were her brains?'

'How could you miss them? They were all sticking out the back of her head.'

I think about a head caved open and brains hanging out. I think about this sort of thing a lot, especially when I'm talking to Mum. I used to want to go to medical school so I could see them do a post-mortem. They make you go to one in your first year, everyone faints supposedly. Mum really wants me to go into further education though, so I'm going to get a job in Burger King instead, to spite her.

When we get to the next stop, there's a lot of yelling downstairs, then Twiggy, Daniel and Kes from Art appear and launch themselves beside us.

'Did you see the deid wifie? We got off the bus to get a better look. Her brains were everywhere.'

'I seen them, I seen them,' screams Rosie.

I can't believe there really were brains and I missed them. Daniel starts going on about a time he saw a man who'd jumped out a third-floor window in Raeburn Place. 'When the polis picked him up, his body just crumpled, like he was a big towel or summat. The blood was aw running in the gutter.'

This isn't fair. I never get to see things like that. I saw my granny dead when I was a wee baby but I can't remember anything about it. She just had a heart attack though, so she probably didn't look much different.

There's this strange, sweet smell and I realise one of them has lit a joint. I see Kes take a few tokes then hand it to Daniel. Fuck, everyone must be able to smell it.

'We're going along the graveyard if you fancy,' Daniel smiles, handing it to me. I quite like him. I don't usually go for guys that young, but he's got big Liam eyebrows and thick dark hair and he looks like he'd have really dark, hairy pubes as well, know, like Robbie Williams.

We all get off at the garage and walk down to the cemetery. As we follow them up to the crypt that gets used as a speakeasy by the drinkers at our school, Rosie and me get the giggles. There's two older guys already there, smoking dope with tins of Irn Bru and plastic sandwich boxes in front of them. They look like painter-decorators. When they see us, the one with the spliff holds it behind him. Kes is spitting as we walk past.

'That's not on. That's our place. Cunts like that can go to a pub, y'know?'

The two guys snigger as we trudge up to the far corner and sit on the grass. It's slightly damp but my bum's sweating so much it doesn't really make much difference. Several joints and a bottle of White Lightning are passed round. Rosie starts pulling horoscope books out of her pockets, chucking them at us according to our star signs. Daniel's an Aries, same as me. Supposedly we're very compatible, as long as I can satisfy his voracious appetite for physical love and not get too jealous.

Something tickles my hand and makes me jump. Holding it up, I watch an ant tramping in between my fingers. We all start gawping at it, open-mouthed, without saying anything. I'm starting to feel really dry, like I've been eating flour, so I ask Daniel for the bottle. Rosie looks shocked, probably because you never usually get a peep out of me in a group. Aw, but the cider's really wonderful. It makes my chest tingle as well, makes me feel all warm and woozy. Lovely.

I watch lovely Daniel rolling another joint. Kes is talking about his dad's new car, really loudly to Twiggy. Twiggy is really into cars, and men who have cars. I'm not sure if she uses the men to get to the cars, or just goes on about cars to impress men. They call her Twiggy cause all her hair fell out when her mum was having chemotherapy. It was like it came out in sympathy. Still, it's no excuse for being boring.

I'm not even listening. Rosie looks like she's about to fall asleep. Staring at Daniel, I fantasise about him taking me behind that tree and doing it to me. He has long fingers and a long nose, sort of foreign-looking, and you know what they say about that. When he's not talking, he bites his lip, or pokes his tongue in the corner of his mouth, sort of like he'd maybe like to be biting and poking somewhere else. I have to remind myself that he's only a year or two older than me. Guys are really immature till they get into their twenties. When I finally get a boyfriend, I want him to be much older than me. Someone that really knows what he's doing and has grown out of slagging girls.

He hands me a joint, to spark up. Did he notice me staring? I'm getting a beamer.

'You did that optical illusion screenprint at Art, eh? The black and white one?'

God, he's noticed something of mine, amazing.

'Ocht, it was rubbish,' I blush, taking a sook of the joint, then handing it back right away as I'm feeling a bit dizzy.

'No, honestly. You should go to college. It was like something out a book, that.'

'Ta.'

It *was* out a book but I'm not telling him that. Some old hippie album cover book Dad has. Nobody else'll have ever seen it.

Rosie's sitting watching us both with a funny smile on her face. Does she know something I don't? Daniel grins at Kes to pass me the cider. What's going on here? Everyone seems to be smiling now, in on something. Then suddenly they're all talking amongst themselves. Rosie leans over to me.

'What's the story with monkey boy? I think he fancies you. Sorry, he definitely fancies you. You like him?'

I can hardly speak for grinning so much. I'm sweating like fuck under the four tops. Not just my bum now, all of me.

'Really, you really think so? He's really nice,' I whisper, leaning close, so he won't hear.

Kes takes a long slug of the cider, then does an enormous belch.

'Someone go an see if they two cunts have fucked off yet, eh?'

Leaping to his feet, Daniel grabs the cider and offers me his hand.

'Want to chum me? You can be my messenger.'

I can't believe my luck. Rosie's giggling, gesturing me to go with him. They all start roaring and whistling as I stumble to my feet.

As soon as we're out of view though, I tense up and can't think of a single thing to say. I dredge my brain for one tiny sentence that might break the silence but there's just a jumble of words up there and a vision of him grabbing me and necking me.

He seems kind of nervous as well. He's sort of hunched up with his hands in his pockets, walking very quickly. We arrive back at the now-deserted crypt without having said a word to each other. He gives me the thumbs-up.

'Right then, go get them. I'll see you in a mo.'

I hesitate for a moment, hoping he's joking and that grabbing and necking are still a possibility. But he turns away from me, unzips and begins peeing against a gravestone. I start running back towards the others, as the sight of him peeing just makes it worse. Even if I pass a complete stranger having a pee in the street it really turns me on. What a pig. He was definitely making out like he fancied me in front of them all. They'll all ask about it when I get back. What a bastard. I fucking hate young guys.

Chapter Two
VIC

I'VE BEEN SITTING in traffic since seven this morning. There's a nagging pain in my right shoulder, well, it started off just my shoulder but is now working its way down my arm. Is it your right arm hurts if you're going to have a heart attack? Jesus, I just want home.

Old Sandy's nattering away to me as he drives. I don't talk while I'm driving myself and it makes me twitchy when other drivers do it. How old is he anyway? Surely way past retirement age. Didn't he start off on the trams?

'Seen these new mirrors? I cracked mine, first day,' he brags as the bus runs a red light onto Morrison Street, right past the cop shop. Old Sandy likes to live on the edge. I almost get off when he stops at the end of Dalry, I just get this bad feeling, but I brave it out and he keeps on talking.

'. . . thing is, I radio in to tell them and they say it's the sixth one smashed that day. They don't move, see,' he continues, one hand on the wheel, the other trying to move a mirror he's just told me doesn't move. By the time we get to my stop at White Park, chills of sweat are running down the back of my neck.

I pop into the grocer's for fags, the *Evening News*, my son's PC mag and a packet of Toffos.

'And where is your beautiful daughter today?' Asif inquires, as I hand over the money and try to get into my sweetie packet.

'D'you want her? Two hundred Silk Cut and a bottle of Tia Maria and she's yours.'

'For how long?' he grins, raising his eyebrows.

'Throw in a box of Toffos and you can keep her.'

As I walk along towards the flat, I count the 'To Let' signs on the shops as I sook on my toffee. I look into passing cars in the hope that the wife's sister will go past and see me. It's often common knowledge before I get home that I've been committing the ultimate sin of chewing a sweetie in the street. She phones and reports it to Angie, she thinks it's so uncouth. Maybe I should let her see me with a kebab. She might disown us. Mind you, we've not heard from her twisted sister since they fell out two Christmases ago. Old habits die hard.

I savour the brief 15 minutes I generally have in the flat at night before everyone comes trundling in, make a coffee, smoke three fags in quick succession, get the fire on, promise myself I'll take the dog out, take off my stiff, sandpapery working trousers and put on my Stilton-crotched cords and smelly, holey jumper. Angie keeps trying to sew it for me, or worse, wash them both. For God's sake, they smell of me, that's the whole point. I complete my domestic outfit with the gorilla-feet slippers my daughter Jo got me last Christmas. They're brilliant. I love them. I think they're a hoot.

There's a loud thud from up the hall. This doesn't alarm me as the walls in here are so flimsy; things have been falling off with great regularity since we moved in. Nonetheless, I go to investigate what's broken now. Our bedroom seems all right, apart from the usual stink of pongy tights and dampness. Next door I find my daughter lying in bed. She shields her eyes when I put the light on.

'Switch it off, switch it off for God's sake.'

What's she on about, it's daylight anyway? However, I do as I'm told, as presently any reaction other than total submission towards Joni seems to antagonise her. I think I smell drink but she'll probably attack me if I mention it.

'What's wrong? You OK? Want an aspirin or something? Is it women's things?'

She pulls the cover up over her face and shrieks, 'Pervert! You're disgusting.'

How can a lassie of 15 be so wounding? I put up with it, like I always do. Being an only child myself, this is my first experience with female puberty, close up. I'm not sure if she is actually psychotic, or if they're all like this. I get a shooting pain in my chest, which I assume is heart-ache, and need to take a Rennie's. I leave Joni to her hormones.

Going through to get the kettle on for her coming home, I stick on the radio for the 5.30 news. Madness's 'Embarrassment' is playing and I think they're singing about me. When it finishes, the DJ announces it's from 1980. Jesus, it cannae be nearly 20 years. Surely he's got it wrong. It can't be 19 years. The whole thing makes me queasy. I feel absolutely ancient and churny and have to take another Rennie's.

The front door goes and I'm joined in the kitchen by my son, Jake, who proceeds to make a cheese sandwich, seemingly oblivious to my presence. I ruffle his hair. He looks at me with pity.

'I've borrowed *Resident Evil 2* off Jason. I'll be too into it by tea-time to stop,' he says, offering the sandwich for clarification.

'What happened to *Fifa 96*? I thought it was the be-all and end-all.'

'Phh,' he splurts, cheese everywhere. 'That's crap. *Fifa 98*, that's what I want now. You can see their faces and everything.'

I have a moment's inspiration.

'How d'you and your pals fancy getting two five-a-side teams together with me?'

'With you?'

'Yeah, you know, trials for Dunfermline and all that? You do more training than Alan Shearer on that bloody computer. You should get out – fresh air, sunshine, real life, you know?'

'You're mental,' he suggests, pushing past me with his sandwich.

'How about fishing? You used to like that. Or ferreting? That's much gorier than *Resident Evil 2*, I bet.'

It's too late. He has vanished into his room with the aforementioned game.

In need of another voice, I reluctantly put on the television. I generally wait for *Channel 4 News*. The other two channels seem specifically designed for patriotic royalists with an attention span of five seconds. I watch Trevor McDonald drooling on about who has and hasn't been to see the Queen Mum in hospital (this is the headline!) and I think, how could you let down your brothers so badly, man?

Then she comes in, wearing what looks like a hula skirt of Somerfield bags. Women love carrying lots of shopping. I'm not being sexist but, you know, it seems to fulfil some basic, we're-not-the-weaker-sex, look-how-much-we-can-carry sort of need within them.

'The manager gave me a lift. I went out at lunchtime.'

'Oh.'

What am I supposed to say? Is she trying to make me jealous about another man taking her shopping? He can take her shopping every day if he likes. I hate waiting on her while she reads the ingredients of every single item in the supermarket, then goes round again collecting loyalty points. She's huffing and puffing round me now, putting things away, making it seem like she's a martyr simultaneously – quite a talent. She puts a bag of Maris Pipers on the bunker in front of me and hands me the tattie knife. I peel as she chops.

'If this manager guy fancies taking you shopping every day, like, I could start going to the football again. I'd do that for you, dearest.'

'If you want to spend £18 watching men with sad haircuts chase a ball about for 90 minutes, then go ahead, Vic. It's your money too. I don't stop you going to the football.'

'But what women say and what they mean are two completely different things. You mean the opposite of what you say, so when you say, "Go ahead, go to the football," what you in fact mean is, "You are the most selfish man on God's earth." Admit it.'

'Actually, I think I'm going out after work on Friday, so if you want to have your wee bit freedom as well, I really don't mind. Stop reading things into everything I say.'

'Who with? This manager bloke?'

'He's not a bloke, he's just a young laddie. It's nothing funny. I think he sees me as a sort of mother-figure.'

'That's OK, cool.'

I honestly do mean that this is cool. I don't imagine for a second that anything might happen between them. All this means is that on my night off, Friday, I can drink a few beers on my own and get my old singles out. Or get Ronnie round, maybe get a five-a-side organised. I've yet to break in the Newcastle top I got for my birthday last August.

Once I've helped her with the tea, I go through and watch the news. My eyes go fuzzy when words come up on the screen, though. What now? What's wrong with my bloody eyes? I had a headache the other week as well. I never get headaches. The doctor's checked me over several times, you know, the full works, and says there's nothing wrong, just keep taking the happy pills. But there is. There definitely is.

She and I eat tea on our own, as Jake is too engrossed in *Resident Evil* as predicted, and Joni is incapacitated with a mysterious, possibly drink-related, illness. They will both no doubt heat theirs up in the microwave, much later on, when I'm starting to get a bit peckish again, then take great pleasure in not offering me any.

We eat off our laps, on the settee, watching *Channel 4 News*. It is, strangely enough, one of my favourite times of the day. She keeps asking me, as she always does, if I like the dinner. No matter how much I enthuse, she just keeps on asking.

'Is it OK?'

'Yes, lovely.'

'Do you like the lime with it?'

'Yes, really unusual. Nice taste, eh?'

'Is the chicken tender enough?'

'Gorgeous, melts in the mouth, mmm.'

'Do you think it needs some salt?'

'No, it's just perfect. It doesn't need salt.'

'Are the potatoes a bit lumpy.'

'No, perfect. Just right.'

You maybe think this is a bit mundane, but you know, it's good to talk, sort of . . .

Chapter Three

JAKE

I SPEND ABOUT an hour trying to run Jason's *Resident Evil 2* on my computer. I've been dying to play it since he said I could borrow it last week but the bastard thing just keeps crashing.

About half-seven, Mum comes through and hassles me to have some tea. I get ten minutes' solid grief about the effort she makes, how knackered she is, how she's not a slave and how lucky I am to have a mother like her. Does she really think that boring me stupid will improve my appetite? Why is she always trying to ram food down our throats? As usual, I have to play the homework card before she finally gets the message and fucks off.

The homework card justifies just about anything you can think of – not eating my disgusting tea, getting to watch a film that has nudie scenes in it, going round to my pal's to study when I'm supposed to be grounded, getting up in the middle of the night to watch an important Open University programme for history the next day (i.e., the Grand Prix). It beats me why kids complain about homework. It's the best weapon you have at my age.

I give *Resident Evil* another go, hoping that the wee rest it had when Mum was nagging me might have helped. Did it fuck. In desperation I open my rucksack and get out my English jotter. I did want to relax for a while before I did my poetry assignment for Miss Barnes, but if the computer crashes again I'll end up trashing it.

Miss Barnes is the relief English teacher from Liverpool. Ever since she said nice things about one of my poems, I've gone really daft for her. She looks like Louise that used to be in Eternal, you know, that hazy-faced, dreamy way you get with really good-looking folk, like there's a glow around them. The last poem we did was to be on our philosophy on life. I did a fucking stotter on putting your real, deep thoughts on the Internet so complete strangers could get to know you after you were dead, sort of like being immortal. She wrote at the bottom, 'Why not tell me about the real you, in the meantime.' Bit of a suspect thing to write on a 14-year-old laddie's homework. Perhaps she wants to initiate me in the ways of love.

I'm really shite at talking to lassies though. If they're ugly it's not so bad, just like talking to guys, but if anyone remotely tidy speaks to me, I shrivel into myself like a tortoise. That's what I don't really understand about sex. How do you ever get off with anyone if you end up going funny like that every time a lassie comes near you?

When I'm happy with the new poem – after several cuts, big words looked up in the thesaurus and a few bits borrowed from other places, I print it out in Germanic font. You can hardly make out what it says, but it looks dead cool. I look through it again and again, trying to imagine Miss Barnes's reaction when she reads it, wondering if she'll realise it's about her. I've thought about sending her an anonymous love poem, but she'd know it was from me right away. I'm way the best poet in the school.

After all the excess thought and exertion, I'm dying for a fag. Shouting through to the living-room that I'm taking Jan for a walk, I jangle her lead till she's hysterical. Jan, what a stupid name for a dog. Dad was engaged to a lassie called Jan, before he met Mum. He was only allowed to get a dog on the condition he got a bitch and called her that, because in Mum's opinion, well, you know? I don't know why he bothered. I'm not saying I'm the only one that walks her, but when any of the rest of them do, everyone starts asking why and wondering what they're up to.

Before the stair door's even had time to shut, Jan lets go this stinking, huge meringue of shite that must have been fighting to keep up her arse all day. Lighting my fag, I watch it ooze out and hope that mum or Joni stands in it, or that Mrs Anderson, the moany old Catholic wifie opposite, who phones the police when I play football on the back green, slips in it and dies. 'Good dog, good girl,' I compliment her on a jobbie well done, before pressing the old bitch's buzzer and nashing round the block. With a little luck they'll be zipping up her body bag by the time we get back.

We sprint the full length of the street, the cold air clear and nippy on my face. I'd probably be brilliant at running, you know, the 500 metres and that, but the guys in the school athletics team are all such wankers.

Squeezing into the phone box opposite MacDonald's, with Jan round my feet, I fumble for change. Jason and me have a pact at the moment. At every possible opportunity, out of school hours, we have to phone our PE teacher, Mr Russell, let it ring three times, then hang up. If you push the next call button, you can do it a few times and still get your money back. Mr Russell's a poof, see? He really ogles the guys' arses during gym and he wears these revolting tight trousers that make his balls look like a ballet dancer's. And see when you're in the changing room? He makes any excuse to come in for a neb, slimy cunt. If we reported him, though, they'd just send him to do it in some other school. So we've taken it into our own hands to drive him out, like they do on the news.

We were posting him scary notes at one point, you know, with cut-out letters. We made out like they were from guys he'd shagged in bogs, but we had to stop. The polis can get your fingerprints off stuff like that. Now our campaign is limited to phoning, doorbell ringing, graffiti about the school, that sort of thing. He must expect it. Why else would he have his number in the phone book when all the other teachers are ex-directory? I've checked.

I do my bit for the cause, but the desperate bastard answers after just two rings and I lose my money. Fucking queer. I can't afford a tin of Irn Bru now.

Jan does another three healthy shites on the way back home. An old dear passes as she's on her third and mutters something, but I just give her the finger. Old wifies are such nosy, whingeing cunts. They should put women down at 18. They just go weird after that.

Skipping along the pavement, I ring buzzers, kick a few bin bags onto the road and gob everywhere. Nobody says a word. The adults round here are shit-scared of kids so we can basically get away with anything.

Mum's on my back to eat something again as soon as I get home. She's sitting watching some crappy Bruce Willis film with a face-pack on. It's an improvement, 'cause it covers the blotches and burst veins but, to be honest, I don't know why she bothers. Bad skin's the least of her problems.

To shut her up, I put some disgusting-looking brown stuff on a plate, shove it in the microwave, taste a bit, nearly throw up and put the rest in the bin. I bang around, making plate scraping noises so it seems genuine, and ask her for a few of her magazines for a project we're doing at Art. She tries to fob me off with *Hello*s but I tell her there's not enough adverts, so she gives me two *Cosmopolitans* and a *Marie Claire*. Hey, hey, this is more like it.

'D'you want a hand? I was good at Art. What sort of ads are you looking for?'

'Nah, Mum, it's OK. I'm supposed to do it myself. I dinnae want to cheat.'

She ruffles my hair. They all ruffle my hair in this house. Ignore me for months then ruffle my hair and think that makes it all right.

'It's better to be honest, right enough.'

Oh shut up. What's she getting all George Washington about? It's even harder than usual to take her seriously with the Halloween face on. I get a glass of Ribena from the kitchen. When I go back through, she tries to kiss me goodnight. It's repulsive. Her periods make her go funny sometimes.

Locking myself in my room, I strip down to my pants, lie on the bed and flick through the sexily plastic-smelling pages. It doesn't take much looking. Just past the index of *Cosmopolitan* is a black and white photo of Kate Moss in her undies. Her simmet is so flimsy, you can see where her nipples go darker. You can even make out the dent in her pants where her fanny goes in. I wish I could see the whole thing. Liam showed us some magazines once that his dad said he'd found beside someone's bucket on his way to the early shift. He told Liam he only took them in case children found them. Aye, sure, Mr Smith. In these, the women's fannies were all opened out, like flowers made of meat. It looked pretty revolting, but they must feel brilliant or men wouldn't be so obsessed with shagging them.

Suddenly inspired, I get a black felt tip from my pencil case. I draw a slit on top of Kate's pants, then some meaty bits at the side and a hole in the middle with a few pubic hairs. For the finishing touch, I draw a willie and balls going into her mouth, the willie with a wee birthmark, just like mine. Putting down the pen, I pull my pants to my knees. I'm so excited by this time, that I do it all over Kate almost right away. It seems to go on for ages and ages. Afterwards, I stare at the thick globules on her face and vest, then crumple her into the bin.

As I thumb the rest of the magazine, looking for my next victim, I'm careful not to touch my face. I'm sure it's that stuff that's giving me the spots. It's amazing. There's loads of suitable nipply photos advertising everything from cars to fanny pads. My favourite is for a hair-removing cream in which you can actually see the woman's pubes. Not so good if you actually want to remove hair, but perfect for me. She's got these big, sooky artificial lips as well, like Julia Roberts. Fuck *Resident Evil 2*.

Chapter Four

ANGIE

IT'S MY DAY off. I've been wide awake for the past hour, but can't bring myself to get up without the incentive of seeing Raymond, my boss at the bookie's. I hear the familiar sound of Joni creating in the next room, followed by a flurry of door-slamming. Vic barges in looking distraught.

'She's phoning bloody Childline on me now. I only pulled the duvet off her 'cause she wouldn't get up.'

Sitting up in bed, I watch him pace the room, flustered, muttering to himself.

'. . . something must have happened to make her like that. Maybe she should be seeing someone.'

Sitting on the bed, he snuggles up to me. I'm in no mood to humour him.

'I keep telling you, you're too soft. See if you just belted her, she'd get such a fucking fright.'

He stands up again and squeezes his shoulder, his useless hippie sensibilities offended. Yanking the duvet out the way, I stamp across the carpet for my robe.

'. . . I'll fucking get her up. Jesus, one lie-in a week. Is it really too much to ask?'

Vic straddles the door.

'Nah, it's OK now. She's locked herself in the bathroom.'

Is he real?

'So what's the fucking problem, then?'

'My daughter accuses me of abusing her and I'm supposed to feel pleased? Jesus, I'm scared to even look at her these days,' he wails, manhandling his clean work-jacket out of our sardine-packed wardrobe.

'Just ignore it. How many times do I have to say? All lassies go a bit Exorcist at that age. You take everything so fucking personally.'

Determined to keep beating himself up about it, though, he ignores me, puts on his jacket and disappears into the hall. The toilet door goes and I hear him pleading.

'Jo, pal, tell me what's wrong. Is there anything I can do to help?'

Another slam, the front door this time. Despite already being late for work, thanks to Jo's carry-on, Vic gives her a ten-minute start before leaving, for fear of being branded a stalker. How did I ever come to marry such a big girl's blouse?

With the flat finally empty (Jake's usually away before the rest of us even wake up. God knows who he gets that off), I shower, then have a coffee with the bar of Bourneville I had hidden in the All-Bran packet.

With the brood out the way, my mind's soon back on Raymond and my unrealistic expectations about Friday night. He let me put money in when my till was under the other day. I said I'd take him out as a thank-you. I've not had a drink since we moved here three years ago, but if I take it easy, I'm sure I'll be OK. It's not like I won't be able to stop again. I just get so much grief off the family, it's easier to avoid it. I'll drink Diet Coke when it's my round so I don't get too pissed. Digging out the Marks vouchers Vic gave me for Christmas, I decide the occasion merits buying a new frock. I'm having a farewell lunch with my pal, Joyce, at one. She's moving down to Hull because of her husband's job. I'll pop in and get something on the way along.

God, I'd forgotten why I hate clothes-shopping so much.

I'm crammed into a tiny changing-room that stinks of cheap, talc-tinged, sweaty bodies and old ladies' pants. Stripping down to my underwear, I survey the awful spectacle in the full-length mirror and feel like crying. I'm like bloody Buddha – all blotchy, boily-backed and cellulite. How can I kid myself someone might fancy that?

I struggle into the first of the dresses – a blue velvet one. On the hanger I envisioned an Isabella Rossellini look but I'm more like a post-ice-cream-addiction Marlon Brando. My whole body shimmers with perspiration as I peel it back off, bursting the zip in the process. Even the mirror's starting to steam up.

I'd picked out a green velvet dress as well but, assuming it'll be as savage on my spare tyres as the last one, don't bother trying it on. I could hardly wear a velvet dress to the bookie's anyway. I'd look like something out of *Oliver*. The third one, a Berkertex, Laura Ashley print, is better. If I don't tie the belt at the back, it hangs loosely over the rolls of fat. It's a bit nippy round my beefy upper arms but it makes my tits look massive. Spinning around in front of the mirror, sweating profusely, I feel a bit better about myself. God, I'd almost forgotten I was a woman.

As the dress is only 35 quid, I decide it's maybe that time of the decade where I buy myself a new bra. My current one's so small now, it gives me four boobs and has a nasty nicotiney tinge that won't wash out. Having no recollection of what size I might be, I have to get measured. The assistant informs me I'm a 36DD and sounds suitably impressed. I wonder if that stands for disgustingly droopy. How the mighty have fallen.

'Do you have any Wonderbras in that size?' I brave, thinking about my flat-chested hairdresser Michelle's new-found cleavage. The woman smirks.

'I don't really think you need a Wonderbra if you're a 36DD.'

Grabbing the first white, lacey bra I see in my prodigious size, I pay for it and the dress, and get out of there before I embarrass myself further.

My lunch with Joyce is a disaster. She finds an inedible lump of something very un-fishlike in her salmon pâté which puts her off the rest of her meal. A large spike of bone in my haddock fillet gives me the boaks. She goes on about her husband's new job so much that, by the time we part, I'm glad to see the back of her. We both promise to write, but know we probably won't bother. We're not that close. At school we were, but we both just seem to go through the motions as adults. Still, another one down in my minuscule social circle.

All in, the lunch costs £21 and I didn't even get to mention Raymond. Fuck friendship, it's far too expensive. At least when I get in, the flat is still that lovely, quiet, empty way and should be for a few more hours.

Making a coffee, I decide to watch my *Body of Evidence* video. It's rubbish, of course, but I adore Willem Dafoe, particularly in the cunnilingus-on-the-car-bonnet scene. I have a small collection of seemingly innocuous-looking videos with good sex scenes that I watch on the rare occasions I'm alone. *Paris Trout* is another favourite. Dennis Hopper plays an old racist who, in one scene, sticks a beer bottle up Barbara Hershey's arse and pours, and it's like, wow. I know I shouldn't find it sexy but I do.

The film's only been on five minutes, when the phone rings. 'Mr Murray?'

'He moved out years ago,' I yell, slamming it down. Fuck, we get more phone calls and mail for the couple that used to live here than we do for ourselves. The husband was a rugby referee so, when there's an International due, it never stops. Vic keeps threatening to pretend he's Mr Murray, on the off-chance he might get asked to do the next Grand Slam.

I crouch on the floor and fast-forward to Willem's first scene.

He was a really sexy Jesus as well. Oh, here we go. He reminds me of Rab, the squaddie I almost married. We got engaged just prior to him being sent off to the Falklands War. My pal and me were working as au pairs in London at the time. At the end of the war, I came home for the weekend as Rab's boat was arriving back at Leith. There was a big welcome-home celebration planned. Thing was, the union wouldn't let the dockers work overtime on a weekend, so Rab was stranded in the Forth for two days. Not wanting to waste a weekend off, I went out on the randan with some of my old pals and met Vic. I'd come off the pill for my forthcoming honeymoon, so that was basically it – bye bye life, bye bye happiness . . . My dad had always hated Rab anyway because he was English, and being a rabid trade unionist, was absolutely thrilled that the Edinburgh dockers' union were responsible for the break-up of our engagement. Yes, Willem looks just like him. I've no idea what happened to Rab.

I've just slipped my hand into my knickers, when the phone goes again. I consider ignoring it, but suppose there might be some slim chance it might be Raymond.

'Yes!'

'Angela, is that you?'

God, it's Vic's dad.

'Oh, sorry, Stewart. I've had people trying to sell me things over the phone all afternoon,' I lie, feeling awful. He's such a gentle old soul.

'How're you doing, love? Is everything well? I'd not heard from Victor for a while, I just wanted to check you were all right.'

'Yes, yes, everything's fine. He's just been a bit busy with work and that.'

I resent having to make excuses for Vic, when the truth is, he's just a lazy bastard.

There's a prolonged silence. I know he's wanting to ask when we're going to visit, but doesn't want to seem like he's hassling us. I have an inspired idea.

'He was talking about going to the match on Saturday. Go with him. Come round for your tea after, if you like.'

Stewart's beside himself. As soon as I hang up I start worrying I've said the wrong thing. Fuck it, though, if Vic wants to go to the football, then Vic can go to the football. I keep telling him to make the most of his dad while he's still got one, but he's forever avoiding the poor bugger.

Again, I attempt to watch my video but, after another phone call for the Murrays, Joni comes tearing in and heads straight for her room. I summon her through. She has a look on her face that says, this better be good.

'What is it? I'm in a hurry.'

'Why aren't you at school?'

'I've just come back for a book. Look, I have to go.'

Skiving little shite. She makes for the door again.

'Hey, I've not finished.'

Tutting loudly, she drums her fingers on the door frame.

'Don't you think you should apologise to your dad for what you said this morning?'

'What?'

'You know what I mean.'

The penny seems to drop.

'Yeah, well he shouldn't pull the covers off me, pervert. What do you know anyway? You don't know what goes on. You're always at your fucking work or getting in strange cars when you're supposed to be at work.'

'What? What're you on about?'

'Just fuck off,' she yells. Out of conversation and out the door. We really are so close these days.

Another disastrous day off nearly over, I go through to the kitchen and start on the tea. Jake appears as I finish peeling a huge pan of potatoes and tells me he doesn't want any. He's got a computer class. Throwing the peeler into the sink, I go back through to watch telly.

I'm still sitting there when Vic comes in at six. I tell him about Stewart phoning and my idea about the football. Letting out a tortured groan, he grabs the *Evening News* and locks himself in the toilet with it. Fucking families? I feel like just telling them all to piss off.

Chapter Five

JONI

DOUBLE ART FIRST thing, the only subject I actually enjoy. Daniel better not be there. I can't face him after running away like that the other day.

'I thought you wanted to shag him,' Rosie reminds me as we wait outside the art block for lovely Mr Gallagher.

'Yeah, so I changed my mind. I got bored and went home.'

'Aye, right.'

'What did he say about it, like?'

'Just that he'd sent you to get us. I knew something had happened. You should have just done it, Jo, he's really nice, that Daniel.'

'Not compared to him,' I purr, pointing at Mr Gallagher striding across the playground towards us with his sexy new hair-do.

Rosie and me gawp at him, with cheesy grins on our faces, then say in unison, 'I really like your hair, Mr Gallagher.' It sounds pathetic, like we've been practising. Rosie and me are like that, though. We often think the same thing at the same time. As he brushes past to unlock the class, I get a waft of really expensive-smelling aftershave. When we follow him in, it mingles with the arty, painty, wooden smell. Sitting at my desk, I breathe it in, watching him, not even listening to what he's saying – gorgeous, gorgeous.

'That's all right with you, Joni? Model for a day?'

Oh God, what's he on about?

'Eh?'

He knows I've not been listening but is cool about it.

'Will you model for us today? You did say you would last week. Everyone's done it twice now.'

Bollocks. I hate modelling in class. He makes me get up on a chair, put one foot on the sink and pretend to hammer a nail into the wall. I can hear them all sniggering behind me. I've got a fanny pad on. I bet they've all noticed. What if it starts leaking?

'That's great. Are you comfortable with that? Break in 15 minutes?'

I make a strange sound that means neither yes nor no.

'Sir, can I get a bigger bit paper, sir? I can't get her arse on this one,' Fartin Martin shouts out. Everyone laughs.

'Sorry, is this a primary class?' says Mr Gallagher, gallantly. Everyone laughs again. They'd laugh at anything. Any sort of noise whatsoever they seem to find absolutely hilarious. They're pathetic.

This is the longest 15 minutes of my whole life. My arm is aching from the stupid pose. As if galleries are full of pictures of schoolgirls hammering nails into walls. It's 20 minutes before I get a break. Having a quick look round, I see their pictures are even more horrific than I'd anticipated. Even Rosie's made me look like Fat Hilary from fifth year. Kes has given me a beard. Fartin Martin's given me loads of spots. In Pete's, my hair is just a big scribble, bastards.

'You're not supposed to look fat,' says Rosie, noticing my distress, '. . . it's just you kept moving.'

I don't want to get up there again, but my break's soon over. By the time the second instalment of my ordeal's over, I'm sweating like a bastard. Mr Gallagher squeezes my shoulder as he helps me down. He's beautiful.

'That wasn't too bad now, was it?'

'It was very bad,' I mumble through my fringe. The finished products are absolutely awful. Just this big, fat, ugh. Three people have given me sweaty armpits. I'm delighted when the bell goes as I'd probably have started crying otherwise.

I chum Rosie to the tuck shop but don't get anything myself because I feel so fat and disgusting. Usually, I have a pie with chippie sauce at play time but I'm not going to eat anything, ever again. Rosie, bitch, gets a sausage roll. The gorgeous meaty, pastry whiff hangs in the cold air around me, even after she's finished it. You can almost taste it.

'See Daniel wasnae at Art, eh?'

'Shut it, right. I dinnae fancy him.'

'Ooh, Miss Sensitive,' she whines, '. . . if you're gonna be like that, I dinnae suppose you'll want to babysit with me tonight.'

'Babysit where?'

'Broomhouse, that woman John knows. Ah said last week.'

'Oh, aye. Brilliant, yeah. I'll do that.'

By the end of play time I'm feeling much happier. Maybe John'll be there. Maybe Rosie'll bring the video with her. I love babysitting. You always find booze.

I try to get Rosie to skive off English and go to the museum or something. You get loads of nice guys in the museum in the afternoon. I bagged off with a boy from St Augie's when I was there once. He had Heineken tongue, if you know what I mean.

Rosie refuses to skive though, because we're doing *As You Like It* and she's playing Rosalind. She thinks she's bloody Winona Ryder. I have to just follow it in the book because there's 37 pupils and only 27 characters. Jamie's playing Oliver in his really dippit, doh-doh voice and keeps losing the place and getting words wrong. Rosie's going for the Oscar, though, getting really actressy. I've absolutely no idea what they're going on about, except when Rosie says, 'But for the bloody napkin' and the whole class starts laughing. I bet they're all thinking about my bloody napkin at Art, bastards.

God, it just goes on and on and on. I hate Shakespeare. It's complete crap. Why do we have to learn all that old shite about crappy kings and queens and rich cunts with poncey, long names you can't pronounce? I can't even understand what anyone's supposed to be saying. Even when the teacher explains it, it's still crap. The *Romeo and Juliet* film was all right. We went to see it with the English class the other week. The Shakespeary bits just spoilt it, though.

Miss Barnes, the relief teacher, is awful too. She wears bright orange foundation and dead tight jumpers. She's just so pattery, you know the type? And she's all over the boys. 'Oh, Pete, that's just fantastic, sooper, fantastic.' But if one of the girls asks her something, she's like, 'Shut up, I'm with my boys.' Ugly cow. And I thought my arse was big.

At last they finish the play. Miss Barnes makes us all clap the people who took part, even though it was shite. I don't mention Rosie's acting to her when the lesson ends as she's really annoying me. You can tell she's wanting everyone to tell her how brilliant she was. As if.

I chum her up to the chippie at lunch-time, still determined not to eat. There's a big queue, though, and as people pass me with their saucy chips, I get hungrier and hungrier. The young Italian guy that works here is really nice, sort of like Johnny Depp, with a double chin. God, I've not eaten anything today and it's nearly 12 o'clock. When we get to the front of the queue, I can't help myself and have to get a bag, a pound bag. Since I'm not going home for tea, I'll make them do me. Then Rosie gives me half her mince pie. I really love chippie mince pies, so I eat that too, then feel really fat and awful again.

We both have double Secretarial this afternoon, which it's compulsory to skive. Telephoning Rosie's, we let it ring 20 times before deciding her mum's at work. She's on the jellies, so you can never be sure.

Her house, as usual, is fucking freezing. There's an electric bar fire, but Rosie's mum takes the plug to work with her because she says it's too dangerous to use when she's out. Honest, she must think Rosie's about five years old. I get the duvet through, for us to sit under, as she rummages the book-case.

'Oh fuck, oh fuck. It's gone.'

'What, what's wrong?'

She rifles the book-case again.

'The video, I put it behind here. If Mum's found it, I'm dead.'

I have to cuddle her, to calm her down.

'Take it easy, she doesnae know it's yours. It could be one of her boyfriends', or her drunken pals. It could be any-one's.'

I get her, still hysterical, over to the settee.

'She'll stop John coming round if she's found it. She'll find out about the other things as well, fucksake.'

'What d'you mean? What other things?'

She looks all coy.

'You know?'

'What?'

Making a circle with her thumb and middle finger, she shakes her hand about. I'm stunned with jealousy. The bitch, the lucky bitch.

'What? Does he do it to himself, or do you do it to him?'

'Both,' she says, all smug.

'God, that's amazing. What's it like? Is it really big?'

She smiles and lets out a little cluck of laughter.

'. . . wow, that's absolutely immense. Is it good, you know, d'you like it?'

'That's what I mean. I really like him. The rest of them

wouldnae understand. What'll I do? Mum's bound to say something.'

Going to the toilet, to try and think of a possible solution, I discover that with all the excitement, my fanny pad's completely leaked onto my pants. Fuck, I don't have another one with me, I'll have to go home. At least I'll be out the way before Rosie's mum comes in. God, it's really exciting. I can find out what happened when we go babysitting tonight. I definitely want clean pants for that.

We agree that I should wait at the bottom of the stair for her at six, in case her mum starts questioning me. As I run along the street towards my house, I feel my knickers squelching. Jan is yelping and trying to squeeze past me as I open the door. I run up the hall, into the bathroom, and lock her out.

Pouring a bath, I strip and stuff the gruesome big whale of a fanny pad down the toilet. Amazingly, it disappears first flush. When I get in the bath, the water turns a dirty, browny red. The blood clots look like little scraps of flesh, like I've been bitten by a shark. It stinks.

I look down at my wet body. My nipples are really sticking out. They're far too big, like the tips of someone's pinkies. You never see models with paps like mine, I'm like a cow. My belly looks OK though, quite flat. I imagine John standing behind me, looking down and seeing what I'm seeing. Running my fingers over my big rubbery tits and down my belly, I pretend it's him, and end up having to X^2.

It's half-three by the time I get dried and dressed. Mum won't be in till about five but I really don't want to see her. I go through to their stinky bedroom.

Pushing the candlewick on top of the bed, I lift up the mattress. There's a pile of little brown envelopes with what they're for written on them – phone, gas, mortgage, Council Tax, computer, holidays, that sort of thing. Mum used to keep it in the bank but she's paranoid about it suddenly disappearing when the computers all fuck up in 2000. Three cheers for micro-chips. At first, I just used to take about a tenner a week but I've been going a bit daft recently – I better watch. The one I usually chory from is right at the back, the most pathetic one – 'Joni – University'. Mum thinks I only exist to do what she was too stupid to do herself, too stupid and pregnant. There's only 80 quid in it as well, bloody cheek. Mind you, I've taken most of it, university of life and all that. I take another tenner, then a fiver out of 'holidays'. I should'nt imagine she'll need either for a very long time.

Mum's going out tomorrow night, so I'm going up town with Rosie. I can buy her drink. Loads of lassies from my class go up Lothian Road at the weekend. We can go to the Barracuda. Supposedly anyone could get a bag-off there. Lying on my bed, I fantasise about getting off with strangers, or John being there tonight, or Robbie Williams bursting in the room and just grabbing me and I X^2 again. It makes my hand all bloody.

I X^2 quite a lot. Sometimes, I think I'm maybe obsessed with it. The magazines all say it's OK, though. I'd been doing it for about five years before I read it was normal, you know, that other people did it too. It must be about the best thing ever invented for humans. I wonder if John's done it to Rosie. Whoargh!

She's waiting for me in the swing park when I go back along at six. Her mum hasn't even mentioned the video, very boring.

'If John's there tonight you can see if she's said anything to him.'

'Where?'

'The place we're babysitting. Isn't he pals with the wifie?'

'What're you trying to say, Jo? She just works for him. What d'you mean?'

Ooh, touchy. Maybe the wifie's been X^2ing John as well.

'. . . look Jo, you better not say anything, dinnae mention it. I'm regretting telling you,' she says, dead serious.

'I'm hardly gonna say anything. I think it's fab. You should run away with him, and take me.'

This seems to calm her down and we're pally again by the time the bus comes. I've never been to Broomhouse before. It's supposedly dead schemie. We go past Saughton Park and Stenhouse and they look not too bad, then it changes and there's these horrid, ugly flats with toaty wee windows the size of cat flaps. It seems completely deserted, as if Red Indians have already been through and massacred everyone. We spend about 20 minutes looking for the right door. Hardly any of the flats have numbers on them. What a dump.

When we eventually find it, the wifie, Jeanette answers, wearing so much make-up she looks like a transvestite. The combined smell of cheap perfume, hairspray and shite is so strong it almost chokes me. A black mongrel puppy yaps round our feet as we walk up the hall. Newspaper covers the floor. In the living room, the shite smell is even stronger as there's only cigarette smoke to disguise it. Again, the carpet is covered in *Daily Record*s.

'Mind yer feet. That wee bastard's shat everywhere. You've no sooner cleaned one up and phoomph, he lets go another. See if yi can keep a coupla clear bits fir me tae walk on when ah git back.'

Euch, it's revolting. There's wee baby shites dotted everywhere, it's like Wardlaw.

Jeanette leads us through to the bathroom to meet Emma, the lassie we're babysitting. I'm expecting a wee toddler. My jaw drops open when I first see her. I've no idea what age she might be, about 16 maybe older, but she's got wee boobs and this big hairy fanny. I can't take my eyes off it. Her head looks a bit twisted, like she's maybe handicapped or something, but when she says hello it sounds pretty normal.

'I'll just get her nightie on,' says Jeanette, shoogling the lassie inside a huge towel. 'Help yersells tae juice.'

I welcome the chance for a breather. Going through to the kitchen, I open the fridge. Rosie's behind me. It's all Kwik-Save cheap rubbish.

'Be all right, eh? A tenner and money for a taxi?'

Big deal. I can make more than that without leaving the house.

'Did you know, y'know, that Emma was like that?'

She stares at me blankly.

'Aye, so what?'

'Och, you know, I'm no being funny, like, but she's got pubes and everything. She's a woman.'

'No in her head, she's no, she's just wee in her head. She's nice, honest, really funny. She just comes out wi stuff.'

I feel like a real bitch for mentioning it. We're stuck here now anyway. Pointing at the cheap juice in the fridge, I pull a face.

'God, you're such a snob, Jo.'

The puppy craps on a photo of Posh Spice as we go through to the living room with our drinks. And I thought our house was bad.

There's a jobbie-brown PVC settee and two black PVC armchairs. I sit on a cushion since cheap plastic plays havoc with my sweaty bottom. The house is so filthy, I'm scared I might catch something. No wonder the lassie's not well.

Jeanette brings Emma through, twitching round the room, quick as a mouse, pulling photos off the mantelpiece, books out of cupboards, ornaments, keys, throwing them all in the middle of the newspapery floor.

'She get's awfie excited with new folk. She'll be wanting to show you stuff aw night. Just watch what she puts in her gob,' Jeanette drawls, skooshing more hairspray on the metallically-solid-looking bird's nest on her head. It briefly disguises the smell of shit. Rosie kneels on the floor and starts looking through a photo album with Emma. Spying a clear patch of newspaper, I get down beside them. Emma turns the pages violently, pointing at photos, saying 'good, good, BAD, good, good, BAD, BAD, BAD.' Jeanette looks down at us, 'She's ay been perceptive aboot the guys in ma life. She susses them oot months before me. Do ah listen taer though? A buckin should.' Bending over, she gives Emma a squeeze.

'OK love, dinnae tire the girls oot too much. Bed by ten.' And suddenly we're alone with this strange girl/woman in her nightie.

We're straight through to the kitchen looking for scran. Oh dear, they have the saddest cupboards I've ever rummaged – all dried herbs, bottles of sauce, and packet sauce mixes, you know, things only good for putting on other things.

'God, Emma, does your mum no buy real food? Biscuits? Custard mix, eh?' Emma goes scampering off, and returns with a box of ginger cream chocolates. I don't know if I like ginger but I take one anyway. Euch, it's disgusting. Like the foosty sweeties they sell in Poundstretcher. Not wanting to upset Emma, I force it down. But then she starts offering me loads, all excited 'cause she thinks she's making me happy. Sick as I feel, I'm worried how she'll react if I refuse. I'm on my tenth when Rosie finally manages to distract her by taking a bleeping Tamagotchi through to the living room. Emma wrestles it off her and sits in front of the TV with the cyberpet right up at her face, showering it, overfeeding it, letting it crap. It's a shame. She'd be a really nice-looking lassie if she wasn't like that.

'If her head's younger than her body, will it still get older, ken?'

Rosie understands, miraculously. 'Aye, I suppose it must do.'

'So when she's 40, she'll only really be 30? And in about ten years, she'll be like we are now.'

'Nah, ah dinnae think so. Ah actually dinnae ken what's wrong with her. I think she was OK when she was wee.'

We both stare at Emma, then at the clock. Only ten minutes have passed. The telly's shite as well. I'm going to be fighting her for the Tamagotchi in a minute.

'Pity about the video. We coulda watched it here.'

'You're just sex-starved.'

Emma's over, flapping around, 'Video . . . video . . . watch a video?' Dragging Rosie over to the TV, she starts pulling tapes out a drawer – all rubbish Disney, Spice Girls, kids' stuff. Eventually she sticks one in the machine and an American film comes on, really bad sound, like one from the 70s. Giggling away, she hits the fast-forward button. Cadillacs speed up streets, crowds rush by like ants, people flash from one side of the screen to another. Then she stops it. There's a blonde woman, about Mum's age, with pigtails, and a lollipop in her mouth. A creepy man in a hat asks her if she likes to suck things. I'm hooked. Emma's killing herself laughing. Rosie knows she should tell her to put it off but doesn't. The puppy is biting at the curtains but we just ignore it. When the man in the hat finally brings his willie out, Rosie and me both do big gasps. The expression 'babies arm' finally makes sense. He tells the woman to shut her eyes, and puts it in her mouth. I'm glad I'm not sitting on the PVC chair as my bum's practically swimming. God, I wish I was on my own.

When he eventually does it all over the woman's tits, I pretend it's John and me. Rosie nudges me out of it, looking absolutely stunned. I wonder how she, of all people, could be shocked, then notice Emma, sitting at the side of the telly, grinning away, legs spread, hand jigging away on her bare hairy fanny. It's horrible, I don't know what to do. We just sit and watch, till the dog, excited by the movement of her arm, starts sniffing around and Rosie has to intervene before things get out of control. She switches the video off while she's there, rotten cow. Emma's still trying to get her hand back between her legs, she's not finished yet. God, she just doesn't care.

Rosie picks up a piggy bank and shakes it above her head to distract her.

'If I give you this you've got to promise to stop that.'

Emma's immediately on the verge of tears, so she hands it over. Emptying it onto the newspaper, she sorts the coins into colours – dirty silver, dirty bronze, shiny silver, shiny bronze. Then she separates the big coins from the wee ones. She grabs my arm, wanting to show me, but when I get down beside her I can smell her fanny really strongly. She tries to give me money but I tell her I have enough. I could help myself, she wouldn't be any the wiser, but I couldn't steal from her. That would just be bad.

Rosie comes over from the sideboard, pointing at an alarm clock in her hand.

'Come on, Emma. Your mum'll be angry if you don't go to bed when she told you.'

I expect her to have a screaming fit, but instead, she comes over, kisses my forehead, then kisses Rosie's and goes off to her room, no fuss, no struggle. When we check, half an hour later, she's out for the count. Disappointingly, Rosie had put the clock forward two hours, to get her off to her bed early so we've still got ages to go. It's not so bad once we've got the video back on, found a bottle of Martini, and started plotting tactics for tomorrow night, though. Rosie is definitely on for the Barracuda.

By the time Jeanette comes back, well after midnight, we've both crashed out on the settee. She doesn't go mad though, just checks on Emma, gives us a tenner and apologises for being late. Although we're both knackered, we walk home to save money for tomorrow. It's going to be brilliant.

Dad's sitting with a face on, when I get in.

'Jo, pet, why didn't you phone? Just phone and say where you are, please.'

'I don't have to tell you everything. I don't ask you what you do.'

He tries to grab my hand but I pull away.

'I'm going to bed. I'm back now, so what does it matter?'

I go to change my fanny pad, then slam myself into my room. Why does he try to make me feel guilty all the time? What's the point in phoning anyway? I could get murdered waiting on a phone box. I wait till I hear him going to bed, before finally X^2ing about the man in the hat in the video. As I fall asleep I think about all the X^2ing I've done, heard about, or seen other people doing today. It just seems odd that I should encounter so much of it in one day. It must mean something. It must be a sign.

Chapter Six

VIC

ANGE IS DOING pig impressions by the time I go through to bed. Stripping to my boxer shorts, I get under the duvet. It's humid. I lie with my back to her, about a foot apart. We used to like a cuddle but she's generally snoring by the time I get through these days and the vibration keeps me awake. This is about the loudest I've heard her. I grapple on the bedside table for my industrial-issue ear plugs. They are black with the ear-wax and blood of excessive usage. Although they muffle the sound slightly, it's still there, too irregular to get used to. Jesus, I just want to unwind. I have all my best thoughts as my mind's losing consciousness. It's not quite the same with that bloody awful din.

As I nudge the tickly bit at her side, her body seems to levitate off the bed.

'Uh, what the fuck?'

I kiss her shoulder. 'You were just snoring a wee bit, love.'

'I was not. I wasn't even sleeping.'

'You were.'

'If it was that bad, I'd have woken myself up.'

I've not even worked out a response when the noise starts up again. It's terrible. I cough loudly to wake her without seeming like it was deliberate. She comes to, but only manages a groan before going limp again. This time, though, she's just breathing heavily. Squeezing my eyes shut, I try to will myself to sleep.

I'm there, I'm almost sodding there when there's a long, loud snort and she's away again. Climbing out of bed, I retrieve my pillows. She wakes up.

'It's OK . . . I'll go through . . . it's my turn,' she says drowsily but, as usual, stays put. I get the spare quilt from the cupboard and go back through to the living room. Hello, sofa, my old friend, I've come to talk with you again. Burst springs jab me in the ribs, but the silence is glorious.

I wake at seven, in a sweaty, cosy ball. When I try to move my head, I get a sharp pain in my neck and my right arm is dead where I've been lying on it. How can I work the hours I do and still end up sleeping on the settee like some dosser? I keep getting blasts of doggy breath and think Jan must be sitting next to me. As it happens, its my own halitosis rebounding off the duvet and hitting me in the face. When did I last see a dentist?

I stand up, stretch and stroke my sore bits, determined to think positive or the day'll just go downhill from here on in. I'll get Ronnie round tonight, have a few beers, then get off to bed before Ange gets back. Sprawl myself across the bloody thing and pretend to be in a coma.

Putting the duvet back in the cupboard, I stick the kettle on and go for a wash and shave, strictly above the shoulders. Not much point in washing the rest of me when nobody's going to be looking anyway.

Jake's up and buzzing around by seven-thirty. He agrees to let me make him some breakfast. I sip my coffee and he sooks a carton of Ribena as I carefully brown an egg round the edges, the way he likes it.

'Have you spoken to Mum about *Fifa 98* yet?'

'Ocht, Jake, you know what she's like.'

'Aaaw,' he groans, as I slide a plate with his breakfast, oozing with ketchup, across to him. He devours it in such mammoth mouthfuls that I take the opportunity to speak to him uninterrupted.

'I'm taking Granda to the match tomorrow. I'll pay you in if you fancy it.'

'What match?' he mumbles through the bread.

'Hearts/Celtic. It should be a good game. Hearts could go two points ahead.'

'Against Celtic? Hardly. I'd like them to beat the Fenian bastards, mind you.'

'Jake, please dinnae talk like that. I've told you before.'

'Mmm, couldn't we go to Ibrox instead? See a proper game.'

Why do I bother? 'Look, it doesn't matter. I'll just go with Granda.'

He grabs his schoolbag. 'Nah, I'll go. Is it all seated now?'

'Yeah.'

'Aye, OK then.'

I give him the thumbs-up and expect him to leave but he stands there, looking at me in an oh-so-familiar way.

'Da-ad?'

'Uh huh.'

'You couldnae give me three pound for my computer magazine, could you?'

'I got you it the other day.'

'Nah, there's hundreds of them now. This one's got a CD with loads of free games on it. Go on. Since *Resident Evil 2* didn't work, eh? Since you've not asked Mum yet?'

I dig three pound coins out my pocket. He swipes them from me and makes for the door. I grab his schoolbag.

'DA-AD! Stop being so childish. What is it?'

I let go and laugh. 'It's just Ronnie's coming round the night if you fancied joining us. I'll maybe even let you have a wee shandy.'

'What for? What are you on about?'

'I dunno, you're growing up, I thought you might like a wee bit adult male company.'

With an offended 'Get a grip, Dad', he's gone. We were together for 12 minutes though. It's a start. And it only cost me three pounds.

Getting the kettle on again for Angie, I stick a couple of slices of bread in the toaster. I hear Joni coming out her room, coughing, and go into the hall to confirm the remarkable fact that she's managed to get up of her own accord. She thumbs through the post, hands it to me and actually gives me a smile. I want to thank her or give her a tenner or something in the hope she might make a habit out of it. Who knows what time she'll crawl back tonight though. Please make it before her mother.

Angie is already up when I take her breakfast through. She appears to have emptied the entire contents of our wardrobe onto the bed.

'Still going out tonight, then?'

She looks at me suspiciously. 'Yeah, why? Do you have a problem with that?'

Why does she have to be so bloody aggressive all the time?

'No, not at all. If you want to chase other men, that's fine by me. I'll just stay in and tidy the kitchen or something.'

She smiles. 'I'd have to run pretty fast with a body like mine, Vic.'

'Nonsense, dear. All women are attractive to men after about five pints. You'll score for sure.'

Biting into the toast, she turns her attention back to the clothes on the bed. I couldn't hazard a guess at the last time we had sex. I've not even managed a stiffie since I started taking these pills. I'm not even sure that I miss it that much. It's one less pressure. I've never felt I was very good at it anyway. I'm all foreplay and no fiveplay. When you come as quickly as I do, you don't really have an option. Women pretend they like all that but they don't. They just want shagged for hours on end.

I do the breakfast dishes and square up in the living room for Ronnie coming round. When Ange reappears, she looks so well-groomed I hardly recognise her. It's like an artist's impression of what she'd look like if she wasn't such a slob. I feel a little pang of jealousy but don't tell her about it. Nothing'll happen anyway. She hates her body too much to subject anyone else to it. She pops an ancient lipstick into her handbag and I give her a lift to work. She seems in a good mood. I'm pleased. It makes a bloody change.

Chapter Seven

JAKE

AS I WALK to school, past the swing park, I see smoke coming out the side of the chute. Jason's under there, firing himself up with his first fag of the day and a tin of Red Bull.

'Here, I brought your bastard game. Can I play it round yours the night? Dad's pal's coming round, so he'll be getting aw his shitey auld singles out. Ah cannae stand it.'

Jason takes the CD out the box and checks it.

'I cannae see how it widnae load. Has your dad got a crappy Amstrad or what?'

He should know, he used our computer plenty before he got his.

'Dad's gettin me *Fifa 98* at the weekend. We're gonnae see your shitey team play Celtic as well.'

Jason grinds his cigarette into the concrete and spits a dirty big greaser on top of it.

'What for? You hate the Jambos. Has your old man's Lottery Instant come up?'

'Nah, I think it's more of a Japanese Endurance-type thing. How long can I watch really gash football for? How much shite can I stand? Be a good laugh anyway. It'll just make Rangers seem even better.'

Jason seems miffed that I'm getting something over on him. Despite the fact he'll probably turn up on Saturday as well now. He's an only child so his mum and dad are forever chucking money at him. Nodding his head thoughtfully, he squirts open another £1.29 tin of Red Bull.

I'm sure dad just pretends to like Hearts to wind Mum and me up. He can't genuinely think they're a good team. They're maybe near the top of the league at the moment, but they'll blow it by the end of the season like they always do. It was Granda, Mum's dad, got me into Rangers. When I was wee, he used to take me to the Orange March in Princes Street. It was brill – all drums and banners and bright colours. You always saw really good fights as well, you know, two people having an argument turning into a massive big pagger. I really miss Granda. He used to speak to me like I was an adult, even though I was only nine when he died. Towards the end, though, he started going strange, telling me he was going to leave the cooker on one night and gas him and Granny. I liked him and I didn't want him to die, or kill Granny, so I told Mum. They wouldn't let me see him after that.

Jason finishes his fag as we walk down for registration. We're in different classes, so I take the long way round to see if I can get a wee glimpse of Miss Barnes. As I prowl towards her class, my legs feel like they're about to give way. When I get up to the door, I pretend to look behind me, so I can stare through the glass panel. She's writing something on the blackboard, but turns round and smiles. I shite it along the corridor and down the back stairs. Fuck, I can't believe she saw me. She'll think I'm a fucking radge. I'm just going to wank for the rest of my life. It's far less scary.

As I get to the bottom of the steps, I feel myself being lifted off the ground. Shug the Slug's suddenly in front of me, breathing his garlic halitosis into my face. Whoever's had a grip of me lets go, and I crunch onto the hard stone floor.

I grasp for my bag, to escape, but Shug stands on my wrist.

'Uyah, uyah, dinnae. Leave eys alone,' I plead, looking round desperately for help. I realise the guy that picked me up is

Adam's pal, Daniel, who we smoked blow up the canal with the other night. He's doesn't even acknowledge me now. Shug gives my wrist a final grind with his size-ten Caterpillars before releasing me.

'Right, you dirty Orange bastard, where's my fucking *Loaded*, eh? It came out yesterday and I don't fucking have it yet. Have you any idea how irritating I find that?'

Shug likes glossy magazines, men's ones, particularly the ones with lots of tits in them. If I don't buy them for him, he kicks my head in. Most of them only come out once a month, but there's so fucking many of them these days, it costs me about six quid a week. And I have to wank on fucking *Marie Claires*!

'Sorry Shug, honest. I didnae get money till today.'

Digging in my pocket, I offer him the three quid dad gave me. He grabs it, but wants more.

'Come on. Interest as well, you little cunt. It's one day late and I'm going to have to go all the way up to the shops and buy it myself. Fucking shocking inconvenience.'

I offer him the money I have left, about £1.33, that I was going to get chips and juice with. He takes it, then grabs my arm and twists it up my back till it feels like it's going to snap. Jo's pal, Rosie, comes down the stairs, glances at us, then walks out into the playground. Shug tightens his grip on my arm again when she's gone. Daniel's still not letting on.

'Right, cunt. It's *FHM* next Monday. If ah dinnae get it before school, I'll bite your fuckin balls off.'

Shug being Shug, I don't doubt this. He pushes me away and gobs in my face.

'Rangers fucking scum.'

As I stumble off, wiping his phlegm from my cheek, Daniel finally comes back to life, slings me a red-card tackle and I slap, face-down, onto the stone floor. As my nose bangs off the ground, this horrible, cold, rushing, pain goes right through my head.

Daniel and Shug strut off, laughing, fucking bastards. Rosie's a cow as well, she could have stopped them. I actually quite like school but cunts like that make me not want to come back.

Blood's plopping out my nose onto the ground. I fumble into the toilets, and check out the mirror. The bottom half of my face is completely covered in blood. It looks sort of cool but my head's so sore it's making me feel sick. I have to lean back and dowse myself with wet paper towels for ages before it stops. I'm still cleaning up the mess when a laddie I don't know comes in and asks if I'm OK.

'Aye, aye, it's fine. I just get these nose-bleeds sometimes. I don't know what causes it.'

He tries to look up my nose.

'Will I take you along to the nurse's? Your face is a funny colour. D'you feel awright?'

'Aye, honest. Thanks, anyway.'

He's still looking at me, but his expression's changed now.

'Is your second name Scott?'

How the fuck does he know?

'Yeah, what about it?'

'I live in your stair, second floor. We moved in last month. Ah'm Sean.'

Oh, my head is so sore. Even trying to smile is painful. 'Yeah? That Mrs Anderson's a cow, eh?'

'Too right. She complained about the noise when we were trying to move in. Her house stinks of cat shit. You can smell it on the landing, eh?'

By the time we leave the bogs, Sean and I have slagged off all the neighbours, he's invited me down for a shot on the Internet and I've enlisted him in the Mr Russell Campaign. It'd be dead handy being pally with someone in the same stair. I'm sure Mum said they were Catholics but he might still be all right.

I walk round to try and catch Jason before he goes into the

next lesson. My head's hurting too much to go to French. I can't understand it at the best of times. Foreign words seem to cause a two-mile tailback in my brain. I mean to say, male and female words, have you ever heard such shite? They teach you useless stuff anyway. If I was in France I'm sure I wouldn't be going about asking folk the time and demanding baguettes and jotters. Things like, where's the nearest cybercafé or when is the next flight out of your stinking Froggy country, would be far more useful.

I stand at the end of the corridor in case the teacher or any of the sneaky lassies see me and think I'm skiving. I'm too embarrassed to say I've got a headache, it's just so poofy. After about five minutes, Jason skits down the main stairs and straight into the class. I holler his name down the corridor but the teacher goes in behind him and shuts the door. Fuck, I wanted him to chum me home in case I blacked out. I've seen it on *Casualty*. If you bang your head and fall asleep, you can go into a coma. Dying doesnae really bother me, but being fed baby-food, having to get Mum or Dad to wipe my arse, just being able to gurgle and not even being able to play *Fifa* doesn't sound too good.

Why didn't I ask that Sean laddie what he was up to? I feel dead alone, like I've maybe only got about ten minutes to live and nobody cares. The pain just keeps getting worse.

As I look out the window, I see Shug, Daniel and a couple of their henchmen coming back across the playground. I run up the corridor and out the main door, onto the street. Maybe I should tell someone about getting my head kicked in all the time. The way I'm feeling, I won't have to worry about it for much longer.

Mr Russell's at the bus stop with swotty Simon from fourth year when I get up to the main road. Hiding in the doorway of one of the derelict shops, I spy on them till the bus comes. They're laughing away together like a right pair of old nancies, in public as well. I always kent there was something funny about that Simon. His dad's a screw, mind, so what d'you expect? As suspected, they both get the same bus, a 33. Mr Russell lives just up the road, Simon's from Longstone, so fuck knows where they're going. Probably to hang about in some public toilet. No point in phoning him before I go home then, I suppose. If I'm not dead by tonight, I'll make up for it. Keep ringing while they're trying to shag.

As I open the door to our flat, I hear screaming and giggling. Jo comes out Mum's bedroom, done up like Marilyn Manson. She looks bored when she sees it's just me.

'What's this then? Home for a wank?'

Bitch, I'm going to do it in the bathroom with the taps on from now on, she must hear. Rosie comes out behind her, looking like a sexy vampire. Maybe it wasn't her I seen this morning.

'I hurt my head.'

'Aw, deedums,' she whines, 'see iz poor wee nose.'

'Poor Jake, d'you want me to rub it better for you?' slags Rosie. I wish she meant it.

'You don't need to do that. Jake's quite an expert at rubbing it himself, aren't you? That's why you've got a sore head. You're probably going blind.'

'That must be how I've never seen you with a boyfriend then, eh?'

With a curt 'piss off', they float back into Mum's room. What's worse? Letting that pair slag me off or going into a coma? I follow them. It looks like the burglars have been round. Clothes are everywhere, drawers are exploding.

'You auditioning for *Scream III* or what?'

'Away and play with your fucking computer.' Jo grins at Rosie. 'You should make some friends, Jake. If there was a power cut, you'd have to commit suicide.'

'Go an fuck yourself. Know what? Your turning into Mum.

You've even started wearing her fucking clothes – Norman! Norman!'

Jo leaps on me and holds my hands above my head. Rosie sits on my legs and starts tickling me. I struggle to be let free, not because I'm not enjoying it, but because I have a shiny patch on my trousers under my anorak and don't want another one in front of my own sister. Then Rosie moves up my body and sits against my willie. It's hard instantly. The more I wriggle to get free, the worse it gets. If Jo wasn't here, it would be fantastic. As soon as I start to put a bit of rhythm into my movements, though, she jumps off.

'We better stop, Jo, He's getting a bit over-heated.'

My entire body feels like it's blushing, as I pull my anorak over my zip. My willie feels like it's about to burst. She must have felt it. If it hadn't been so embarrassing, it would have been about the best thing that's ever happened to me.

Rosie and Jo start putting things back into drawers, not folding them, just stuffing as many in as will fit. As my excitement subsides, my head starts throbbing again. Rosie smiles over as I rub my temples.

'Did I see you with Daniel this morning?'

Jo spins round and glares at her.

'. . . aye, Jo, your Daniel. I seen them.'

How the fuck do they know that cunt?

'What about him?'

'Jo fancies him rotten. She knocked him back, but it was just to make him more keen.'

'Fucking shut up. Dinnae listen to her, Jake.' Then she comes and sits beside me. 'Do you know him, but?'

'Sort of.'

This isn't real. My own sister fancies the guy that just tried to kill me. What if she starts going out with him? What if him and Shug start coming round here?

'What's he like? Do you know where he stays?'

This isn't fucking true. If I tell her Daniel's a bastard, it'll just make her fancy him even more. She's funny like that.

'He's all right. In fact, I really like him. He's a brilliant guy.'

Jo looks repulsed and I know I've done the right thing for everyone's sake. Rosie looks like she believes me too, so maybe she just didn't realise what was happening this morning. I think she really likes me. She would have definitely stopped them if she'd known.

Jo tells me to disappear cause they want to get changed. Why can't Jo just fucking disappear? Rosie probably wouldn't have minded me watching. I go through to the bathroom, look at my stupid purple nose in the mirror, then turn on the taps.

Chapter Eight

ANGIE

WORK'S FUNNY PECULIAR. Being completely over-dressed in my new outfit and full face doesn't help. The punters all look like they notice something's different about me, but nobody bothers to comment. Worst of all, Raymond doesn't mention anything about our drink tonight. It's like we're just pals again. Again? Who am I trying to kid? I've been thinking about it so much I've already convinced myself we're more than that. I'm chain-smoking just so I have something to fidget with when he's talking to me. It's ridiculous. I can hardly bring myself to look at him. He probably thinks I've gone off the idea, the way I'm acting.

Just before closing time, he comes up behind me as I'm cashing-up.

'You're not going home dressed like that.'

My head's in bits. Running through the figures five times, I get radically different totals. All I can focus on is Raymond drifting about behind me, coughing, humming, smelling gorgeous. On my seventh attempt, the totals tally with my first shot, so I hastily staple the two sums together and chuck them on his desk. My whole upper body is trembling.

Scurrying to the loo with my make-up bag, I huddle on the pan for a few minutes, trying to pull myself together. I can't even make a fist. I'm jittering so much the application of make-up is extremely perilous and I almost put my eye out, twice, with the mascara brush.

Raymond gives me a slow once-over and a wink of approval when I go back through. Fuck, I forgot to pluck that hair on my cheek.

'I'm sorry, Angie, but come out with me looking like that and I will not be responsible for my actions.'

Christ, a new frock and a layer of lippy and he thinks I'm Michelle Pfeiffer.

We go to the pub up the road. He points me to a seat in the corner and goes for drinks. I ask for a vodka but remind myself to take it easy. A vodka, amazing. It's good just to say the word again. I can taste it before he even hands me it.

The first sip, I swear, gives me a rush, right up my spine, that explodes inside my chest like my air-waves are all reopening. It tastes so strong, it must be a double. Right away, fuck, what a feeling. I am come home.

Raymond's talking about the post-Grand-National party Head Office have arranged next Saturday. I've avoided the last two as the thought of sitting beside a free bar with Vic without drinking or speaking to each other didn't really inspire.

'We should go. Honest. Wear that. Ian Dawson'll probably come in his pants.'

Stuck for words, I swallow my voddie in one and stand up to get Raymond another and me a Diet Coke. He's having none of it.

'Sit on your arse and put your purse away, woman. Your no out with your old man the night.'

I'm going to get steaming so quickly, I better watch it. Or maybe Vic's just made me neurotic. I'm sure I'll be fine, I always was. It was them was the problem. The next one slips down so painlessly, so gloriously, that it more than confirms that this is the case. Raymond doesn't fart around with mixers so he's knocking them back himself. The more I have, the stupider I feel for letting myself be scared off it for so long.

With each drink, we get increasingly tactile with one another and the more inevitable it seems that something is going to happen between us. Suddenly realising we're sitting holding hands, I stroke the bulging blue vein in Raymond's wrist and glance my fingers up and down his arm. After 17 years of nothingness it still comes naturally.

'I've wanted to do this for ages,' he whispers, 'I didn't think for a minute you'd be interested.'

Holding his cheek, I kiss him gently on the lips, just like that, no fucking about. He responds, his warm, soft pillows pecking gently round the side of my mouth. The boozy smell on his breath evokes all sorts of deeply buried memories and needs. These are the best bits in life. The brief moments between knowing you're going to fuck someone and actually doing it. That ache. All life comes from that ache.

A drunk woman at the next table suddenly prods us, demanding a light. Raymond uses the enforced intermission to get more drink. As I gaze at him waiting to get served, I imagine him fucking me on the bar, the bar stool, the floor. I could eat him. Handing me my drink, he slides back in.

'Why do I never fucking learn?'

'How d'you mean?'

'Married women. You're the bane of my fucking life.'

I'm slightly taken aback.

'You make a habit of this?'

'Nah, no like that. It's just my main big fuck-off relationship was with a married woman. You always hear women saying, "He kept saying he'd leave her", you know, all that shit? That was me. Don't get me wrong, it was amazing, really intense, but four years in, I'm wondering what the fuck I'm doing. Two years after we split up I was still trying to get my head back together. I'm still not out the woods. I just had this feeling I'd nothing to look forward to any more, till now.'

'That's exactly how I feel too, Ray. Can I call you Ray? Oh, all right then. You know, what did I have to look forward to – an "I Am Forty" badge, varicose veins, lung cancer?'

What am I on about varicose veins for? Am I trying to shag him or what?

He starts kissing me again. The booming jukebox just adds to my wonderful, happy, confident feeling. How could I let Vic deprive me of this for so long?

My glass is empty, disconcertingly empty. I try to go up to the bar, but Raymond intercepts again and gets us another couple each.

He looks rather forlorn as he sits back down.

'I need to tell you something, Angie. I've got a confession to make. You're too nice to bullshit.'

Oh, God. I knew it was too good to be true.

'Does it involve my husband . . . or Jeremy Beadle?'

Taking a long drink, he suddenly can't seem to look at me. Oh shit, what's wrong?

'Please, tell me, I'm starting to get the fear.'

'Fuck, Angie, I don't know how to say it.'

'Just say it, please.'

He circles my fingertips with his thumb.

'It's just . . . you know what I was saying about married women?'

'What about it?' Christ, talk about dragging it out.

'Fuck, Angie. I'm married as well, there, I've said it . . . and before you say, I know, I'm a bastard.'

I feel such relief, I want to hug him. That needn't change anything between us, need it? It just puts us in the same boat.

'And how long have you suffered from this affliction?'

He bows his head.

'Three years . . . well, four actually. I'd like to try and explain what it's like to you but it'll just sound like male bullshit, you know?'

'Can I decide that for myself?' I ask, depleting the first of my two drinks.

'It's embarrassing, though, it's such a cliché. I dunno why we got married. I was on the rebound, see, the married lassie, I didn't make that up. It wasnae fair of me. We're good pals, but there's nothing else there, no attraction, never has been.'

'At least you didn't say she didn't understand you.'

He's too into his spiel to hear me.

'. . . it's not just me though. She's got a degree, you know, in textile design, but she can't find work up here. She's just temping. It's like I'm holding her back. She thinks so too, I know she does. She just doesnae want to hurt me.'

I'm flattered that he feels the need to be honest with me, but by the end of my next drink, tales of his poor saint of a wife are beginning to grate a bit.

'I think I get the picture, Ray. I'm hardly one to talk.'

Wiping a wet Diet Coke patch from my lip, he kisses me again. Out the corner of my eye I see the two barmaids smirking at us but I don't give a damn. When he goes to the toilet again, I rush up for more drink.

'Same again?' asks the blonde one, pouring two doubles before I have time to reply. God, we really have been drinking doubles all along. I should be worried about being pissed but, at this precise moment, I don't fucking care any more. It feels like my life's been on pause since I stopped drinking.

Raymond swallows his in one when he gets back, without even realising I'd got another round in.

'That's why I'm so into this stuff. I'm here till closing every night, just avoiding going back. Trying to work up the balls to end it.'

'Is it that bad?'

'I'm in here lunch time as well. And when I've been doing the banking. I'm having swifties all the time. The money I spend avoiding her, I could get another flat, you know. It's fucking stupid.'

'You never seem pissed.'

Waving a packet of Extra-Strong Mints at me, he stumbles out his chair, supporting himself against the table to get his balance. He didn't seem drunk until he started talking about it, but to be honest, I quite like it. Drinking seems to give men a bit of depth, a sort of tragic quality. Raymond walks slowly and carefully to the bar, slipping money in the jukebox as he goes past. It's been silent for about ten minutes now. He makes a few selections as the barmaid milks the optics. Bringing them over, he leans on the table and kisses me.

'You're brilliant, Angie, you know that? I actually used to think you were a bit stuffy, you know, but you're brilliant,' and he skulks back over to finish picking his records. The intro to 'Stairway to Heaven' starts. He strums an invisible guitar on his way back.

'How do you mean, stuffy?'

He rolls his eyes as he tries to think what I'm referring to. His face seems to be going in slow motion.

'Eh, no, y'know, not so much stuffy . . . more like just unattainable, untouchable you know . . . slightly intimidating, I suppose. But you're not. You're the same as me.'

I'm not sure whether to take this as a compliment or an insult.

'So does your wife know you come here? Does she drink much?'

He roars out an exaggerated laugh. 'You're fucking kidding. She doesnae drink, oh no, not her. A poncey bottle of Chardonnay every fucking night, no, but that's not drinking, see. She's English, see. It's all right for her.' He shakes his glass in front of him. 'I'll tell you something. I get a damn sight more from this than I do from fucking marriage any day.'

I take a deep breath.

'I've been sober for three years. I dunno, tonight just seemed like the right time to finally say, "fuck it".'

I've actually admitted it to a new person. I can't believe it. Raymond drapes his arm across my shoulder and droops against me.

'You did that for me? You came off the wagon for me? Ma fucking wife wouldnae do that.'

Just as I start to feel fate has led us to each other, they start calling last orders. Jesus, it's 20 past 11. We've only had about five or six drinks. Raymond goes back to the bar, weaving slightly. When he returns this time, though, there's a sense that the end is nigh, for tonight anyway.

'Ah dinnae want to go home,' he whines, cuddling me again. We kiss, more desperately than before and I start to feel quite fraught. We're soon getting hassled by the bar staff to drink up. They seem slightly annoyed with us for some reason. I want to tell them I've not felt like this for years, I've not felt so fucking good. What would they know about it, though?

When we finally stumble out onto the street, the door is immediately bolted behind us. Raymond pins me against it, growling into my hair. His hands are up, squeezing at my breasts, nipping my nipples through my new bra.

'This isn't a one-off, Angie, is it? You won't go all cold on me on Monday?'

'I don't think that's likely.'

He kisses my forehead and takes a step back.

'I want it to be special the first time, though, not like this.'

I'm a bit puzzled.

'. . . well, you know. More special than against the door of a pub.'

The sentiment is lovely but, to tell the truth, I don't really care about it being special. I just want him to fuck me. It's only just starting to sink in what's happened tonight. I can't believe I'm not going to see him all weekend. I must tell them I want to start working Saturdays again. I'm starting to miss him before he's even gone. Could I finally have met my soulmate? Christ, wait till he sees me with my kit off.

Chapter Nine

JONI

WHOEVER TOLD ME the Barracuda was great was a fucking liar. We had to pay to get in, bottles of K cost three times what they do in the Paki shop, and the men here are all absolutely minging. It's not fair. The two Jackies from French got off with a couple of gorgeous Norwegians here a few weeks ago. They showed us photos and, honestly, wee Jackie's one was Christian Slater's double.

Typical, the night Rosie and me decide to come, it's crap. There's hardly any other women here, and the ones that are all look like hairdressers or footballers' wives, real old boilers. They stare at us like we're open sores.

The men are mostly greasy Arab types, hanging about in wee groups, not drinking, just standing staring at everyone in a really creepy way. The few white men are all either ancient or hackit, or have indentations on their wedding fingers where their rings usually are. Honest, Rosie pointed one out to me and I've spotted about five since.

Rosie gets chatted up right, left and centre. The Arabs are round her blonde hair like flies round shite. The music's so loud, and their English is so bad. She's just sitting insulting them – 'Is it against your religion to use deodorant?/Won't you get your hands chopped off for coming in a place like this?/Do you have your own corner shop?/Do you share a bedroom with your granny and seventeen sisters?' I just sit with my drink and listen to her. It's like I have a sign on my head that says, 'Please ignore me', not that I'd get off with any of these smelly bastards anyway. It'd be nice to knock someone back nonetheless.

We give it till half-ten before deciding it's not going to improve. Twenty quid down the drain and not a Norwegian in sight. When I get outside, Rosie's got her perfume out and is spraying it all over herself.

'Fuck, these bastards don't half stink. I'll never get a bag-off smelling like this.'

'So what'll we do now then? Just walk about till someone tries to get off with us?'

We try a couple of pubs opposite the ABC but they won't let me in 'cause they say I don't look 21. Rosie goes in a huff because, being a blonde, she can get in anywhere. That seems to be what it comes down to. I'd dye mine but, with my luck, I'd end up looking like Jimmy Savile.

We wander round to a pub in Bread Street, but come straight back out as it's tiny, the barmaid looks like a prostitute, and a group of drunken schemie pensioners are flirting with a topless go-go dancer.

This is getting desperate. We decide to try the Grassmarket but hear loud music coming out the Cas Rock Café on the way down and decide to give that a shot. It's more like it. A couple of Irish guys accost us almost immediately and buy us drinks. Mines is gorgeous, sort of like Sean Hughes – big Bambi eyes, beautiful pale skin. Rosie's is a skinhead – a wee bit overweight, OK-looking but no Ewan McGregor. She doesn't look too happy but, fuck it, I've just sat through two hours of the Arabian Nights. It's my turn now.

We go over to the corner and they try to chat us up over the racket of the band. I just sit smiling and agreeing with God knows what. They get us more drink. Sean's barking something in my ear but the music seems to be getting louder. The band must think they're really brilliant. I shout that I can't hear what he's saying, but he just smirks and grabs me. His kisses are nice and gentle at first but, as he gets more excited, he plunges his tongue deeper and deeper into my mouth until I can hardly breath. I try to push him off, but it just makes him worse. I try putting my tongue in his mouth to stop his getting into mine, but he bites it and laughs.

The fat one hasn't even attempted conversation with Rosie and is trying to push her down onto the seat. She's punching his arms and telling him to fuck off. I lean over to try and help but Sean grabs me again and puts his hand right up my dress. I squeeze my legs together, really tight to try and crush his fingers, but he's much stronger. I plead with him to stop, but he just keeps probing and biting at me. It's disgusting, I can feel his slavers running down my neck.

Suddenly the table with our drinks on it collapses onto its side and Fat Boy rolls, wailing, onto the floor grabbing his balls. Bouncers start running over and Sean leaps off me and starts pegging it through the crowd. I think they'll chase him but instead they grab Rosie and me and drag us outside.

'Aw, mister, that's not fair. They fucking attacked us. They tried to rape us in the middle of the pub.'

The bouncer gives us both the finger.

'Sorry, girls, we have a no-slapper policy, I'm afraid,' and the door slams. Loads of folk are looking out the windows at us, laughing. I wish I had a brick to throw so the glass would splinter in their stupid faces. I'm fucking raging.

'That's fucking terrible, that. It's like *The Accused* in there.'

I hear the pub door being unlocked again.

'It's OK boys, they're waiting for you,' and Sean and Fat Boy are suddenly about ten feet away from us again. Fat Boy's eyes are bulging. He comes limping towards Rosie like he's going to pull her head off.

We both take off, running into the path of a car on the way across Bread Street. The driver slams on his brakes and Rosie seems to stumble for a minute, like she's been hit. I hesitate, terrified, as I see them catching up with her.

'Hurry, hurry. Fucking Rosie, c'mon,' I scream. It seems to shock her back to life. We nash all the way down Bread Street, past the hotel and the paintball place, up an alleyway beside the vet's and squeeze behind a big industrial dustbin. Rosie is nearly crying and I'm so scared I'm getting a headache. Their big clumpy footsteps echo nearer and nearer, then run past. I'm really breathless but I try to hold it in, till we can't hear them any more.

'You're a fucking bitch. How could you lumber me with that fat ugly bastard?'

'I didn't know. I couldn't even hear what they were saying. My one put his hand right up my skirt. He was really slobbery. It was disgusting.'

'Big deal, Five-Bellies was trying to get me to wank him off. He had his cock out in the middle of the pub. I just yanked it as hard as I could. Did you see his face?' She starts laughing and I'm relieved that we're not going to fall out in this time of great crisis. Jesus, how do guys always want Rosie to X^2 them? How do they know? It must be her suggests it, it's too much of a coincidence otherwise. When I work up the nerve to look out from behind the bucket, the alley seems clear.

'What if they come back down again? Maybe we should just go home.'

'Aw, Rosie. Dinnae be like that. Just 'cause you've already got John. What about me? Just a wee bit longer. I'll take you for a pizza.'

'Where about?'

'I don't know, I've never taken anyone for a pizza before. There's loads of places round the corner though. Go on.'

'One pizza, then, but that's it. I've gone off the boil now,' she says, hobbling out onto Bread Street again. I notice blood running from a gash on the back of her leg but don't mention it or she'll definitely want to go home.

Instead, I grab her hand and drag her into the first place I smell garlic bread coming out of. This Italian guy with really dreamy eyes comes over and leads us to a table. He's really polite, pulling our chairs out for us, calling us madam and everything. Foreign men really know how to treat women. It's dead busy and there's this great racket of plates being clinked, diners talking, pizzas being thrown in and dragged out the oven, vegetables being chopped and meat being slapped about the place. There's hundreds of different lovely smells – garlic, peppers, steak, chips, all hanging together in the air. The waiter hands us menus, then goes over to another really nice Italian guy who's standing beside the cheesecakes. They both smile over at us.

'Look at the fucking prices. Fourteen pounds for a pizza. Ten pounds for a bottle of wine.'

I check my menu. 'Aye, but it won't be the same stuff we get. It'll be posh stuff. Will we get a bottle?'

'I thought you only had 20 pounds?'

'Nah, I took another 30 from Mum's electricity envelope this afternoon. There was nearly 200 quid in it. And Dad gave me money for us to go to the pictures the night.'

'Won't she notice? You better not say I knew if she catches you.'

'She won't catch me, she doesnae even check. I'll just blame it on Jake if she finds out.'

'Can we have a starter as well, then?'

I get Rosie to do the order, as I feel really silly. It's like we're just playing at being out for a meal. He takes ages to bring the wine but, when it arrives, it's worth it. Much nicer than the cheap stuff we nick out Scotmid, really cold and refreshing. We knock back our first glasses in one, then belch in unison and start giggling.

'Oh, beamer, that nice guy beside the cheesecakes heard that . . . naw, it's OK. He's smiling over. Aye, I love you too, darling,' and I blow a kiss at him. Rosie guffaws, splurting wine everywhere. A snobby older couple at the next table start giving us the evil eye. When I point this out to Rosie, it just makes us laugh all the more.

Before long I bring the conversation round to John. She's not even mentioned him since the video went missing. So much for us all living together.

'Mum's just being her normal awful self, but she's going out tomorrow and she hasnae asked him to come round yet. I don't even know if she's spoken to him. I havnae seen him.'

When the waiter brings our starters, I take one look at them and tell him he's brought the wrong things. He checks his notebook.

'Wan tamat moassarailla an wanna seafoot cockteel, yuh?'

We look at our plates in confusion, then Rosie tells him it's OK.

'I thought it was going to be all gorgeous stringy melted cheese. What the fuck is this? I only like tomatoes in a sauce,' she whines, picking up a bit cheese, trying to take a bite and throwing it back down on her plate in disgust. 'Fuck, it's raw. It doesn't even taste of anything. It's like chewing on a rubber.'

'What about me,' I say, lifting something up on my fork that looks like a washing-machine part. I try to take a bite. It tastes like a washing-machine part. I spit it onto my plate. The rest of it's mussels, which I really hate, and white things that are just like big lumps of fat. There's a few prawns in there but I can't bear to go near them as they're touching the washing-machine parts.

'I don't believe this. I thought it was going to be shrimps and nice wee bits of fish.'

Rosie's looking worried now.

'What'll we do. We cannae just leave it all. They'll think we're stupid. It must be real food if it's busy like this.'

I hand her across my napkin. 'Here, put some of the cheese in that. Heat it up in the microwave when you get home.' She does as I say.

'Really, you think it's the same stuff you get on pizzas? It's in wee bits, though, is it no?'

She's actually being serious. What a dippit.

'It's grated. Wee bits . . . fuck . . .'

She stuffs it in her bag. 'Aye, OK, OK. So you think I'm an idiot.'

I spoon some of the yuck off my plate and under the table. Rosie yelps and grabs the spoon off me.

'Stop it. One of your intestines just hit my leg. That's fine. They surely cannae expect you to eat any more than that. It's disgusting.'

The snobby couple are nebbing at us again. I wish they would just fuck off back to Corstorphine. We're paying the same for our food as they are. I nudge the waiter the next time he goes past and ask him to take our plates away. If I have to look at the entrails in front of me any longer, it'll put me off my pizza.

'Was efrything hokay?'

'Mmh, yes, lovely,' we say in one of our psychic duets as we stare up at his big dreamy eyes.

The snobby man at our side grabs him and starts moaning on about having to wait 20 minutes for his pudding. The waiter tries to explain but the snobby man won't let him get a word in.

'It'll take even longer if that wanker keeps holding him up,' says Rosie really loudly.

The waiter gives us both a smile. The snobby man turns to us, his face all purple and wrinkled with temper. 'If I require a running commentary from a couple of inebriated Lolitas, I'll bloody ask.'

It really gets us giggling again. What's he on about? Then he's back on the waiter. Eventually Cheesecake Man comes over with two absolutely enormous knickerbocker glory type creations, with sparklers showering out the top.

'Wis are comblimends.'

'Fucking hell, they're giving him it for nothing,' yells Rosie. 'That's no fair. Our things were rubbish but we didn't go on about it and we have to pay.'

I pour her some more wine, to shut her up. I can't understand the justice of it myself, but posh man looks like a bit of a nutter. We don't need another radge chasing us about.

When they bring over our main courses, it silences us completely. Rosie's ordered fish and chips. I was really embarrassed when she asked for it, y'know, it's a bit insulting to the Italian guys to order the one Scottish thing on the menu. Now it's arrived though, I'm sort of regretting getting a pizza 'cause, although mines looks great, there's just one of it. Rosie's got chips and salad and peas and bits of lemon. Desperate not to be outdone when I'm the one paying for it, I order a side portion of chips.

Oh, my God, it's absolutely the best pizza I've ever tasted. It's about twice the size of the family ones you get in Iceland. There's tons of cheese and it's really greasy and buttery on top. I see Rosie eyeing up my mozzarella a few times but since she doesn't offer me a bit fish, I just ignore her.

By the time he brings my chips, I'm stuffed. I've only eaten the cheesy bits in the middle and left the crust, but I can hardly move. Rosie's left her salad, peas, eaten the chips, and picked all the batter off the fish. It's a waste but, to be honest, it's the only bit I like myself. As soon as he realises we've finished, Cheesecake Man's over, trying to entice us with his puddings. We both lean back in our chairs and rub our bellies, but he keeps trying to tempt us and eventually takes Rosie's hand and pulls her over to the sweet trolley. She seems to be over there for ages. I finish the Leibfräumilch.

When the bitch finally comes back over, she's beaming and looking really pleased with herself.

'Did you give him a pull for a bit Black Forest Gateau?' I mutter, emptying my glass before she has a chance to ask for some.

'Be like that if you want. I've just arranged for us to meet them both outside when they go on their breaks in ten minutes. If you dinnae want to come, though, that's fine by me.'

'Who, the nice waiter as well?'

'Uh huh,' she grins, blowing on her nails, '. . . just call me the queen of lurve.'

God, I feel rotten for having drunk all the wine now, although they probably both fancy Rosie. The waiter's the best-looking but I don't know if I'd want to go out with someone as attractive as that. I could never trust him. Cheesecake Man's a bit fat and baldy but he's got a really kind, smiley face. He'd be much less likely to go with other women. And he's older too, probably about 30.

'Which one do you fancy?'

'I don't mind. Take your pick. It's my thank-you to you for getting all the drinks tonight,' she says magnanimously.

Handsome Boy brings over the bill. Fucking hell, it's 32 pounds, for the middle of a pizza and some fish batter. I didn't even touch my chips, they'll probably just stick them in the microwave and give them to someone else. I count the money out onto the wee saucer. The last four pounds I have to give them in bronze and silver. Hopefully the two Tallies'll buy us drink.

We go and stand outside. The street is absolutely teeming with people moving on to nightclubs, well-pissed – fighting, singing, peeing all over the place – nice. Fuck, why didn't I steal more money? I want to go to a club. You have to pay to get in, so you maybe don't get as many head-cases there.

'So what did Cheesecake Man say? Did he mention me?'

'Just that they wanted to meet us. He's hardly going to say, oh, and by the way, I fancy your pal. They're Italian, for God's sake. They're the most romantic men in the world. Shh, here they're coming. Try not to seem desperate.'

'Rosie, Rosie, I've only got 90 pence left. I can't afford to get them a drink or anything.'

She looks annoyed.

'Fuck, I don't even have a bus fare. You should have said before we went for the meal.'

The restaurant door swings open. Cheesecake Man puts his arm round Rosie's waist. Handsome Boy and me straggle nervously behind.

'I Antonio,' he announces as we turn into Morrison Street. He is so gorgeous.

'I . . . I'm Jo . . . Joni,' I stammer, pathetically.

'Ah, Joni Forster, I see . . . *Silence ov Lambs.*'

What's he on about?

'Not Jodie, Joni, Joni.'

'Ah Joni, Joni, OK, s'foney, you look juslike Joni Forster.'

Jesus, thanks a lot. He thinks I look like a 40-year-old lesbian with a face like a bag of spanners. Cheers, pal. I knew it. He does think I'm a dog.

Walking past the pub I'm expecting to go into, Cheesecake Man leads us into the car park. Brilliant. Most romantic men in the world, right enough. Then bloody Rosie and him get into a car and just leave me and Antonio standing there. He takes my hand.

'We walk. The buildings all lit up. Ferry beautiful.'

Great, I'm going to get a boring lecture on Edinburgh architecture from a man who thinks I'm a pig while Rosie gets shagged by the bloke I fancy. What's so fucking irresistible about her? Just 'cause she's got blonde hair and a strong wrist.

We walk to the back of the car park and sit down on the grass verge.

'How-long-do-you-get-for-your-break?' I say very slowly so he'll understand me.

'Fefteen minute hoanly. Then we on till two. You wait till two?'

Fuck, I've only got 90 pence left and this stunning creature wants me to meet him after work. Maybe that's why he's not making a move now. We can't possibly sit about for another two hours, though. It's getting freezing.

'We're going home soon. I could give you my phone number.'

Antonio laughs and I feel really stupid. Then he pulls a huge joint from his inside jacket pocket, lights up, and I don't feel quite so bad. Ha ha, spew Rosie. He takes ages in between tokes and has about six before he hands it to me. It smells really, really strong, like I've never smelt before. He maybe has Mafia connections. Lying back on the grass, he lets out a loud, smoky groan. I take three puffs, pausing in between each like he did, and feel really pleasantly numb. It's nice to spend time with a guy who doesn't jump on you right away. Maybe Rosie and me could go and sit in a bar till two and share a Diet Coke.

We have one more hit of the joint each, then walk back towards the car. The windows look a bit steamed up as we approach. That jammy bitch better not have done it. Antonio opens the driver's door and there's a bit of a scramble within. Cheesecake Man emerges, smiling, takes a few tokes on the joint and stands on it. Rosie comes out the other side with a big grin on her face. I'm so glad she missed the spliff.

Then, with a sudden, 'See yiz later, girls,' they walk quickly back towards the street, deserting us. Were they taking the piss out our accents? I'm absolutely gutted. Why didn't I say I'd meet him? What a stupid bitch.

'Well?' asks Rosie as we walk through the maze of cars.

'Well, what?'

'Did anything happen? Where did youz go?'

'We just had a joint. It was amazing stuff as well, I'm fucking wasted. He wants me to meet him later.'

She ignores the mention of my potential date.

'You coulda kepties a bit. Specially since I got money for more drink.' She produces a tenner from her cleavage.

'Fuck, what did you do? Did you shag him?'

She looks offended.

'What, for a tenner? Cheeky cow.'

'Well, what then?'

'You know.'

'Know what?' I'm starting to get annoyed now.

'I gave him a gobble. I told him the meal cost more than we thought and we'd no money left and he said if I sucked him off he'd give me a fiver. I must've been good eh, he gave me twice that.'

I'm stunned with envy.

'But that's like being a tart.'

She grabs my arm and pulls me back towards Lothian Road.

'Is it fuck. I didn't shag him or anything. We needed money and I got us it.'

'You should have shagged him. We could have gone to a club.'

'I haven't got any on my face, have I?' she asks, dead cocky, as the green man beep-beep-beeps. I ignore her. I'm going to tell John she's two-timing him, slag. Still, at least we can afford more drink now.

'What about the Rutland? That's pretty bag-offy, is it no?'

'Aye, if you want to share a drink and walk home. It's

really dear. And folk steal your drinks as soon as you've bought them.'

'And how are you such an expert?'

'John sometimes goes there.'

Oh John, see, she's rubbing it in again. How am I ever supposed to get a boyfriend when she's got about two dozen?

'Aw, come on, I just want to go somewhere and have a seat. I feel a bit funny.'

I am feeling a bit funny. Sort of dizzy and scared and really clammy.

'Serves you right for not leaving me any.'

We stop outside Century 2000 and have a look at the posters to see what's going on. There's a huge queue outside, though, and it probably costs money. I try to look inside to see what it's like, then the bouncer opens the door to let people out and suddenly Sean Hughes and the fat skinhead are in front of us again. I freeze for a second, as I don't believe what I'm seeing. As soon as we make eye contact, though, it becomes very real. When I turn round, Rosie's already bolting down past the queue. I look behind to see if they're following us. They are, at speed.

When I get down to King Stables Road, Rosie's vanished. I don't have time to look for her as that pair are in hot pursuit. I just sprint through all the milling, drunken people, screaming. When I get to the bottom of Lothian Road, I look back. The fat guy is waiting for a car to go past, Sean is only a few feet away, but suddenly trips up and falls onto the pavement. He's so pissed he keeps running. Nashing down some steps, I run away round the back of the church. I stand, panting, against the bricks for a minute, then hold my breath and listen for any sound. Nothing. Then it starts to register where I actually am — in a fucking graveyard. I'm alone, I'm wasted, it's late on a Friday night and I'm in the middle of a fucking graveyard with two mad Irishmen chasing me. They could be murdering Rosie at this very moment. Where the fuck did she go? Fuck, she's got all the money as well. I can't even afford the night bus now.

Chapter Ten

VIC

THE PHONE RINGING wakes me at quarter to one. A bad feeling washes over me as I jump out the chair to answer it.

'Dad . . . help me, Dad.'

'Jesus, what it is, Jo? Are you OK?'

'Aaaww, Dad, um scared. Come and get me, puleeease.'

'Where are you?'

'The phones outside the Caley Hotel. There's a scary guy saying he's got AIDS. Hurry.'

Think, think, where should I meet her?

'Dad, please . . .' and the line goes dead. I'm shaking as I dial 1471 and return the call. Christ, I can't believe I fell asleep. It rings one . . . two . . . three times.

'Who's that?'

'Joni, sweetheart, what happened?'

'I was away to wait on you.'

'OK, OK, just hang on. I'll be there soon. Stand somewhere safe.'

'Like where?'

'I dunno. Find an adult . . . no . . . dinnae. Just stand next to the hotel. Dinnae speak to anyone.'

Putting down the receiver, I'm confronted by six empty Beck's bottles. I'll be way over the limit. It is my bloody daughter we're talking about here, though. As long as they stop me on the way back.

Bursting into Jake's room, I put the light on. There's a frantic rustling and smoothing of the duvet.

'Aw, Dad, knock first, eh?'

I switch it back off and look the other way.

'Look, I'm sorry. Jo's up the town bubbling and greeting. I'm just going out to get her. Is Mum back?'

'She's your wife,' he whines.

Shutting the door, I check my reflection in the hall mirror. God, I look half-cut.

It's hard not to speed. Once I'm onto the Western Approach Road, I take it up to eighty, but the steering goes to buggery. The lights at the junction with Lothian Road seem to have an aversion to turning green. I'll end up getting there a minute too late. A purple-faced ox in a suede jacket bangs another man's head against the Shakespeare. As the lights start to change, I go from 0 to 60 in about five seconds.

There's crowds of people outside the hotel, but none of them is Joni. Deserting the car, I start pushing through them, staring at all these drunken mental faces in a complete panic. A couple of blokes get shirty because I've parked in the taxi lane but I don't care, I just want to find my baby. If she's not here, I'll kill myself. Then, right at the back, from one of the benches, her eyes meet mine.

'Aw, Dad, get back in the car. What an embarrassment,' she wails, before turning to apologise for me to a black guy at her side. What the hell is this? He looks like her pimp. Her eyes are Jim-Morrison-droopy as she slurs at him. Joni – my baby, my angel – is out her bloody tree.

'Come on love, come home,' I say, extending my hand to her.

'Stop it. I'm OK now. Just lend me money for a taxi?'

'Jo, will you get in the bloody car, now.'

I grab her wrist, trying to get her away before I panel the

bastard. I'm not racist, but the sight of my 15-year-old daughter throwing herself at some dodgy darkie is pretty hard to stomach. Pulling free, she launches herself through the crowd. I'm too old for this sort of shit.

By the time I catch up with her she's, thankfully, already sulking in the back seat. One of the guys that moaned about my parking bangs his fists off the bonnet and screams abuse as we drive off. Taxi-rank rage, I assume.

'Go on then, Joni, enlighten me. Was that the guy with AIDS?'

'Eh?'

'Lover-boy on the bench.'

'Oh you would assume that, eh? He's black, so he must have AIDS, charming.'

'Well, I don't know, do I? Who was he, then? What are you doing up town, dressed like that at one o'clock in the morning? You're 15 years old.'

'Use your imagination,' she drawls, pretending to yawn.

'You've been drinking, eh? Have you taken anything else? Jesus, Jo, you look like a junkie. Should I take you up the hospital and get you checked out?'

'For God's sake, Dad, chill out. I'm not exactly OD'ing, am I?'

'Why, what've you taken?'

'I was at the pictures.'

'You don't get in a state like that at the pictures. What did you go to see, like?'

'Stop picking on me. You're always picking on me.'

How come no matter how badly she behaves, I always end up feeling like the bastard of the piece?

We pass behind the Conference Centre. The whole road is lined with new buildings I didn't even notice on the way along.

'Changed a fair bit round here, eh? See where that big

mirrored building is now? We bought the living-room carpet there.'

For some unfathomable reason, this comment reduces her to tears.

'Shut up about it. I saw it earlier. Can't you just take me back there. I'm supposed to be meeting someone at two.'

'Who? What sort of person arranges to meet a 15-year-old lassie at two in the morning?'

Another long silence. As I come off the motorway at the top of Ardmillan, an over-zealous old dear in a grey Volvo runs a red light and almost crashes into the side of us. Slamming on the brakes, I hear Joni let out a loud groan, followed by frantic retching sounds.

'Aw, hang on, sweetheart, we're nearly home. Not in the motor, please.'

Bleaugh! I grab a plastic bag out the glove compartment, but by then the horse has well and truly bolted.

Dropping her off at the flat, I open all the car windows and try to find a parking space. The powerful stench of garlic vomit is making my eyes nip. After a couple of minutes, I have to drive back to ours and double-park before I start hurling myself. As I climb the stair, I anticipate a massive scene with Angie and Jo. It'll be all my fault, no doubt. There's no sign of her. Jo has collapsed on her bed, still in her vomity prostitute outfit. What is it with women and drink?

'C'mon, sweetheart. You cannae go to sleep like that.'

Groaning, she looks like she's about to throw up again but has turned to rubber. I practically have to carry her to the toilet. God, the whole house'll be stinking. Plopping a couple of Disprin into a glass, I wait for her to stop puking. They say you should drink plenty if you've taken ecstasy, so I make her swallow two pints of water, just in case.

I look at her semolina complexion and red zombie eyes

as she washes crusted sick off her chin. She notices me in the mirror.

'Stop staring at me like that. You're giving me the creeps.'

'Why do you hate me, Jo? I'm on your side.'

'And other clichés.'

She stumbles past me to her room and slams the door. I stand outside, listening to her banging around, trying to get undressed. Waiting till I hear her getting into bed, I go in to check on her.

'Feeling any better? Look, dinnae lie on your back in case you're sick again. I don't want you doing a Jimi Hendrix on me.'

She grunts onto her side and I start to leave.

'Dad?'

'Uh huh?'

'Nah, nothing.'

'Are you sure?'

'I'm trying to get to sleep.'

As I close the door, I hear the bed squeak as she turns onto her back again. I have to fill a basin via the kettle and a few saucepans to clean the motor out. I used all the hot water earlier, bloody waste, having my biannual bath, to sit and drink beer on my own. By the time I got round to phoning Ronnie, he'd arranged to go out and play pool. He said he'd phone me back so I could join them, but didn't bother his arse. Also, when I phoned up about tickets for the football, I found out it's an away game. I've not had the balls to tell Dad or Jake yet. How come everything I touch turns to shit?

It takes 40 minutes, and three jaunts upstairs for fresh water, to eradicate the smell of cheesy, garlic alcohol from the car. It's in between the seats, down the doors, everywhere. I bet it was deliberate.

When I finally get back in, I get a crushing band of pain across my chest, as I stick the three stinky towels I've been using on a quick-wash. Sod the neighbours. I'm not explaining it all to Ange in the morning.

When I check Joni again, she's asleep. As I roll her onto her side, she grunts, but doesn't wake up, thank God. Angie is snoring through the wall. Fantastic, just fantastic. Jan pees on the hall carpet as I get the duvet out the cupboard. I hum 'Perfect Day' to myself as I go through to the settee.

Chapter Eleven

JAKE

I'M ABOUT TO go through for *Live and Kicking* when I hear Mum shouting. God, she's started early this morning. This'll be the week for sure that Zoe Ball gets her kit off in the first five minutes. Zoe is a babe. I listen to her radio show under the duvet every morning, before I get up, and pretend she's under there with me. It's quite a challenge trying to come in between the records.

The front door slams at ten past nine, so I brave it through to the colour telly. Dad's sitting with a tube of Superglue and his Arthur Scargill Toby jug, which is in several pieces. It is, was, his pride and joy because some old Commie gave him it during the miners' strike. Dad thinks the miners' strike was the most significant thing that ever happened in the history of mankind. It sounded pretty stupid to me. The miners went on strike, so they closed down all the mines. What's so great about that? They must have hated being miners. If all the kids went on strike, would they close down the schools? Maybe it wasn't such a bad thing.

'Mum's gone to her pal's for a couple of days. I made her a coffee. It seemed to antagonise her,' he mutters, trying to work out what way up the dismembered jug handle goes. I wish he'd piss off and leave me with Zoe. She's wearing a really tight top that shows off her tits in a way that shouldn't be allowed on children's TV. Why couldn't Dad've married someone like her? Imagine that tucking you in at night.

He goes to make breakfast but his timing is awful and I'm left watching a stupid cartoon with a stiffie. By the time Zoe comes back on, he's back through with two bacon rolls and a glass of Ribena. Sitting back down with his ugly Arthur mug, he stares at my nose.

'What happened to you? You look like W. C. Fields.'

Shit, I forgot to check my face when I got up.

'Eh, oh nothing. I got hit by a football.'

He looks hurt and surprised.

'Football? What about my five-a-side?'

'Nah, not playing, I was walking through the park. Anyway, what happened with Jo last night? What did she do?'

'Apart from spewing all over the car, I'm not at all sure.'

'Was she drunk?'

'From the evidence I've gathered so far, my professional opinion would be, yes, she was guttered.'

'Is that why Mum was shouting?'

He pulls a strange face. I check the front of my jammies, then he lets out an 'oof' noise and grabs his chest. This doesn't alarm me. Dad does it all the time. He's always imagining there's stuff wrong with him – cancer, brain tumours. Heart attack is his current favourite, since Father Ted died. Dad loved Father Ted and cried when it said on the news he was dead. For days, all he could say was, 'Forty-five . . . God . . . only forty-five,' as if that was young or something. If you just ignore him, he tends to forget about it after a few minutes. I ignore him.

'I've buggered up on the football I'm afraid. It's at Parkhead. I don't know what I was thinking.'

Wasn't that the whole point? A day in Glasgow at a massive big stadium? Who wants to go to poxy Tynecastle? They've maybe got the new stand, but you can still see Gorgie outside, it spoils it. He's really apologetic and gets another pain in his chest. It's starting to bug me, so I take my Ribena and go through to annoy Jo.

Taking a run across the room, I launch myself onto her bed, then, brilliantly, manage to squeeze out a really loud, smelly fart. Chucking me onto the floor, she's immediately on top of me, slapping me round my sore head.

'Bastard, bastard, dirty little bastard.'

Dad comes in, shakes his head and says, 'Jake, stop bothering your sister, or she'll stab you,' then shuts the door again.

Jo grabs me by the throat.

'I will as well, you clarty little shit. Stop acting like a fucking five-year-old.'

Wrestling free, I cower over to her swivel chair.

'. . . you better not fart again, I'm warning you.'

I spin round and round.

'So what happened last night? Dad said you spewed in the car. Were you on eckies or summat?'

'You're too immature to discuss it with,' she says smugly, getting back into bed.

'Aw, c'mon Jo, tellies. I winnae say anything.'

'Use your imagination. You're good at that.'

I go over and jump on the bed again. Her face turns greyish-green and she runs out the room, with sick bubbling between her fingers. The toilet door slamming is followed by long, loud puking sounds that make me feel sick as well. When she comes out ten minutes later, she looks like something that's been dead for a week.

'I was just bringing up bile.'

'Cheers, Jo. I really wanted to know that.'

Dad appears with a glass of fizzing somethingness, fussing over her. She grabs it off him without even saying thanks and goes back to bed. I decide to play the computer. Dad follows me through. I play Solitaire to illustrate just how desperate my current computer game situation is.

'D'you still want to come and see Granda with me? We could go for a run. Stop off and have a fish supper.'

Whoopee! I didn't want to see Granda, I wanted to go to Parkhead. Granda's a wimp, like Dad. It's depressing being with them, 'cause it makes me think I'm going to end up like that, too.

'Nah, Dad. It's OK.'

'Aw c'mon. We could maybe stop into PC World on the way back.'

'Mmh, well, I suppose it has been a while since I've seen him.'

Bollocks, I'll have to go now. He's gone all shiny and happy. At least I'll get my *Fifa 98*.

I go to clean my teeth and check out my horrible purple nose and the graze on my cheek. If it was just the cheek, it would look all right, quite hard, but the nose makes me look like something out an Askit commercial. Jo better not start going about with that bastarding Daniel although, hopefully if she does he'll beat her up too.

The car's absolutely minging. I refuse to get in until Dad does something to get rid of the stink. He gives it the once-over with a bottle of aftershave, but then it smells like Mr Russell and it's almost worse. Even the dog looks offended as we force her into the back seat. Once she's found a stray bit sick to lick, though, she's fine. I try to lose myself in my Game Boy, to take my mind off it but Dad's so pleased we're out together he won't stop talking.

'Jake, will you answer me something honestly. You won't get into trouble.'

Oh, here we go.

'Mmh?'

'You know, at school, has anyone ever offered you or Joni drugs? Like, if you wanted to get drugs at school, would you know who to ask?'

'Why, what are you after? Speed? Eckies? You'd have to ask the headmaster about that. He does Class As.'

The radge looks like he actually believes me. I can't stop myself laughing.

'It's not funny, Jake. Y'know what I mean. D'you know anyone that takes drugs? Does Joni?'

'Mr Russell, the gym teacher, he's on crack. So are a few of the relief teachers, but they only let you try it if you take biology.'

We stop at the lights and he gets all intense.

'Look, Jake, has Joni ever said anything to you about drugs?'

'What are you asking me for? She's the one that puked everywhere. Ask her.'

'And she'd tell me the truth? C'mon, she'll batter me if I ask her.'

'Ditto.'

The lights turn green and we drive past McDonald's. There's a brief silence, very brief.

'Seriously though, Jake. Has Joni said anything to you whatsoever about drugs?'

'Aw, Dad, if you're gonna keep going on about it, I'm going home.'

This finally shuts him up. What's he on about anyway? As if he never took drugs in the 70s. And look what Mum used to be like. It's all so centred round him worrying about Joni as well. It makes me want to go out and do a River Phoenix.

Granda's at the end of his path, waiting, when we turn into the street. He goes back in the house when he sees the car.

'Bugger, he's got his Hearts scarf on and everything. I haven't told him about the match yet, shit.'

We go through the open front door, to the back of the house

where Granda is standing, looking out the window. He pretends to get a big surprise when Dad says hello and Jan sticks her nose up his arse. Poor bastard, he's done up like he's going for his knighthood. He always looks really, really smart, even though he just sits round the house on his own. Today, seriously, for the football, he's got on a grey suit, white shirt with matching hankie, silk tie and camel overcoat. This with a manky Hearts scarf. Giving me a yucky big cuddle, he tells me how grown-up I'm looking. He doesn't seem to notice my purple nose, but he's half blind anyway. Then he starts fussing around, digging things out, trying to give me things – old Hearts programmes from the 60s and 70s, a pile of computer magazines I've already got that he picked up for me in a second-hand shop, a big bag of mini Mars bars, a tenner. Dad has to tell him to stop eventually, says it's embarrassing. Speak for yourself, I think, with my arms full of booty.

When Dad explains about the football, he just smiles and slides his scarf off.

'Don't worry about it, that's fine. A drive with my two favourite people'll be just smashing.'

God, why do people do that all the time? Pretend to be happy when they're sad? How has the human race got this far when everyone says the exact opposite of what they mean?

Granda screws up his face when we get in the car.

'That's rather an unusual aroma, son. Is there a dead homosexual in the boot?'

Dad laughs at his attempted joke. So do I. It's a shame for the old codger.

'Jo got a bit carsick. Sorry, does it smell really bad?'

This is the understatement of the year but Granda just grins and opens the window. Dad puts on a rubbishy rock-and-roll tape and gets Granda to guess who all the groups are. I only know a couple of them, from films, but Granda should be on *University*

Challenge, honestly. He knows who's singing each one, the year, who sang the original. It's just a pity the bands are all dross. It's so obvious why there's been a revival of everything except rock-and-roll. It's fucking gash.

We don't seem to actually be going anywhere. Dad's just going round in circles, pointing out all these new buildings and saying how wonderful the crappy old shops and car parks that used to be there were. I think they look great myself, really modern and Bladerunnerish. After an hour of it though, I'm bored shitless.

The awful bop-shoo-wop tape finally finishes, thank fuck. Then dad leans over and sticks in something even worse – the tape he used to play in the car when we were wee. It was OK when I was five, but it just makes me cringe now. What if the polis pull us over when we're listening to 'Puff the Magic Dragon'? They'll think we're on a day trip from the Royal Ed. Dad sings along to the first verse, but gets so many words wrong he gives up while he still has his dignity. Granda's lapping it up, but he's just a big bairn anyway.

Next up is 'Calling Occupants . . .' I used to crease myself every time they sang 'Interplanetary crapped'. The singer gave me the creeps though. She looked like she'd actually come off a spaceship.

Dad wants to show us where the new Parliament's going to be but I'm getting sick of his shitey guided tour and start complaining. We make a detour towards Portobello instead. That really awful 'Superman' song by Black Lace comes on. I make Dad fast-forward it. Joni and me used to do our own stupid wee dance to it when we were bairns. Dad made us do it in front of the whole family, three Christmases in a row. No wonder Auntie Jean doesn't speak to us any more.

Oh, fuck, it gets worse. Next up's 'Born Free'. As we drive along the seafront to Eastfield, Dad and Granda start singing their lungs out, really giving it laldy. Dad knows all the words to this one, and wants everyone to know it. It's like the sort of music they play in shopping centres. My God, he's even singing the bits where it's just the orchestra. It's a shame, really. He's about as free as a goldfish.

'Mind you took me to see the film when I was six? I wanted to be a vet for years after,' Dad says to Granda. What a memory he's got.

'Aye, till you tried to practise on Mrs McKenzie's cat and it clawed you in the face, mind? I'm sure it didn't even need an appendectomy,' giggles Granda.

Dad parks the car next to the toilets and we get Jan out the back. Exhausted by the journey, she collapses in a heap and we have to drag her along the prom. Once she's sniffed a few shites and found a used condom to chew, though, she seems to get her bearings. There's a cold wind blowing across the sand but the place is completely deserted, which is the way I like it. I'm still wondering what could possibly have been going through Dad's mind when he was singing that song. It's probably easier to be born free when you live on a massive nature reserve in the middle of Africa and have lions for pets. Maybe Dad tortured small animals because he resented not having that. How did he end up so boring?

When we get along to the arcade, Granda empties his pockets and gives me about four pounds in loose change. Dad takes Jan back along to get the car. I'm straight over to the clay-pigeon-shooting machine. The graphics are crap, but you get to hold a real gun and it feels really heavy and sexy. What did they have to ban guns for, just when I was nearly old enough to own one?

Eeeeeh, bang, eeeeh, bang, eeeeh, bang, shit, missed them all.

I'd like to take a gun to school and waste anyone that tried to give me a hard time. Why couldn't that Thomas Hamilton guy have come to our gym when Mr Russell was taking Shug's class?

Imagining the next three lights are Mr Russell, Shug and Daniel, I only manage to hit Daniel. Granda gets behind me and tries to show me how to hold the gun properly. I hate when people touch me but I have to let him, because he's old. Doing it how he tells me just makes me even crapper and I miss about 15 in a row. Granda puts in another pound, takes the gun off me, and has a go.

Eeeeh, bang, eeeeh, bang, eeeeh, bang. Bastard gets them all first time, then the second time, and the third. I cheer and pretend to be pleased for him but inside I'm pissed off. He shouldn't even be having a shot. It's supposed to be for kids. He offers to pay for me to have another go, but I don't want to now. I'll just look crap.

Leaving him with his gun, I go over to the fruit machines. I get five holds in a row, but don't know what to do with them, so win nothing. Granda's over at my side again, pumping coins into a two-pence machine. Almost immediately it starts chugging out money. For fuck's sake.

'I should come here more often.'

'It's only two-pence pieces,' I say sarcastically. I just want to go home. This is so fucking tedious.

Sticking my last pound in a simulated driving game, I crash on the first corner. Not wanting to watch Granda win the arcade pentathlon, though, I just stay there, staring at the Game Over sign.

By the time Dad comes back, Granda's having a coffee in the arcade café, chatting up the tea lady. You can tell he doesn't get out much. He never even asked if I wanted something to eat.

I tell Dad I want to go home. He looks all hurt, but I've been humouring them both for bloody hours now. Why did I agree to this? I want to go and see if that Sean's in, and get a shot on the Internet.

'Dad, we better get going if we want to get to PC World.'

He puts his hand up to his face. 'Oh, shit, I forgot all about it. D'you mind if we give it a miss today? I think Granda's a bit puggled.'

Great, absolutely fucking marvellous. I've been cheated out of a whole non-school day of my life for nothing. I could have been surfing the Net. I could have been Rangers against AC Milan, 45 minutes each half, and beat them 100–0 three times, by now. But instead I've spent a whole day looking at poxy buildings and having to listen to these two old farts. Lying bastard. I hope I die before I'm 16, I never want to end up selfish like that.

Chapter Twelve

ANGIE

IT'S QUARTER TO six. This time yesterday, it was all about to begin. Caroline, my friend on community care, is sitting opposite me. We went out for lunch, then a couple of drinks, but, now we're back at hers, the conversation has dried up. The last three times she was sectioned, I never visited. Her last two overdoses, she phoned and asked me to help her do it properly, but I didn't. When she was being bullied in the women's refuge and asked me out for a drink to get it off her chest, I pretended I was going on holiday. But this is important, this is about me. So I phoned her up despite all that and said, 'Caroline, sorry I've not been in touch. Why don't I come round for the weekend and make it up to you? Howya doing anyway?'

'How d'you think I'm doing?'

I'd have put the phone straight back down again, but who else is there? Where else can I be the person I was three years ago without anyone noticing? Besides, Care in the Community means use me and abuse me, I don't have anyone left I trust enough to complain to. Perfect.

Lunch wasn't too bad, with people to look at and other conversations to eavesdrop on. I let Caroline ramble on about all the awful things she'd been trying to tell me over the phone for the past four years. I'd heard most of it before, so I suppose it must be genuine. It's the only way I can gauge what's true and what's imagined with her nowadays. It was an excuse to get wellied into the Chardonnay, if nothing else.

After, I took her to a pub, with the intention of drinking myself stupid enough to get a taxi to work. In the end, I got sick of paying two pound a time for tiny measures and I couldn't shake Caroline off when it got time to go, so now we're back at her place with a bottle of vodka.

I'm pouring drinks through in the filthy kitchen because she's stopped taking her medication, so I don't want her getting too pissed. Since I made her go halfers, I make sure my drink isn't three shades lighter than hers or she might get a bit touchy. How come there's 28 pub measures in a bottle of vodka but when you pour them yourself you only get about six?

When I go back through, she's put the radio on. Repetitious rave-type music. It sounds really uppy and high but Caroline's face looks like it should be staring through the fence at Belsen.

'This programme used to gear me up for Saturday nights. Now it *is* my fucking Saturday night.'

'You could still go out. People go to clubs on their own. If you just want to dance . . .'

'Oh no no no. Too many bad people out there.'

Why does everything have to be a conspiracy with Caroline? I'd like to tell her about Raymond but she might start using it to try and get me to come and see her more often. Mind you, she doesn't appear to have the confidence left to do something that decisive, but you can never tell.

Trying to lose myself in the monotonous music, I imagine writhing around on top of Raymond to the constant thump, thump, thump. Then I'm aware of a conflicting noise and realise Caroline's crying. Oh Christ. Going over to comfort her, I stop short of a cuddle as her clothes stink.

'You shouldnae really be drinking. Want some Coke?'

She just keeps wailing.

'. . . maybe you should take some medication. D'you still have any?'

'I dinnae need medication. I need Nick,' she snivels, throwing herself into my arms, smelly clothes and all.

God, is she still banging on about him? They split up over two years ago. She was bonkers long before that. That's what drove him away. This is ruining my little vodka haze.

'Look, you dinnae need a man. It's hellish being tied down. I'd love to have what you have.'

'What've I got, like?' she asks, gesturing to her junk shop of a living room, '. . . go on, tell me, apart from an intimate knowledge of British television schedules?'

'Freedom. Y'know . . . you can take my boyfriend but you cannae take my FREEDOM. You don't have to consult about a dozen other people before you make a decision.'

At least I've stopped her crying.

'But what's the point in being free, if you've nobody to share it with?' she says in all seriousness, before breaking into her first smile in decades. We start laughing, both of us. I wish I had the power to keep her like this, but I don't.

'Honestly, Caroline, nobody gives a shit about me either. The kids hate my guts. Vic winnae even share a bed with me any more. I've forgotten how to let people like me.'

This desperate admission seems to tickle her, somehow. Swallowing down the remainder of her drink, she hands me the glass.

'Get us another, I actually do have something to tell you. Something good.'

Intrigued, I go to the kitchen for replenishing. There's only enough for one big and one small one left. Pouring myself the big one, I knock back half the small one and top it up with Coke. She's still smiling when I get back through. She's even turned the radio down.

'There's this guy I met, just before I got discharged, I think maybe quite likes me . . .'

She pauses for my reaction.

'That's great. Who is he?'

'You've got to swear no to tell another living soul. We could both be in danger if you do.'

'I swear.'

She gets so close I can smell her again, and have to sniff at my glass to block it out.

'He's really nice. He sort of looks like Ian McKellen but not poofy, y'know. He was high up in the civil service but he lost his job, heavily into coke and that, and he basically ended up with nothing. Ended up in rehab.'

'Ian McKellen?'

'Well, y'know, better looking than Ian McKellen. A bit younger. Not snobby at all. Really easy to talk to.'

'Give him a ring. Get him to bring some Bolivian marching powder round.'

She doesn't even hear, she's in full flow. It's like someone's unlocked the talk in her.

'He's told me so much, y'know, with him being a civil servant. Like, d'you know how many suicides there were in Scotland last year?'

I wait to be enlightened by her cheery bloke's statistics but she wants to turn it into a party game.

'No, come on, guess. In one year.'

'I don't know, a hundred and sixty.'

'Five hundred and ninety-nine. Nearly twice as many as died in road accidents. Fucking freaky, eh?'

'It's a fair whack,' I say, but really, in comparison to the number of people who must regularly feel like topping themselves, it's toaty.

'And it's people like me, people like Clive and me.'

'Clive, is that his name?' As I stifle a chortle, a smile slips out. She ignores both smile and question.

'Really, Angie, I'm no joking. It's like Marilyn Monroe. Clive was involved with it himself, y'know, with Scottish Republicans. They pretended they were drug killings. That was his job.'

'Oh, right, so he was a hit man?'

'Aye, sort of, I suppose. He was dealing more with terrorists, but they do it to anyone who costs too much. Y'know, pretend it's suicide. Say they've been playing Nirvana records backwards.'

She pauses, to give me time to take it all in. It's disconcerting not knowing what sort of face to pull.

'So is he, like, still an assassin or what?'

'No, no, that's how he ended up in the hospital. He couldn't do it any more. He's ashamed of what he's done. It's tearing him apart inside.'

What am I supposed to say? How should I react? I don't know if it's good she's got a bit of company with Carlos the Jackal, or if it'll just make her madder. There's no vodka left and it's only half-seven. I was planning to stay till Monday but I can't listen to much more. Why can't you just will yourself into a coma at times like this?

'Come on. We need more drink. I'll get it this time. Fancy getting a video?'

'There's none I can watch any more, without them terrifying me.'

Aw, gie's a break.

Taking her to the shops is a bad idea. She keeps hesitating, looking round cars and making me run ahead to check behind hedges. She refuses to come in the grocer's because of the situation in Iraq but doesn't want to wait outside on her own. Is she doing this deliberately because I don't visit her enough? Once we get back to the flat and I have vodka to pacify me, I hog the conversation so she won't start raving on again. Besides, me talking about my own unhappiness seems to cheer her up.

'. . . I mean does anybody actually bother to have kids any more? I'd rather have a career, you know, a bit of fulfilment but it's like I missed the new way of thinking by about four years. Joni and Jake fucking hate me, really. And Vic's so fucking straight it's not true. Honestly, Caroline, marriage's like basic training for terminal illness.'

Why did my life take that cruel turn? What is Rab, my jilted squaddie, doing now? A bit of me will always love him because it ended so inconclusively. You should never end relationships at their peak or they just eat away at you forevermore. How is it that on the rare occasions in life that I've taken other people's advice, they've always been wrong? Everyone said Rab was a cunt, he'd shag a split heid. Vic was honest, dependable, worked hard and all the other Calvinist bullshit. All Rab had to offer me was a huge cock and a filthy mind. That would have been enough. That would have been almost too much in comparison. Never listen to other people. Live and die by your own decisions.

Getting myself another vodka, I bring the bottle back through. It's time to stop fannying around and do some serious drinking. Rab was a drinker, too. My family were scared we'd encourage each other, just like Raymond and I are going to. Good old Vic, eh, practically teetotal, lovely family man and about as exciting as watching concrete. IFUCKINGHATEHIMIFUCKINGHATEHIM!

God, I almost forgot Caroline was here. She's staring at the back of my chair rather intensely. I look behind me, but the stained bean bag doesn't seem to merit her expression. Or is she just looking at the merry-go-round of bluebottles, buzzing about the lampshade à la Bangladesh?

'It's your dad. He's right at your side,' she whispers, smiling into nothingness. That's not funny. It's sick.

'Come on. Don't say stuff like that.'

But she keeps staring.

'He's wearing blue trousers and a cream raincoat.'

She knows he used to wear that. This is not amusing me in the slightest.

'Don't, Caroline. Please.'

'I can't help it. It happens to me all the time. Speak to him.'

Fuck this! Storming through to the bathroom, I sit on the pan, seething. What a sick bitch. Why do mentally ill people always try and bring you down to their level? I'm leaving if she's going to head-fuck me like this. Then I realise I've left her alone with the drink, and worry she might be helping herself.

When I go back through, I ask if I can borrow a jumper. The temperature's really dropped since it got dark. Caroline can't afford heating as she gives all her money to charities, just so she'll get some mail. The jumper she gives me has the same socky smell that seems to pervade the whole house. Still gittering from my stint in the Arctic bathroom, I suffer it.

She puts the radio back on. It's still the same mindless music but increased vodka consumption makes it sound a bit better. I dance around with my drink, trying to reactivate my circulation. Caroline knocks up the volume and starts dancing with me, really into it, thrusting her arms violently, with a strangely sublime look on her face. Putting down my drink, I try to let go a bit myself, to work out some aggression. By the end of the first record, though, I'm getting chest pains and need to sit down for a drink and a fag. Caroline remains lost in it. I told her she was free.

Before long, her frenzied air-thumping develops into relentless spinning round. She wails as she does it. The image is slightly frightening and I have to stop her, as it's freaking me out. By this time, though, her balance is completely fucked. She swaggers about the room, knocking into things, eyes all over the place. Oh, Christ.

'D'you mind if I go to bed? I'm starting to feel bad again. Please stay, though. Dinnae leave me.'

Hallelujah!

'I won't, I won't. That's fine. I shouldn't have been forcing drink on you all afternoon.'

'No, honest, Angie. It's been great. It's the best time I've had for years,' then she looks a bit woozy, '. . . too much excitement for one day, though. We've still got tomorrow.'

I start worrying about how I'm going to ditch her in the morning. Sod it, I've got time on my own now, just enjoy it. As I get the spare duvet from her room, I notice she sleeps in her clothes. No doubt in case the CIA turn up in the middle of the night, with a bottle of paracetamols and a spoon. No wonder the place stinks.

I put the radio off when I go back through, but if she starts crying out in the night I don't want to hear, so I stick on the telly, and let it hum away in the background. It's ridiculous. I'm starting to feel guilty for thinking about Rab tonight. Like I was being unfaithful to Raymond in some way just by thinking it. They've actually got a similar sexy confidence about them. Cuddling up in the duvet, I imagine every possible sexual scenario that may occur on Monday.

I wake up entwined in a sweaty heap at ten the next morning. My head's throbbing but the unfinished vodka in front of me dulls it slightly. We drank less than half the second bottle – fucking waste. Since there's no sign of Caroline, I go through to the kitchen, wash out a virtually empty sauce bottle and siphon in some of the surplus drink. She shouldn't be boozing on her own and, besides, I paid for it.

I'm on my second vodka by the time she surfaces.

'I'll make breakfast. I can never be bothered when it's just me.'

I raise my glass.

'This'll do me. I'm not a great eater in the mornings either.'

She starts sooking on a Mars chocolate drink from the fridge. Just the thought of it makes me nauseous. Then she makes revoltingly greasy French toast in the dirtiest frying pan I've ever seen. Escaping through to the living room, I decide to have one more drink, then leave. I can't be noticeably pissed when I get in. They can't stop me drinking, but I don't want them to know, they'll just give me grief.

Finishing my final drink in conjunction with her French toast, I go to get my bag. She's at me immediately.

'Aw, Angie, you arnae going are you? I thought you were staying till the morrow. We could go down the Botanics. Please, dinnae go.'

Despite her efforts to pull it off me, I manage to struggle into my jacket.

'I'd love to, but I've got stuff to do for work, I'm sorry.'

'You work in a bookie's. What kind of stuff?'

'Oh, you know, washing, ironing, shit that free people don't have to worry about.'

'I'm not going to see you for another four years, am I?'

'No, honestly, it's been great. We'll make it a regular thing now, definitely.'

I'll promise her anything if it'll get me on the other side of that fucking door.

'I've really missed you, Angie. When you phoned, I'd just decided I was going to rent a car, and take it into the country to gas myself. It's amazing you called when you did.'

'OK, then, I'll give you a ring, maybe see you next weekend.'

She insists on a cuddle before letting me go. Smelly clothes aside, it's a small price to pay. Hopefully, by next week my life will be transformed to such an extent I won't need to resort to Caroline and her squalor any more. I mean to say, what's the point in wasting valuable drinking time and money on a miserable fucker like that?

Chapter Thirteen

JONI

THANK GOD I finally feel better. I was holed up in this dump, puking my guts up, all day yesterday. Even last night, when I'd recovered a wee bit, I had to stay in my room cause Granda was round. He interrogates me about boyfriends and stuff. It gives me the creeps, he probably gets off on it. Why do old people have to be so fucking nosy anyway? I don't give a shit about his sad life, so why should he concern himself with mine? He could rob banks and shag his budgie, for all I care.

Rosie phoned in the afternoon. Apparently, she bumped into young Jackie in the queue outside Century 2000, while I was getting chased the other night, and they ended up going back to the Barracuda. Cheers, y'know, just leave me to get murdered. Then she had the fucking gall to say she's never going up Lothian Road with me again after what happened. Making out like it was all my fault. I ended up putting the phone down on the jealous bitch.

Going through for a wash, I almost put hair-removing cream on my toothbrush by accident. Mum's left the tube lying next to the toothpaste, stupid cow. It was probably deliberate. Mind you, I do have a bit of a moustache. It's fair but you can still notice it. As I rub a thick layer of the lotion onto my upper lip, I suddenly get a shooting pain in my stomach. I just manage to make the pan before my bottom explodes. Where is it all coming from? I haven't eaten since Friday. I'm never touching seafood again.

By the time I stop crapping, my tache is stinging like fuck. Shit, I was only supposed to leave the cream on five minutes. Diving over to the sink, I wash it off, then throw cold water on it to try and soothe the nippiness. In the process, I take off about ten layers of skin and I'm left with this big, sore, burnt patch, like Tom fucking Selleck. I try putting foundation over it, but it looks even sillier. Mum's make-up's about twenty shades darker than her skin so it makes me look like I've got a big fucking birthmark under my nose. Dad'll probably think I've been snorting cocaine. Sometimes I just wish I was dead. Thank fuck nobody's in.

To take my mind off it, I go through to their bedroom to nick more money. Paranoid about how much I've been taking from the holiday envelope, I take tenners out of electricity, gas, telephone, Council Tax and birthdays instead. God knows how much there must be altogether, hundreds of pounds. Obviously not too much, though, or they'd notice it was disappearing.

I sniff the five crisp tenners in my hand. How come money always smells the same, even though thousands of different people have touched it? What's it made out of that makes it stink like that? Hiding it inside an old radio I've taken the batteries out of, I go and wash my hands. If they smell it off me, they might realise what I've been up to. I try Rosie again.

'Aw c'mon. I go babysitting with you. We don't need to go to pubs, just a pizza, please, Rosie.'

'Please stop going on about it. It makes me feel really slaggy. If I ever see that guy again, I'll die.'

'Aw Rosie, I think mines really liked me.'

'Come off it, Jo, y'ken what Tallies are like. They'll try it on with all the young lassies that go in there. They were really greasy anyway.'

How dare she say my beautiful Antonio was greasy.

'Please, pal, I'll give you a tenner, I'll get you that Catatonia CD. Please, just this one thing.'

'Oh stop acting so desperate. You'll never get a man if you act desperate like that.'

The fucking nerve.

'I'm desperate? I'm no the one shagging my uncle. I'm no the one that sucks off strangers for money. Just 'cause Antonio respects me and nobody respects you.'

There's a silence. Fuck, what did I say that for? Even if it is true.

'So that's what you really think of me, eh?' Her voice is shaky.

'Ocht no, Rosie, y'know what I mean, but. Why should I no be able to see him, 'cause of something you did? It's no fair.'

'OK then Jo, tell you what. Go and fucking see him. Dinnae waste your time on a slag like me. Go an' get AIDS off some whoory Iti and stop buggin me.'

Brrrrrrrr.

Throwing the phone across the room, I kick it against the wall. It's still working when I pick it up. I'm so useless I can't even break the poxy thing. See Rosie? She can fucking poke it, I don't need her. I'm going to get Antonio on my own.

Jan comes sniffing through to find out what the commotion is. I hate that fucking dog. She makes the house smell, and everything's covered in about an inch of her hairs. Rolling up the dish towel, I smack her across the nose so she'll piss off but she just sits there, whining, wanting out for a shit. I briefly consider crapping on the carpet myself and blaming it on her, but that's too gross even for me. Dad's left a note reminding me to feed her. Opening the tin, I scrape its contents into the bottom of the bucket as she wails at my side. It makes me feel slightly better. Locking her in the kitchen, I go and switch the telly on.

The *EastEnders* omnibus has just started. I've stopped watching it because every time I start to fancy one of the characters they leave – mad Joe, the black guy Michelle used to go out with, nice Alan ... Nick Cotton was my first love, though. I used to X^2 about sitting on his lap and us peeing on each other. I've no idea how I knew sex was sort of like that, when I was just a bairn. Maybe something happened when I was wee that I can't remember. That would be typical. Actually having lost my virginity years before Rosie, but not being able to mind.

Fuck, I'm so bored. I retune all the channels on the telly so each one is a crackly mess and it looks broken. If they can't watch telly, they'll all be as miserable as me. Serves them right for not getting cable.

I'm so desperate for something to do, I go through to Jake's room for a neb. He's such a boring little twat I won't find anything remotely interesting but the fact he'll be annoyed I was looking at his stuff is enough. There's Rangers posters all over the wall. Studying the team shots, I pick the three players I'd most like to do it with and end up X^2ing about Jorg Albertz getting sent off and shagging me in the dug-out. Maybe I should go to the football with Dad. I'd probably be the only woman there. Surely I'd be able to get off with someone. How is it always Jake gets to go to things like that? Dad's such a sexist.

Getting up, I spy a giant whisky bottle full of coins over by the window. Emptying it onto the carpet, I take all the pounds and 50-pence pieces. Not that I need them, but I just want to piss Jake off. As I'm putting the other coins back in the bottle, I notice a pile of magazines under his bed. *Marie Claire*, *Cosmopolitan*, *New Woman*. What a wee poof. I hide them in my room. He'll be too embarrassed to admit he had them in the first place and it'll really do his head in.

Jan is howling away in the kitchen. I go through and give her another slap with the dish towel, then put my All Saints CD on loud to drown her out. As I lie on my bed, thumbing through the magazines, my mind keeps returning to Antonio. Maybe we could run away to Italy together. Mind you, I'd have to chory some decent clothes first. They all wear designer stuff over there. He'd pack me in if I looked scruffy.

Euch, fucking hell. Loads of the magazine pages are stuck together and Jake – sad, perverted little bastard that he is – has drawn hairy fannies over the models' knickers. And I thought I was desperate. Tearing one out, I put it face-up on his bed and the rest of the spunky magazines back where I found them. When I go to wash my hands, the burn on my face looks worse. How could I even think of going to see Antonio with a puss like this?

There's a bang from up the hall, then silence. Mum's not back till tomorrow. Dad's note said they wouldn't be back till after six. Maybe we're being burgled. You read all the time about burglars being disturbed while they're burgling and ending up raping someone. I check my scabby face in the mirror, put on some eyeliner and go out to investigate.

The flat is dead silent as I tiptoe up the hall, check the bedrooms, then creep into the living room. Fuck, it's just Mum. I'm so disappointed I feel like punching her. She jumps about a mile when I tap her on the shoulder, though, which is quite amusing.

'Christ, Jo, it's you. I didn't think anyone was in.' She's standing in the kitchen, chopping onions, drinking Diet Coke with her coat on.

'Why have you come back?'

She puts down the knife and looks hurt. 'Oh, thanks a lot. I've really missed you too.'

'Y'know what I mean. I thought you were away till th'morrow.'

'Caroline hadnae been taking her medication. I feel really sorry for her and that, but it was too gruelling to handle two days of. I tried to . . .'

'Aye, OK, Mum. I get the idea.' I go back to my room in disgust. Her pal Caroline's not sick-ill, it's just in her head, like

Emma. Mum's making out like she's such a martyr for going to see her, but I bet she's about a hundred times easier to get on with than Mum is.

Putting on my Pulp CD, I lie on the bed, and pretend I'm all the women Jarvis is singing about. Their songs are nearly as depressing as my life and I'm soon sniffling into my pillow. Why is life so awful? I can't believe someone finally likes me and I can't see them. It's like *Romeo and Juliet*. By the time the CD finishes, I'm on such a downer that when I hear Jake's voice in the hall I actually feel glad.

When I go through, Mum's ladling soup into bowls and bragging about how quickly she can drum up a pot of home-made tattie and leek, trying to imply that this means she's a good mother. She's acting a bit weird, pretending to be friendlier than she actually is. It's like she's been abducted by aliens and replaced by a replicant. I wish. Much as I want to K.B. the soup, after her going on about it so much, I have a bowl as I'm absolutely starving. When Mum asks what I think, I say it's so-so.

She starts boring Dad about her pal. I think she only went to see the poor woman so she could go on about what a kind, caring person she is. If I was mentally ill, the last thing I'd want is for her to turn up and start nipping my head.

'. . . a shame . . . blah, blah, blah . . . really felt sorry for her . . . blah, blah, blah . . . too gruelling . . . blah blah blah.' Oh, give it a rest, for God's sake. Someone give her a Blue Peter badge and be done with it.

Dad's sitting supping his soup, nodding away mindlessly with one eye on the Italian football. Bastards, they've re-tuned the telly again. They're not even going to give me the satisfaction of them blaming me. I suddenly get a bit gristle in my soup, which makes me go breenjy and I have to throw the rest away. Jake follows me through and puts the remainder of his in front of the dog. Jan and me lunge for it simultaneously, but I get there first.

'I just fed her a wee while ago. She'll be sick,' I lie, scraping it into the bin as the stupid mutt starts crying again. If I can't get what I want, why should the fucking dog?

I follow Jake through to his room. As he opens the door, he pounces onto the Kate picture and crumples it into his pocket.

'What's that? What did you hide?'

His face is beetroot as I try to get it out his pocket. He suddenly seems to have about ten times his normal strength and soon has me pinned to the floor. Grabbing a clump of my hair, he pulls really hard till I think it's going to come out. I kick out wildly, trying to get him in the balls. Eventually he stands up with tears in his eyes.

'Fucking stop it, Jo. I dinnae want to fight you. I wish you and your pals would just leave me alone.' Picking up a PC World bag, he makes for the door.

'What're you on about? Where're you going?'

'Downstairs to see Sean. He doesnae beat me up.'

'Who the fuck's Sean?'

'Ma pal downstairs. You better keep away from him. You deliberately turn folk against me.'

The front door slams, and he's gone. I'm in shock that he's actually stood up to me for the first time. What did he mean about me turning people against him? Fuck, even he hates me now. And where did this fucking Sean suddenly spring from? My wanky wee brother's got more friends than me, it's pathetic.

I go back through to my room, in tears again. This is the most I've cried since I was about two. Everyone hates me. Even Dad's sick of me. He's taken Jake out the last two days and not even asked me. Nobody even noticed my scabby moustache. I start to fantasise about my funeral and Mum, Dad, Jake, Rosie and everyone else that hates me standing round, crying, feeling really bad about how they treated me. The organist could maybe play something by Elton John. That always gets them going. Or maybe

Antonio could sing 'Nessun Dorma'. Thoughts of hanging myself in the stair, or swallowing all Mum's pills or cutting my wrists in the bath, cheer me up slightly. It would be worth it just to get at them. I end up having to X^2 again. I must be a pervert.

Chapter Fourteen

VIC

ALTHOUGH MY ROSTERED back-shift's three-thirty till one, I had to go in early today due to an epidemic of sickies. It's always the same at this time of year. The racing at Cheltenham and Aintree seems to have a bizarre effect on bus drivers' abilities to fight infection. Personally, I've never succumbed to the gambling bug myself. The thought of being served by someone like Angie is enough to put anyone off.

Usually, I can see in my whole shift on three buses; however, today's shortage of staff has me farting about all over the place. Splitting up the routes is supposed to offer us variety but, you know, if I wanted variety I'd be MC at a comedy club, not driving a bloody bus. Give me the same faces at the same stops at the same times every day. It's mindless and, this being Edinburgh, I'm well aware that no amount of familiarity will ever get the conversation beyond the 'sixty-five, please' stage but there's a strange sort of comfort in the predictability of it. Christ, listen to me. What sort of dull bastard have I become?

When I get to Haymarket, I see the crowlike figure of Brutal, the Inspector, perched outside Ryrie's. Please make him wave me past. If he gets one whiff inside here, he'll be straight onto the depot, reporting me. A gang of laddies got on at Wester Hailes Centre to Gorgie and it's still reeking from their exotic fags. You're supposed to radio in the police for stuff like that but I never bother. What bloody harm are they doing?

Bollocks, I've just caught Brutal's eye. If ever a man's read too much into his job title, Inspector, it's that ugly bastard. If he gets on, he won't let me go till he's found something to give me a hard time about. Y'know, he's only supposed to check we're on time, but it's generally him makes you late in the first place with all his petty crap. Yes, you beauty. A tanned, blonde lassie with a back-pack the size of a fridge-freezer accosts him for directions as I pull away from the last stop in Dalry. The lights change and I escape onto West Maitland Street. He'll probably report me for insolence now.

Oof, I just got one of my pains. It's the strain of avoiding that bastard. As a blind man manoeuvres himself onto the bus, I take the opportunity to have a good cough. My phlegm is semi-solid and all the colours of autumn. I'm obviously riddled with infection. Maybe the doctor can't see the point in telling me because, since I'm a smoker, they won't treat me anyway. I wipe the slime under my seat beside the rest of today's specimens.

A bairn starts screaming up the back and I hear the mother effing away, smacking it. Where do they get the idea that hitting children stops them crying? The hardest part of this job is not intervening when I see the way some of these young lassies treat their kids. If that's what they do in public, God knows what they're like in private. The bairns, invariably, have suspiciously scabby faces, but what can you do? This one carries on greeting, in between smacks, all the way through the South Side, right up Gilmerton. By the time mother and child finally get off, three stops before Gorebridge, I feel like my nerve endings are on the surface of my skin and if someone touches me, I might explode. They should introduce it as a new kind of punishment therapy for repeat offenders. Manacle them in a bus with screaming kids and drive them round in horrendous traffic. A few days of that would be far more effective than nine months in an open nick, doped out their skulls. Jack Straw's such a wanker, he'd probably think it was a good idea.

When I get to the terminus, I shut the doors and sit up the back with my flask and the *Herald* crossword. My record for completing it is 22 minutes, which I'm sure is pretty shit-hot. I'm wasted in this job. I wanted to be an architect when I was at school, then, having passed all my exams and got an unconditional for St Andrews, I got baw-heid up the duff. I'd be quids in as well. Edinburgh's like a massive bloody building site at the moment. When I was a kid, I used to take games and books on bus journeys because I got bored. Now I'm just bored by nature.

I've three clues left by the end of my break. It pisses me off when I don't do it in a oner. I actually prefer the *Scotsman* crossword but it's so anti-Scottish I'm going to stop buying it. The *Herald*'s a bit more positive but, then, most of the journalists are English. And as for the *Record*, it's not fit to wipe your arse with – racist, destructive bullshit that it is.

I start back again at 5.17. The serious congestion doesn't start until Clerk Street, where I spend 25 minutes staring at the Queen's Hall. Several people ask to be let off between stops. I wish I could go with them and just leave the bloody thing here. Once we finally move, it takes a full hour to get back to Haymarket. If the roads were clear, I'd do it in about seven minutes.

Then back to dear old Gorgie for 35 minutes. Where do cable TV companies get the idea that the rush hour is the most prudent time to dig up the roads? There's temporary lights and only three cars are getting through at a time. For every three that go through, another four come out of McDonald's car park and jump in front.

By the time I get past Luckies, it's started pissing down. An army of drenched, angry people scowl at me as I pull in at the stop.

'Is there a fucking strike on or what?'

'Call yourself a public service.'

'Cunt!'

'Is this a Sunday service?'

'I've just watched five 65s go past. Why is that?'

How am I supposed to know? If they've all been standing here as long as they're making out, then surely the reason for the delay must be obvious to them. How is it my fault? Thank God I've just got to go to the depot.

I crash out during my dinner break. It's horrible waking up and realising I've still got half my shift to do, but it's seven by the time I go out again, so the roads are marginally quieter. I do my next two runs almost to the minute. Does anyone appreciate this? Does anyone congratulate me on my Christ-like avoidance of red lights? Do they hell.

It rains for the rest of my shift. I love the rain. It gives all the buildings really amazing definition and reminds me of Christmas when I was a kid. Every year we'd pray for snow, and every year, without fail, it'd either be pissing down or subtropical on Christmas Day. It also seems to soak up some of the pollution. This is probably my imagination, but I almost feel like I can smell the air when it's raining.

The bus, as usual, is empty by the time I get back to Westfield at quarter to one. I generally sprint up to the depot at this point as there's rarely anyone waiting. As I drive past McDonald's for the sixth time today, though, there's a woman in the shelter with her thumb out. I'm only going a few more stops but she gets on anyway and sits next to me.

I give her a smile in the mirror, but she looks so nervous, I regret it. You have to be so careful how you deal with women these days. And there's something about this one that starts to put me on edge. She has a disturbed look about her. Each time I glance at her reflection, she's staring at me intensely. Thankfully, it only takes a couple of minutes to get to the last stop before the depot.

'This is it, love. I dinnae go any further.'

Still, she just stares.

'. . . you OK? You'll have to get off here, I'm afraid.'

She wants to go to the garage with me, though. She must live round here. Rather than see her walk up there on her own, at this time of night, I shrug and head back to base.

When I next check the mirror, having parked and cut the engine, she's hiked up her skirt and has her legs open. I just gawp at her. I'm no longer equipped to deal with things like this but I just can't stop staring at the unfamiliar minge in front of me.

'D'you want some?' she whispers.

Jesus Christ. As I frantically check the windows, I half expect Brutal to suddenly swoop towards us. There's only a few guys just finished their shift at the far side of the garage. Switching all the lights off, I get out my little box.

'Look love, ta for the offer, but you better go.'

The legs spread a little wider.

'Go on. You know you want to.'

She must be a junkie or something. Even if my cock wasn't frazzled with Prozac, I wouldn't touch that. I wish she'd cover up her bits and get off my bus, but I'm scared to touch her. A tiny crumb of my DNA on her skirt and I'd be buggered. Retrieving the cash box, I open the door and get out.

'No offence, love. I'm a married man. I just want home to my cocoa.'

I'm smiling, trying to keep it friendly, but she lets out a wail and marches off the bus, towards the group of drivers. By the time she realises the exit's in the other direction, they've spotted her. Once they start laughing and shouting, she can't get out of there quick enough.

I get back on the bus and pretend to check things to give

her time to leave, then walk across towards the rest of them to thunderous applause and whistling. A driver I only know by sight drops his trousers and starts running after her, shouting, 'Me next, me next.'

'Weh hey, who's been despunked on the 33 tonight?'

'Did you make her take her falsers out first?'

'What's on the end of your prick, Vic?'

What is this? I nod my head as I approach.

'Nah, nah, nothing like that. Sorry to disappoint you boys.'

'Aw c'moan,' says young Stevie. 'Everyone's had her. Did she spread her legs and offer it to you? That's the usual routine.'

'Dunno what you're on about,' I smile.

None of them believe me.

'C'mon, we winnae tell the missus. Did you fire a quick one up her or what?'

'You saw me pull in just a minute ago. Even I'm no that quick.'

'C'moan, tell us. It's the only excitement we get round here.'

'I've no idea what you're on about, Stevie. She asked me to drive her to the depot, then she got off, end of story. Who is she, like?'

Angus, a grandfather, elaborates. 'You no hear? It's been in the paper and everything. She's been doing it about a month now. She has an insatiable appetite for bus drivers' cocks.'

'What, have you shagged her?'

His yellow teeth shine out from his white beard. 'I couldnae really say.'

The other four men start pissing themselves laughing.

'You're kidding me, Angus. She's a junkie. She looked mentally disturbed.'

'What woman isnae? Look Vic, a lassie half my age offers me it on a plate. I'm 57 years old, ken. Ah cannae afford to be too choosy.'

Stevie lights a fag and starts swaggering about. 'Me and another two guys had her up the back ova 44. Y'kin do anything w'her. She's mad for it. I cannae believe you didnae poke'r, man. God sent her down for our morale.'

Is it just me? I can't believe it. Bloody Angus as well. I thought he was just interested in his pigeons. Who am I working with here? I need away from this.

'Ocht well, I just hope she doesnae have the virus or we're due for a bit of a staffing crisis.'

This silences them briefly, but they're back exchanging gruesome anecdotes by the time I leave. Jesus. When I finally escape into the fresh air, I almost puke behind a car. Do none of them have daughters? What if Joni did something like that? Would they all get fired into her just the same? I definitely wouldn't have done it, even if I had been capable. I'm sure I wouldn't. The whole incident turns over in my head as I try to get a taxi. Whatever way I look at it, though, it still seems just awful. The human race goes down another notch in my estimation.

Chapter Fifteen

JAKE

I'M GOING DOWN Sean's for a shot on the Internet before school. Well, to tell the truth, it's his sister, Eva, I'm really interested in seeing. When I was down last night, she kept putting her arm round me, pretending to show me things on the computer, so close I could smell her chewing gum. She looks a bit like Demi Moore, except not so fat and she's got these amazing turquoise eyes. It wouldn't surprise me if she was a beautiful alien from the planet Babe.

As I walk down the stairs, my head's fizzing with ideas about how I can touch her without it looking obvious, and clever things I can say to impress her. When it's her that answers the door, though, I almost collapse with nerves. As I stumble towards Sean's room, I pretend to suddenly be fascinated by the paintings and canvases that line the hall. It's mostly modern what-the-fuck sorta stuff with splashes of colour and crucifixy-type bits but it must be good, 'cause their mum doesn't have a proper job, but they've got plenty money. God knows why they're living in a poxy place like this.

Sean's banging the desk in a rage when I go through.

'The fucker's crashed. I was printing out stuff on spontaneous human combustion – barrie photos of half-burnt legs with the shoes still on, fuck.'

We try everything to get it working – shake the keyboard, swing the mouse in the air, then whack it off the table, punch the monitor – but the error message's just frozen on the screen. Pushing herself onto Sean's seat, lovely Eva comes to the rescue.

'No, no, no, you've got to be gentle,' she whispers, pressing it off, then on again, running her fingers across the screen as if it's a face she's about to kiss. The machine, like me, responds to her coaxing, grumbles, then tinkles the Microsoft tune. I start to think that she's maybe an angel. When she tries to get us back online, and it's too busy for us to get through, I'm sort of relieved. An angel would never get off with me anyway. She tells us it's impossible to get on, once America's woken up. See fucking Americans? Even in a boxroom in Gorgie, they still run your fucking life.

Eva gives us half a packet of Marlboro Lights to make up for it. Is she trying to impress me? Imagine Joni doing something like that. She'd be more likely to stub fags out on me.

As soon as we're out the stair, Sean starts chasing me in and out the cars, through shops, into old ladies. I'm Mr Orange and he, Mr Blond, has just found out I'm an undercover cop. We were planning to have a shoot-out in the swing park, but when we get along there's a bunch of pukey wee second years sharing a fag without inhaling. They all look up, expecting a fight. We stop in our tracks and try to look cool. Sean lights a Marlboro for me and I hold the smoke in as long as possible to show them how it should be done. Jason keeks out from under the chute and we go over.

'No seen you around,' he mumbles, staring at the railings.

'I've been at Sean's.' I gesture to Mr Blonde. 'He's got the Internet but we cannae get into it. He was trying to print out photos of folk who'd exploded.'

'Oh, good for Sean,' he whines. What's his problem? He's not still in a mood about me chucking that baby rat at him in Biology, surely.

'Aw, c'mon Jace, dinnae be like that. What're you doing after play time? I've got poofy-baws for Gym, I cannae face it. We could take Sean up the farm. It's dead funny, Sean. We chuck stones at the cows. They fucking hate it.'

Jason scowls at him.

'What team d'you support? Celtic?'

'The Hibees.'

A lump of phlegm lands about a foot from Sean's trainers. 'Fuck, that's even worse. Youz winnae even be in the Premier Division next season.'

Sean shrugs.

'I dinnae support teams just 'cause they're winning.'

'Obviously, Fenian shite,' Jason gobs again, before disappearing down the street, singing, 'Hello, hello, we are the Gorgie boys.' Proddy wanker.

'Was that your pal? You better go after him.'

'Nah, it's awright. He's just in a couple of my classes. I dinnae even know him that well.'

We take our time walking down to school, so we don't catch up with the tosser. What's he on about anyway? His old dear's shagging a Paki so he's hardly one to talk.

We've just walked in the main door when Joni suddenly accosts us from nowhere. She skives so much it's weird seeing her here. It looks unnatural.

'You havnae seen Rosie, have you, rat-face?'

'I thought you'd fawn out w'her.'

'Aaaaye, I have. That's why I'm looking for her, doh.'

'I suppose that makes some sort of sense,' says Sean. Immediately, Joni's all smiley and flirty and giving him fish eyes. When she discovers he's the boy downstairs I've been going to see, it makes her even worse. I'm glad someone I know's finally being nice to him but she's like a dog on heat. She better not try to steal him off me, he's my pal. I pretend we've got someone to meet, just to get him away from the slag.

Sean's got double Geography and me English. We arrange to meet outside the library at lunch time. As I walk along, into the class, Miss Barnes is suddenly there in front of me, looking so much better than I remember. It actually looks like there's a halo round her.

'Morning, Jake.'

Managing only a red-faced grunt, I crash into my seat and hide behind my jotter. God, I've been concentrating so much on Eva, I've not even had time to think about Miss Barnes. Life suddenly seems full of possibilities. She drifts around, handing back poems from last week. She usually reads out her three favourites, so I'm praying she doesn't give me mine. She'll definitely have liked it. It'll make her understand me more. The very idea causes a flutter in my pants. God, not here, please.

Fuck, she's just put mine on my desk. I look round, not quite believing it, trying to work out whose she's holding onto. Fucking typical – diabetic Elaine, Paki Geena and Todd 'three girlfriends' Mackay. Turning back to my rejected poem, I read the comments and just want to die.

'Well written, with plenty of feeling, but slightly *déja vu* for a Radiohead fan like myself. 65%.'

Fuck, I only copied a couple of lines out of 'Creep'. I was listening to it after I'd finished the poem and just thought these two bits would make it better. I can't move. She'll think it's all choried bits now. Her liking Radiohead's made me like her even more, though. I usually concentrate when she reads out her favourite poems, so I can guess what she liked about them, and try to copy it. I'm in too much of a daze to take anything in, though, fucking lazy-eyed bastards!

When the lesson finally ends, I try to sneak out behind a group of lassies, but she calls me back. I have to stand at her desk, shuffling and sweaty, until everyone's left. Closing the door, she turns to me.

'Don't look so frightened, Jake. I just want a wee word.'

'Please Miss, I didnae know it was Radiohead, honest. I've maybe heard it somewhere without realising and it's gone into my subconscious or something but ah didnae ken.'

My bum cheeks are trembling. I'm going to fart if she doesn't stop staring at me.

'At least you made an effort. The rest of it was so good, though, that's the thing. You don't need to copy other people. I want to know what you have to say, not anyone else, OK?'

'Aye, Miss, I'm sorry, I'm really sorry . . . sorry,' I mumble from inside my invisible shell. She tells me to relax, but as I make for the door it's like I've never realised how complicated walking was before. *I want to know what you have to say, not anyone else.* What did she mean by that? Was she trying to tell me something? What a babe. I wonder what her first name is?

Skipping along the corridor, I check the main entrance, before going to Gym. I thought Jason might have changed his mind about skiving. No such luck. That bastard Daniel's in my class as well.

We were supposed to be doing gymnastics, but someone's vandalised the vaulting horse, taken the top of it and pulled one of its legs off. No doubt a revenge attack by some laddie Mr Russell's tried to shag. We play basketball instead, which is much better. I get picked last on Daniel's team, but that's because he's a bullying Celtic bastard. I'm actually better at basketball than any of them and he knows it. I end up playing really shite, though, because I keep getting tackled while trying to avoid going near sphincter-boy and his disgusting poofy aftershave. I'm scared if I breath it in, I'll turn into a poof as well.

By the end of the first period, there's no score and we're all playing so badly the queeny bastard stops the game and insists we spend the rest of the lesson practising throws. It's not fair. Just because the rest of them are crap. When he's in the store cupboard, getting more balls, Daniel slams the door and locks it. The sight of the wiggling handle and the sound of the old fanny banging to get out is all it takes to turn everyone ballistic. Everything remotely moveable – balls, bollards, bean bags, chairs – gets kicked about the gym to the chant of 'POOF, POOF, POOF, POOF.' Even a couple of lassies start paggering – tearing at each other's hair, scratching like angry cats. It's brilliant. It's like a prison riot.

As the gym's separate from the rest of the school, nobody hears, so this goes on for most of the lesson. By the time the bell goes, I think most of us have forgotten the jobbie jabber's even in the cupboard. Daniel shushes us down and puts his ear against the door. It's gone completely silent. Fuck, will we all get the jail if he's had a heart attack? It was Daniel that done it. The rest of us were just too scared to stop him. It was brilliant, though. Even more so when, as it is, in fact, lunch time and we only get an hour, we decide to leave the bastard in there. I'm sure someone'll find him eventually.

Chapter Sixteen

ANGIE

DESPITE SHOWERING THIS morning, Raymond's smell is still oozing out of me as I watch him settle dog bets.

'Is that me? D'you want more tonight?'

Nodding, I look down at the settling desk we had our maiden fuck against last night. It was all over in about 60 seconds but Jesus, was it the most exciting, uncontrollable 60 seconds I've ever experienced. Just to be taken like that, almost like rape. To be treated like some kind of slut. Sooner a frenzied minute than a passionless, predictable 15 of marital banging that I have to dredge my distant memory for fantasies to enable me to remain awake throughout. Marital banging, which is, in itself, a distant memory.

It was only a matter of time. Practically all my relationships, prior to getting hitched, were work-related. It's more civilised than picking up strangers in clubs, you know. The last time I did that, I met Vic.

With the fibreglass screen to disguise our drinky breath from the punters, Raymond and I take it in turns to go for swifties at lunch time. A Chinese guy's in for most of the afternoon. He wins three in a row, over a grand, but keeps betting till he's lost it all. The addicts are like that – it's the losing, not the winning, that really matters. Today, it is Lady Gabriel in the 4.37 at Sunderland that renders Charlie Chan finally penniless. He leaves, exhilarated.

As I make for the loo, with my bag, in the break before the 4.45 at Nottingham, Raymond grabs my hand.

'Take your knickers off,' he whispers as old Sid staggers up with a 10-pence reverse forecast, 'I can't smell me any more.'

Slipping them off as I pee, I'm slimy by the time I wipe myself. He can do that to me just with his voice. I take a slug from the quarter-bottle I bought at lunch time, before I'm calm enough to go back through. As I take a, by now, irate Sid's bet, Raymond pushes his hand up my skirt and fingers deep into me. Sid's still whingeing about missing the last price when he takes them out again. I give him ten to one, and everyone's happy.

A big, purple-faced, intense-looking man slaps down a £500 win bet on Largesse in the next race. I hand it to Raymond to clear with Head Office in line with their crusade against betting syndicates. When I attempt to serve the next customer, the purple-faced man blocks his way.

'What's the focking problem? Where's me bet?'

I explain the procedure to him as calmly as possible, but he keeps interrupting. Why are the stroppy ones always fucking Irish? Catholic too, no doubt.

'Just put d'focking bet on, will yah.'

'Take a seat. It won't take a minute to check.'

Again I try to take someone else's bet, only to have them knocked to the ground by the thug.

'Look, youz of got me focking money. What sort of focking Mickey Mouse shop is this that you can't just take a focking bet without crying to d'boss?'

Raymond finally gets through to Head Office, but can hardly make out what they're saying for this stupid Irish twat blowing a gasket. Slamming the phone down, he puts the bet through the till, slowly counts the wad of 50-pound notes, runs them through the camera, then defiantly thrusts the underside of the man's bet under the barrier.

'Look, pal, I don't need to serve you. Speak to a member of my staff like that again and I fucking won't.'

The man gives him the finger and goes and sits at the back of the shop to watch the race.

'He better not fucking win,' Raymond whispers, looking pale. 'I banked all the money earlier. We don't have enough to pay him.' He retrieves the bet from the camera to check it's win and not each way. 'Bugger it. Fall, you bastard, fall!'

A crowd of regulars gather round the Irish git, shouting on his horse, even though they've all bet different runners. Just because he's had a go at us, two-faced wasters. Largesse, seemingly spurred on by their yelps of encouragement, romps home at twelve to one. Irish boy's up for his winnings before they've even declared. Raymond phones our nearest branch to try and scrape the money together. Then he phones a taxi for me to go and pick it up, ignoring the man, who, by now, is tearing up piles of unused betting slips as he kicks a stool around. Some of the more half-witted regulars start to get wound up as well, yelling abuse at us, calling us robbing bastards, accusing us of not giving them good prices. Fucking lemmings. It's like *Spartacus*.

By the time the taxi arrives, Irish boy's gone storming off, apparently to get a gun, having issued very convincing death threats to us both. Raymond phones the police, then sees me out to the cab. I beg him to lock up till I get back, but he refuses. Head Office really frown upon such losses of revenue. As I pull away, I'm terrified that the next time I see his face, it's going to be splattered across the form for Sandown in today's *Racing Post*.

The taxi hits all seven sets of red lights as we travel less than half a mile to the other shop. Once I get there, they make me fill in about a dozen different forms and insist on counting the ten grand twice in my presence. By the time they finally free me, I'm fit to be tied.

There's no sign of Paddy or the police when I get back and most of the regulars have shown their support by leaving. Only the Chinese guys remain – too focused on losing to have noticed anything happening in the first place.

'Christ, I could murder a drink,' Raymond mutters, alcohol perspiration running down his face and neck. I know that greasy feeling so well. As he counts the money again, I go to the kitchen and splash some of my quarter bottle in a mug, slugging back a mouthful myself. He sniffs and whirls it about before knocking it back in one. Almost simultaneously, four cops burst through the door in a overdone stake-out sort of way. When they realise there's just us and the Chinamen, two of them leave again. Raymond chomps frantically on Polo Mints.

They seem to swallow up all the space when I let them behind the counter. Why do coppers always have such huge feet and enormous arses? The older of the two sniffs at the air and winks at his colleague. Christ, it probably smells like a brewery in this enclosed space.

The younger one takes my statement, but my mind seems to seize up on every detail, like it's already blocking it out. They spend less than ten minutes with us and make no attempt to hide their irritation at being called out on something so inconsequential. The older one's Irish himself, which doesn't help. I was sort of expecting an armed guard till closing time, whereas they only seem bothered with descriptions. Probably so they can pick the cunt up quicker once he's shot us.

As they're leaving, the guy comes waltzing back in, gunless. Raymond knocks on the glass, making unsubtle shooting gestures at the departing cops. The older one looks alarmed, then realises what he's on about and begins explaining our complaint to the bastard as he walks meekly up to the pay-out.

'Ocht, I'm so sorry. I should never mix drink and horses. If you put a bet on, though, you'd expect to get paid if you won, no?' Oi wasn't aware that complaining about second-rate service was a criminal offence.'

As I count the money yet again, securing grands with elastic bands, the younger cop watches with his gob open. It no doubt reminds him of the last bung he took. As I slide the wads under to Irish boy, he tears a 20 off and slips it back through. The older copper tuts and they escort the man out, laughing and joking. It's ridiculous. Someone threatens to kill us and we end up being made to feel like we've deliberately disrupted the peace process. Fucking Masons.

There's still another two races to go but the fuzz have scared everyone off. There's a mouthful left in my quarter bottle for us both. Slightly settled by it, we start cashing up early. Despite having hardly any money left, we're 40 quid over.

'Fuck this for a game of soldiers,' Raymond says after our fourth attempt, stuffing the offending notes in his pocket. 'We'll check it again in the morning. I can always put it back.'

I go through to the kitchen and put the money in the safe. Raymond's leaning back on the counter with his legs open and lip curled when I go back through. Anyone else would look ridiculous in such a pose but him doing it gives me a bolt of desire like an electric shock.

'Did you put your knickers back on?'

'No.'

The taste of drink and Polos on his warm lips is divine. His hands seem to go everywhere at once as he hoicks up my skirt and throws me, face-first, over the desk.

'D'you want to go home with wet knickers again, Mrs Scott?'

Reading my mind, he subjects me to a short, sharp shag, the settling machine rattling on the desk in syncopation. I don't orgasm but it doesn't bother me. If I concentrate too much on coming during sex, I tend to lose track of what's going on. Besides, it's fodder for a thousand future wanks. Raymond was right, I do like to go home with wet knickers. These foolish things and all that.

We make a beeline for the pub as soon as we've fucked, same as yesterday. Unfortunately, Ronnie, the manager of the rival bookie's round the corner, is in, and insists on buying us a drink. Raymond puts his hand on mine to stop me drumming my fag packet on the table. Ronnie looks down, waiting for him to remove it but he doesn't.

'Dangerous, dangerous . . .' Ronnie warns. Obviously, William Hill's indoctrinate them in the relationships-at-work-are-evil ethos better than our lot do.

I drink slowly, even saying no to a couple of rounds. It's inconsequential what Ronnie might think of me but I don't want him passing silent judgement on my alcohol consumption. They rabbit on about the Irish git and compare punters-throwing-wobblies stories. My rage intensifies behind a fixed grin, until he finally fucks off at quarter past eight.

Another couple of double vodkas and one of Raymond's lovely whisky kisses soon melt my stiff sulkiness, however. It feels as if the world is something insignificant that revolves round the pair of us. All I want is here with me now.

By nine-thirty, we're half-cut and all over each other. The barmaid keeps wiping our table in a bid to embarrass us into behaving. We ignore her. I'm becoming obsessed with the idea of going back to the shop for afters. Raymond's worried about the alarm going off and the police coming back but I'm feeling so fucking horny I'd probably ask them to join in.

Last orders are called. They let us get two drinks each but as soon as the second bell's rung, they want our glasses. I resist a terrific urge to kick over the table, only because we have nowhere else round here to go to. Besides, I'm still at the pretending-to-be-demure-and-submissive stage of my relationship with Raymond.

You can't afford to let men see the real you until they're too smitten to object. If that blonde barmaid calls him 'sweetheart' one more time though . . . I get myself out onto the street before my violent fantasies become reality.

We stand hugging, kissing and lamenting in the pub doorway until the blonde bitch comes out, looks at us with contempt and stops a taxi. I wonder if she knows how close she's just come to losing her eyes.

It's five to twelve. It's been easy with Vic working late this week but next week's going to take a lot of explaining. We agree that we'll have to sort something out by then. It's only been a few days but it doesn't seem to matter. Reluctantly hailing me a cab, Raymond tries to make me take a tenner for the fare. Pushing it back in his trouser pocket, I give his shank a goodnight stroke.

We arrange to meet back in the pub before work tomorrow, then suddenly there's a slam and he's gone. I feel like fucking Cinderella. I had more freedom when I was 15 and living at home.

Joni's sprawled on the settee when I get in, scowling at figure-skaters on TV. It's like landing without a parachute.

'I didn't know you were into that sort of thing,' I say, more to hear if my voice sounds OK than in an attempt at conversation.

'I'm not. It's crap.'

'Is your brother in?'

'He's downstairs at his boyfriend's.'

I let this one go as she's probably just trying to start something. So what if he was gay anyway? The sooner this family's genetic line is no more the better.

'No Rosie tonight?'

She tuts, as if I'm some sort of idiot.

'I fell out with Rosie ages ago. You just aren't interested enough to notice.'

Ditto.

'What about your other friends?'

'What other friends? They're all Rosie's pals. I lost all my pals when we moved here.'

I'm in no mood to be made a scapegoat for her unpopularity.

'Have some folk round for your birthday next week. Dad can go to Granda's, I'll go to the pictures or something, so we don't cramp your style.'

Oh no, am I trying to be too nice? She'll know I'm pissed.

'Aw, yeah, brilliant idea, Mum. I'm not seven years old any more, you know?'

'I'm not suggesting jelly and ice cream. I could maybe stretch to a bowl of punch. And I am aware how old you are. Believe me I've felt every year of it.'

'Thanks, Mum. I feel a lot better now,' she drawls, switching off the television. I pray she's going to bed, but she hesitates at the living-room door.

'If you really wanted to do something, though, there is somewhere I fancy going.'

'Surprise me.'

'Well, there's this Italian restaurant in Lothian Road. The food's supposed to be really good and it's quite reasonable and that. You, me, Dad and Jake could go.'

Surely she's not that desperate. I wouldn't even be able to drink.

'A meal?'

'Yeah, that's a pretty normal thing to do on someone's birthday, isn't it? I thought you'd be pleased.'

Oh yes, I'm delighted. Little bitch.

'But why, Joni? You can't even stand to eat in the same room as us. You can't speak to me without that whiny sarcastic tone in your voice. You batter your brother and accuse your father of abusing you. Why in God's name would you want to go out for a meal with us?'

Pushing me out the way, she makes for the hall. 'Oh, don't bother. I wouldn't want to disrupt your hectic social life.'

'What are you on about?'

'Bookie's aren't open till midnight, you know. Where have you been?'

She chooses now to start taking an interest?

'A man went mental in the shop, said he was going to shoot us. The police were in for hours, then I had to take the relief cashier home. I think she was in shock. I didn't want to leave her on her own.'

I'm scared to stop talking in case she interrogates me but there's no need as she merely screams, 'Aye, right!' before slamming herself in her bedroom.

I hate fucking kids. They never stop nip, nip, nipping from the day they're born. Why is wanting some kind of life for yourself after you've had kids a sin akin to granny bashing? Joni'll get pregnant. That'll be the next thing. The next generation of misery. This awful idea reminds me to keep taking the pill next week when it should be my week off. My relationship with Raymond is too intense for menstruation at the moment.

With Moaning Minnie out the way, I pour myself a vodka from the vinegar bottle at the back of the kitchen cupboard. It's ridiculous, sneaking round like this when I never had a serious drink problem in the first place. If I had, I wouldn't have been able to stop for three years, without going to the AA. Gulping it down, I rinse out the glass before someone comes in. It's like being in Cornton Vale.

I go through to the bedroom, to find something to wear tomorrow. My wardrobe is like a museum piece on frumpiness. What's the point in making the effort, though, if your husband can't get it up in the first place? Oh, no, please don't make God have been listening there. It would be grotesque if Vic suddenly started wanting it again after all these years. Praise be to Prozac.

Chapter Seventeen

JONI

I'M TOTALLY FUCKED UP. I've been moping round the house for days. This morning, I couldn't even face school. I told Dad it was period pains but it's my personality that's the real problem. It must be, otherwise I'd have pals. I can't even sleep, which makes the days even longer and more awful. Dad's on the back-shift, so I stay in bed till lunch time, X²ing over Richard Madeley, planning my apology to Rosie, wondering what my family would be like if I'd never been born.

When I get up at half-one, Dad's still not left for work. He apparently has the shits, so he's chain-smoking and drinking black coffee to try and empty his bowels before his shift. Exactly why he thinks I might be interested in this revolting fact is beyond me.

We sit watching *Neighbours*, even though it's been rubbish since Joe Mangel left to become a crap comedian. For some reason, most of the cast are round Helen's house, watching a video of Jason and Kylie's wedding. Surely this must be the ultimate in boredom – watching people on telly watching telly. Then a character I've never seen before comes to the door, looks at Helen and announces she's dead. Really, they've all been sitting round watching a video with a corpse. It's bizarre.

Dad's got tears in his eyes. For fuck's sake, why is he such a sap? They play the theme tune really slow at the end, like they do in soaps when one of the old cunts dies, or someone leaves to have an embarrassing stab at pop-stardom. It's ten past two.

'Shouldn't you be going to work?' I ask, hoping it's just slipped Dad's mind.

'You want rid of me, like?'

What does he think? Naw, I want to sit round watching crappy soaps with my wimpy father all day. He goes through to the bathroom to shave. Following him through, I try to sweet-talk him into taking us to the Antonio restaurant for my birthday.

'I'm game for that. When is it again? Friday?'

Charming, my own father doesn't even know when my birthday is.

'Aye, but I've already asked Mum. She said I don't deserve it cause I don't eat in the same room as you. She thought it was a shite idea.'

He looks at me in the mirror as he slices through the foam.

'Rubbish. She'll be dead chuffed.'

'Naw, Dad, honest, she said she'd get bevvy for me and my pals and you could go to Granda's.'

He finishes shaving, wipes the surplus foam from his ears, and slaps himself on the face. I follow him through for his jacket.

'Sorry, Joni, you've lost me. What is it you actually want? I'm not buying you drink. You want to have a party here?'

Is he thick or what?

'Naw, Dad, listen to me. I want to go for a meal. It's Mum wants me to have a party. Go an speak to her? It's my 16th, I should get to do what I want.'

He agrees, but I know he'll chicken out of asking her. At least, it finally gets rid of him, though. As soon as he's out the door, I tear off my nightie, put on my black Levi's, stolen tight, white v-neck top and patent leather platform ankle boots.

Going through to the money mattress, I have to do some shrewd arithmetic. There's only £30 left in the Joni envelope, so I put in 20 each from Council Tax and telephone. Then I have to put 30 from gas into electricity as the bill arrived yesterday. I only get ten each from the Jake envelope and holidays, for myself. Jesus, when did Mum last put any money in? It's going to run out at this rate.

Since Rosie should be back from school by now, I decide it's time to have friends rather than principles. When I get round there, her mum answers. Rosie's not in yet. I say I'll wait in her room, but she directs me into the lounge. The interrogation starts before I've even sat down – when did I last speak to Rosie? What did we fall out about? Has Rosie said anything about John? Have I met John? Did I go babysitting with Rosie the other week? Did Emma say anything strange? Fucking hell. I deny everything, including having fallen out in the first place and ever having met John.

When Rosie finally does come in, she doesn't exactly look pleased to see me. She just looks scared.

'What is this?' she squeals.

'I just came to see what you were up to. Fancy coming round mines?'

She looks hugely relieved and we both make for the front door. Her mother shouts after us to keep away from John. Oh fuck, the shit must have finally hit the fan.

'What's happened? She was asking me loads of questions. I didnae tell her anything, though.'

'Sshhh, no here,' she says, as if the whole street might be bugged. I'm not even allowed to mention it until we get back to my house. This must be mega. Lighting up one of Dad's fags, I chuck her the packet. She sits on the rug, takes one and shakes her head at me. 'There's really heavy shit going on, Jo, it's been really bad.'

'What, what? Tell me. What's happened?'

Once she starts, I can't take it all in. Every sentence is more unbelievable than the last. John's spent two nights in police cells because Emma, spastic Emma, said he'd been interfering with her.

As if. And Rosie's mum confronted her with the video tape. Rosie said she'd never seen it before but they know she's lying. They know I know too. Oh, fuck.

'They want me to go to court, to say stuff against John.' She starts crying. 'I winnae do it, Jo. He hasnae done anything I didnae want him to. Emma's lying. Folk like her dinnae ken what's real.'

What if I have to go to court because Rosie told me what was happening?

'Maybe she made it up 'cause she's jealous about John and her mum.'

'What about them?'

'Well, they're shagging, aren't they? Maybe she got pissed off 'cause she fancies him.'

'He isnae shagging that old bag. I told you. She just works for him.'

Jeanette's thick make-up and tarty clothes suddenly make sense.

'What, is John a pimp?'

'What are you on about? He's a care assistant. How could you think he was a pimp? You're as bad as them.'

I don't know how to respond so I shut up and let her ramble on.

'I've been trying to phone him since the police let him go on Sunday. That's how I was funny with you. It's just constantly off the hook. I cannae go round there 'cause the neighbours aw ken me. They'll tell Mum. I wish I was dead, Jo, I really do.' And she starts doing big sobs. I've never seen her like this. Shuffling across the carpet, I give her a cuddle. She sniffles into my ear.

'You wouldnae do me a huge favour, would you? I'm sorry we fell out, I really missed you. There's nobody else I can talk about this with.'

'Anything, pal, just say.'

She hesitates, like she thinks I'm not going to like what she has to say.

'You wouldnae go round there for me, would you? Find out what's going on? It's a stair so nobody'll ken you're going to his house. Please, pal.'

It's hard to keep the grin off my face. I'm practically peeing myself. I've finally got an excuse to go round and see John on my own. The most brilliant excuse ever.

'Of course, pal. No problem.'

Yes, yes, yes. She's so grateful she even agrees to come looking for Antonio with me. Fuck him, though, he's just a laddie.

I practically dance along to John's in Dalry. My breathing's dead fast and I can hear my heart beating in my head. I find myself smiling at strangers because it's a shame their lives aren't as exciting as mine. I'm completely hyper when I get into his street, knowing he could come out at any moment. He'll like me so much for having taken such a risk. Also, if he's not allowed near Rosie, he'll be absolutely bursting for it.

Shit, the nameplates on the intercom have all been burnt with cigarettes so I can't tell which one is his. I squint at the two bottom buzzers as I know his flat is in the basement. The door opens as I lean against it. It must be a sign.

There's an odd smell in the stair, not pissy like the stairs in Gorgie but a sort of damp, dirty smell. The lights down to the basement have all been smashed so I have to go by the tiny chink of light from the stair door. I count the steps down, taking about four deeps breaths for each one. When I get down to the two flats at the bottom there's a scary sort of buzzing silence. It feels like I'm miles from civilisation and, if anything happened to me now, nobody would ever find me. Then I see his name on the door – J. Goodfellow, a big red door. Please God make him be in. Rubbing my mouth on the back of my wrist, so my lips go all inflamed, I give the doorbell three short rasps. Still just the silence. I wait a minute, with my ear against the door. I'm sure I can hear a television whispering away in there. I ring again, four times, each longer than the last. I can hear someone moving around. Crouching down, I peer through the letterbox. I've only just made out the pair of legs on the other side of the door when it opens, and John's standing there, naked from the waist up, scowling down at me. He seems about two foot taller than I remember.

'What are you playing at?' he snaps, then seems to recognise me.

My voice comes out all funny.

'I'm Rosie's pal. She made me come.'

'Jesus Christ!' Grabbing my arm, he checks there's nobody outside, pulls me into the house and shuts the door.

'Go through there,' he orders, pushing me towards a room at the top of the hall. It's roasting in there. The heating must be on full belt, but the curtains are drawn and the only light in the room is from the television screen. There's racing on.

'Did anyone see you come here?'

The telly's casting all different sorts of light and shadows on his face, each one making him look sexier than the last.

'I was careful, honest,' I lie. Really though, there could have been a bloody parade in the street and I wouldn't have noticed.

His body is completely hairless, like a little boy's, but his shoulders are broad and he has a slight paunch where his jeans meet his body. It's identical to what I've always imagined Richard Madeley's body to be like.

'Fucksake, if anyone catches you, I've had it. What's Rosie said? She's no outside, is she?'

'Naw, naw, she just wants to know you're alright. Why are they saying that stuff about you?'

'What stuff?' He leans so close to me, I can feel his words on my face.

'Y'know . . . what the police said. Has Rosie's mum mentioned the video?'

'Fucking hell. See that fucking lassie. Tell me, tell me what she's said.'

'Nothing.'

'TELL ME!'

Why is he shouting at me? I'm trying to save him.

'The video . . . y'know . . . her mum found it. Did you say it was yours?'

'Did I fuck. And you two better not either.'

I just keep talking now I've started. What have I got to lose, apart from the obvious?

'Why's Emma saying these things? What's going to happen? Will Rosie have to go to court? She says she winnae.'

Folding his arms, he smiles for the first time since I arrived. I immediately feel in with a chance, just the look he's giving me.

'It's aw shite. Emma's mum made her say it 'cause she owes me money. Disgusting, eh? Using a lassie like that to get back at me. She's the sick one. As long as Rosie keeps her mouth shut, though, they can't make Emma speak in court. I swear, I've done nothing wrong. Sorry, what was your name again?'

'Joni.'

'Joni . . . Joni . . . that's a nice name. Did I no meet you at Rosie's last Hogmanay. I remember your eyes. Lovely eyes.'

He slowly looks me up and down as I stare at the horses on the telly. I'm so glad it's dark. My face is burning up.

'So what else has Rosie said, eh? Come on, give me all the gory details.'

I feel like I'm standing in the middle of Princes Street, naked.

'Och . . . y'know.'

He shrugs. 'Know what?'

'Oh dinnae . . . I cannae say.'

He touches my chin and makes me look up at him.

'D'you cream your knickers when she tells you about it?'

Oh no, I just want to go now. I've never been so embarrassed. I can't believe he's just come out and said that. Is it so obvious?

'. . . eh? Do you like watching dirty videos, too?'

He's speaking in throaty whispers, like Jarvis Cocker. I feel scared but don't know why.

'I suppose so,' I mouth, but no sound comes out.

'You suppose so?'

It's happening. This is what I wanted. Why am I shitting myself?

'Um . . . erm . . . I dinnae ken.'

He puts his face right up to mine, like he's going to kiss me, then makes a clicking noise with his lips on his teeth and starts walking towards the door.

'Look, you better go. I shouldnae've even let you in. How old are you anyway?'

'Sixteen next week. My birthday's on Good Friday.' My voice is working again but it's too late.

He lets out a long groan as I follow him up the dark hall. I keep waiting for him to turn round and grab me but he opens the door and I walk out into the stair. Shit, I can't believe I'm leaving. He fancies me, he really does. Why is he letting me go? I want to beg him to do it to me before my birthday, before it's legal. But he just stands with his thumbs in his belt loops, giving me his stare. I want him so much.

'So what should I tell Rosie?'

He puts his index finger to his lips and says, 'Ssh,' that's all, 'ssh,' then blows me a kiss and shuts the door. What a waste. He fancies me and he's stuck in there on his own. I'd die just to go in and spend an hour with him.

I'm too stunned to move. I want to ring the bell again and offer myself to him. Threaten to spill the beans if he doesn't shag me. That'd just make him hate me, though. A door slams on one of the other landings. Scared it might be the police, I bolt up the stairs and out the main door. I don't want to get him into any more trouble. I think I'm in love with him.

The brightness outside is like a cold shower. I'd lost any sense that it was still daylight. It was like a secret underworld place. John's street suddenly seems so familiar, like I belong here in some way. I'm sure it's a sign.

As I get on the bus, all sorts of emotions are swimming round my head. I wish Rosie wasn't back at my house. I'm feeling dead jealous and I just want to X^2 myself silly. When I get back and see her, I want to tear her hair out for not taking me round there when we had the chance. She was just trying to keep him for herself, selfish bitch.

'You fancy him, don't you?' she suddenly says after I've raved on about what a cow Emma's mum is for about ten minutes.

'Do I fuck.'

'Yes, you fucking do. Did he try anything on with you?'

'Did he fuck,' I say, trying to look disgusted by such an idea.

She smirks. 'I didn't think he would.'

At this moment I make it my ultimate mission in life to steal John away from her. Nothing will get in the way. If I devote all my energy to getting him, I will. I must.

Chapter Eighteen

VIC

THIS BEING MY only day off this week, I'm determined to spend it with fishing rod in hand. To prevent Angie issuing a list of chores to take up my day, I feign sleep till she's left for work, then accidentally put the Yellow Pages on top of her subsequent note of instructions. As a token gesture, I stick her stinky bed-clothes in the machine.

The sky's clear at the moment, but this doesn't count for much with the weird weather recently. Blizzards that last three minutes then disappear without trace, the temperature like a bloody lift. I'm sure it usually stops snowing before April. April the second? Why is that date so familiar? What have I forgotten now?

Snapping the *Scotsman* from the letter-box, I squint in dismay at the back page. Rangers can't get ten in a row. It's always good to see Hibs get beat but not by Rangers when they're vying with Hearts for top of the league. The fact that I sired a Rangers supporter is a constant source of shame and ridicule to me. I tried to bring Jake up as a Jambo but Angie's father brainwashed him with all his Orange shit. Bollocks, that's why the date's so familiar. It's the anniversary of her dad's death. What was it, 1993? Shit, the fifth anniversary as well.

Angie's dad died on Kingsknowe golf course. One minute he was whistling the Sash as he teed up on the eighth hole, the next he was turning blue. Angie lost her licence whizzing up to the hospital, at 11 in the morning, three times over the limit. She remembers nothing about it now – the hospital, the funeral, nothing. Just one day, about two years later, she finally sobered up and realised her dad was gone.

To cheer her up, I dutifully decide to pop into her work and take her for lunch. She's laughing with a colleague when I go in. It's weird seeing her with a smile on her face. I stand, waving like a prick, but she serves two punters before noticing me. God, what sort of a look was that? A mix of terror and loathing. My sense of well-being pisses out of me as she over-rings the next customer. As I walk up to the counter, she scowls and mutters something. Pardon me for breathing.

'What're you playing at? What's wrong?'

God, is it so long since I've taken my wife for lunch she assumes I'm the bearer of tragic news.

'I just realised what the date was, sorry. Have you had your break?'

Staring at the calendar on the wall does nothing to allay her apparent confusion.

'. . . your dad. It's been five years.'

Her mouth drops open.

'Oh, shit, of course.' She stands awkwardly, then whispers something to the laddie at the desk. He gives me the thumbs-up as she gets her coat. God, why did I bother? I could be down the Water of Leith with a bucket of maggots by now. She blusters out into the street with me in tow.

'I can't be long. The relief cashier didn't turn up.'

'Remind me never to be spontaneous again, will you?'

'I'm only saying.'

I suggest the pub next door. A jumbo sausage and chips would just go down a treat, but she seems to take this as an affront.

'Not a pub, eh? How about an Indian? Or I think the Chinese does business lunches. I'm not even hungry, to tell the truth.'

'What's the point in going for a meal then? Come on, dinnae be silly.'

Taking her arm, I try to pull her in but she stands rigid, like some sullen child.

'Fuck off, I don't want to. You can't turn up at my work and drag me to the pub.'

'C'mon, restaurants take ages. I thought you didn't have much time.'

'Don't do this to me, Vic.'

'Do what? I thought you'd be upset about your dad.'

She flutters her eyelashes helplessly, then yells, 'OK, OK, do it your way, as usual. I'm sorry, you know, I'm sorry I'm such a bitch and you're such a fucking saint.'

I start to walk away but she grabs my jacket.

'Come on. You want to go in, so let's fucking go in.'

Ordering a Diet Coke and bowl of soup, she goes to the back of the pub and sits in the corner. The barmaids are smirking at us, no doubt having heard the carry-on outside. It's put me right off my jumbo sausage, so I just have a fresh orange.

When I take the drinks over, she's mellowed slightly.

'Sorry, Vic. The dad thing has been preying on my mind. I don't want them asking about it at work. It's private.'

Lighting two fags, I hand her one.

'D'you want to talk about it? Five years, eh? I could hardly believe it.'

Inhaling deeply, she blows smoke rings at me. She's actually looking quite attractive. Perhaps I just haven't looked for a while.

'I'd rather try and block it out. I don't have time to think about it.'

'I went through it with Mum. It comes to the surface when you least expect it.'

She lets out a smoky sigh.

'Please, Vic, don't get all deep on me, eh? I've got opening day at Aintree this afternoon.'

A marital silence descends upon us. I find myself struggling to think of things to say that can't possibly offend her. I tell her what Joni said about Friday.

'Bullshit. It was me suggested we go out somewhere as a family.'

'She said you wanted to buy drink for all her pals.'

'Oh c'mon, she's taking the piss. Y'know how she plays us against each other.'

Is this a puzzle I'm supposed to solve?

'So you do want to go for a meal?'

She says yes, but her face says no. I give up. I will never try to understand women again.

The barmaid brings her lunch. I'm grateful for the interruption. A look of utter displeasure returns to Angie's face. God knows what I'm supposed to have done now. I tell her about the woman getting gang-banged up the back of the bus, but she's too busy trying to get soup to her mouth before she trembles it down her front.

'God, it's so long since I've eaten at a table. It's much easier on the settee with the bowl under your chin,' she laughs, before giving up. 'What you doing tonight?'

I shrug. 'What do I do every night?'

'Go and see your dad while you've still got one.'

'I saw him at the weekend.'

'So? He's not got anyone else.'

Tell me about it.

'Come with me then? He was sorry he missed you the other day.'

'I'm going late-night shopping with Vicki, to get something for Joni. Anyway, I'll have to make a move. First race is at two.'

I finish my drink as she puts her coat on.

'So how many work in that shop? Just the pair of you?'

She doesn't speak till we get out onto the street.

'So are you going to your dad's tonight?'

'I shouldn't think so.'

'So you'll be in all evening?'

'I was going to go fishing. Why? Do you want me to get something for the tea?'

'What's the point. Nobody's ever in to eat it. I'll probably just grab something with Vicki. Anyway, I must go.' She's really champing at the bit to get back to work.

'Isn't there another cashier? You're entitled to more than 20 minutes, surely.'

'I've told you. The relief cashier didn't turn up. The usual lassie's off with stress after that fucking nutter the other day.'

She does look good – younger somehow, slimmer. When I peck her on the cheek, she looks at me as if I'm some over-zealous dirty old uncle.

'What's wrong with you?'

'See you later, Angie,' I mutter as she hurries away.

When I get back to the flat, Joni shoots into the corner of the living room, like a disturbed mouse.

'Erm . . . hi, Dad . . . I've to hand in an essay. I forgot it this morning.'

'Oh, yeah?'

'Got it now anyway. My next lesson's not till half-two. I'm meeting Rosie.'

I follow her into the hall.

'I just had lunch with Mum. She's fine about going for a meal. She said it was her idea in the first place.'

'What's she on about? Honest, Dad, she was dead against it. Fucking hell, lying about her own daughter. She needs a shrink.'

That's it. I'll just have to stop trying to work this one out or it'll do my head in.

'So that's it then? Meal on Friday?'

She shrugs. 'Actually, I'm not that bothered any more. I don't know what I'm doing yet.'

'Fine.'

They're trying to make me go insane. That's it, they're going to get me sectioned and sell the house.

'Da-ad.'

'Yeah, how much?'

'What?' she scowls.

'Well, usually when you look at me like that it means you want to borrow money you don't intend paying back.'

'Fuck off. You're wrong actually. Don't be so sarcastic.'

'Sarcasm and stating a fact are not the same thing, dearest.'

'Don't call me that. Naw, Dad, but seriously, d'you know how old you have to be to give evidence in court? Y'know, can kids be made to do it?'

God. What now?

'What's happened?'

'Oh, it's not me. I'm doing a story for English and I don't want my 16-year-old giving evidence if it wouldn't happen in real life. D'you know anything about it?'

'What's he supposed to have done?'

'Nothing. I meant, could he give evidence against someone else?'

Typical, she finally asks me a normal daughter-type question and I can't answer.

'I dunno. I'd think you'd have to be 18. You couldnae serve on a jury if you weren't old enough to give evidence. I'll find out. Can I read it when it's finished?'

'I suppose, but I've still got a lot to do. It's not to be in till next term.' She echoes, running down the stairs.

Hanging the washing out, I get my fishing gear together and walk along to the fishing shop. I spend about 20 minutes chatting to the manager, trying to impress him with my knowledge of fly-tying in the hope he'll offer me a job. He, at least, humours me.

Once I'm down by the water's edge, with a hookful of juicy maggots, breathing in the vegetation, my mind starts to clear. I get lost in the bubble and rush of the strong, black current, utterly focused on the five-pound trout I know lives nearby. There's plenty one-pounders to be getting on with but I let them go as they're generally full of sewage from the bakers and food factory. I could take them home and stick them in the oven ready-stuffed, so to speak, but the sight of diced carrots when you cut open a fish, conjures up all sorts of unpleasant explanations.

I sit there for hours. Even when it starts to get dark, I keep going, not wanting to stop. It's much better once the sun's off the water anyway. I spot a fox on the other side, sniffing, prickling and cowering about in the bushes. It starts to rain, but I still sit there, letting it run down the back of my collar and seep through my cords. I wait till I'm completely sodden before reluctantly calling it a day. I walk, blindly, along the pathway with only the light of the moon and the slight illumination from the lamp-posts high up on the other side to guide me. I take small, delicate steps for fear of treading on toads. I see birds snuggled into balls of sleep where the moonlight shines through arterial trees and bushes. I smell wet grass, mud, wild garlic, leaves breathing, wonderful, wild, indescribable smells.

Then I'm suddenly out in the concrete again, staring across at the Wheatsheaf. I cross the road. The clock in the chippie says quarter to ten. Jesus, I've done just about a full shift down there. Immediately, I start feeling guilty about not getting anything for the tea. My damp clothes start to annoy me.

In a moment of inspiration, I phone the house to see if anyone wants chips brought in. There's no answer. During the few seconds I'm in the phone box, the rain turns into hard driving hail. It stings my face and forces me reluctantly to seek shelter on a bus.

Angie's in the kitchen, pouring herself a Diet Coke when I get in. She apparently got back at quarter to eight and was in the toilet when I phoned. Her coat is hanging on the kitchen door. There are dark wet patches on it.

'I felt bad about snapping at you, so I came back early. Fuck knows why.'

'I said I might go fishing.'

Her hair's wet too. Why is she lying? I wasn't going to mention it but she starts on about how I'm a selfish bastard who doesn't give a shit about his own father but tries to make her feel guilty about hers. Only Angie could make a man feel like a villain for taking his wife out for lunch and going fishing on his day off.

'Hang on a bloody minute, here. If you got back in at quarter to eight, how come your coat's soaking, eh? I've been out in the elements all day and there wasn't a drop of rain till an hour ago. What time is it now, eh? Five past ten.'

Oh no, bring on the pointy finger.

'So what are you saying, eh? You don't fucking trust me, is that it? For your information I went downstairs for fags. I got caught in the rain on my way back. Suspicious bastard.'

She's lying.

'Give's one, then.'

I don't know if she looks alarmed because I've caught her out or because she think's I'm propositioning her.

'What?'

'Give me a fag. If you've just bought a fresh packet, let's see them. Give me one.'

Grabbing her bag, she hurls an unopened packet of Marlboro Lights at me. Shit. The first time in years I've actually stood up to her, I'm in the wrong. Bloody typical.

'Go on, then, fucking smoke one you bastard, you were so

fucking desperate for them a minute ago, smoke one.' At least I think that's what she says. Her voice is so shrill and hysterical now, I can barely make her out. '. . . where the fuck d'you think I'd been, eh? Getting it elsewhere? Did old soft dick think I'd finally had enough? Would you blame me? Would you fucking blame me?'

The neighbours must be able to hear this. Great, now everyone in the stair'll think, 'There's that guy that can't get it up,' when they see me.

'I guess I don't have much to stimulate me.'

'Oh, it's my fault, is it? Well, hey, Vic, don't worry. I wouldn't screw you again if you had a gun at my head. I mean to say, *come and watch Hissing Sid get big*, you know, I'm not a fucking four-year-old.'

I let her go on, in the hope she'll eventually get round to chucking me out. She just has to say it. I'll take the kids. See how she likes living on a bookie clerk's wages. I make twice what she does and still she grudges me the occasional bloody football match.

'. . . look at you, sitting there taking it. You don't even attempt to act like a real man. What was I fucking on the day I met you, eh? I must have been fucking pissed.'

'You always were.'

I see her arm go back, then in slow motion, the big glass ashtray come hurtling towards me. Unfortunately, I'm also moving in slo-mo, so don't manage to get my hand up in time to divert its course to my face. Thunk! Right on my eyebrow, right on the button. The pain goes shooting down to my stomach and I feel like I'm going to throw up. She just watches, no doubt hoping she's fractured my skull. Putting my hand up to my eye, I let out a long, delayed groan. Blood tickles down my wrist.

'Jesus, woman. You're completely insane.'

My eye's starting to close already. I can feel it swelling and throbbing but she just sits laughing.

'Tell you what,' I say, getting the duvet out the airing cupboard and lobbing it at her, '. . . you have the bloody settee tonight.'

'Oh, you're so masterful,' she whines, as I thunder through to our room. Blood's still dripping from my eye as I tear my clothes off. The bed-clothes are still on the washing line, so I can bleed all over the naked pillows and duvet. I don't give a damn, I paid for them anyway. As I stumble blindly into bed, the pain is unbelievable but if I go through for painkillers, it'll just start her off again. I lie there for ages, thinking that it must stop hurting eventually, but it doesn't. I wish I was dead. The way I'm feeling, I will be by morning.

Chapter Nineteen

JAKE

WE'RE SUPPOSED TO go to church – aye, fucking church – with the school at 11 this morning. It's a yearly punishment they make you go through before freeing you for the Easter break. As it's a Proddy church, though, Sean's not going, so neither am I. The churchy bit of religion's really boring anyway. It's the football that matters.

We agree to meet at the main door after registration, then just bugger off. It only takes five minutes but I'm gimping to get back to Sean's before Eva goes out. As I try to make my exit, however, the headmaster drags me into his room.

'A word, please, Mr Scott.'

Here we fucking go. Closing his office door, he tells me to sit down. As he usually makes me stand with my hands behind my back, for a second I think he's maybe come in peace. Then he starts on about the Mr Russell cupboard incident. Just recalling it makes me smirk, but I say nothing.

'You obviously find it very amusing. Does it make you feel big, to treat someone like that?'

Bloody hell, don't tell me old Muirie's a shirt-lifter as well.

'Honest, sir. I was at the back of the gym, practising ma throws. I didnae even realise what'd happened.'

'Come off it, Jake. He was put in there half-way through the lesson. If the janitor hadn't been so conscientious at locking-up time, the poor man would've been in there all night.'

Fucking beauty. I wish I could stop smiling. He'll think it was me.

'. . . come on. A teacher vanishes in the middle of a lesson, the pupils stage a mini-riot and you don't find anything strange in that?'

'But that's what it's usually like.'

He tries to stare me out as he squeezes a squash ball. I bet that's it. They're just a bunch of poofs covering up for each other. I'm sweating with the strain of clenching my bum cheeks by the time he shows me the door. I always thought he looked a bit like Dale Winton.

'I'll need to speak to everyone again. I have to establish the facts for my report to the Occupational Health. I don't know, another good teacher lost through stress whose wages we still have to pay from our budget. And your parents wonder why there's not enough books to go round.'

Aw, deedums!

'Sorry I couldnae help you, Mr Muir.'

'Well, if you do remember anything, slip a note under my door. Anonymously if you must. It's easier to intimidate people into talking once I know who the ringleader is.'

Fuck, it's the perfect way to get back at Daniel. Then again, why should he get punished for the one decent thing he's done in his whole life? That's the thing. He's maybe a cunt, but Mr Russell's the real bad one, the real sick fucker. Why do only the male teachers fancy the young laddies round here anyway?

Pulling my jacket over my arse, I run down the main stairs. I'm relieved to see Sean still there, despite me being about 15 minutes late. As I near the bottom, though, I realise who he's with – the fucking man himself, Daniel, and Shug. Backing against the wall, I peer through the railings at them. I should probably go and help, but the more I watch the less it looks like he's actually in trouble. In fact, they're all looking pretty fucking pally, laughing away, about me, no doubt. It's suddenly so obvious they're all in it together, to get me good. How could I have fallen for Sean and all his shit? Still, I just stand there, praying that one of them will suddenly hit the other, but they don't. I should have listened to Granda. Never trust a Catholic.

Skulking back up the stairs, I go out the back way. All my barrie plans for the next fortnight are fucked now. As I run up the middle of the road, I hope some joy-riding radge will come speeding round the corner and kill me. For once, though, there's not so much as a fucking cyclist.

To avoid bumping into the three treacherous fuckers, I jump on the first bus that comes. I'm only going three stops, but the driver makes me go upstairs as it's absolutely stowed out with kids obviously allergic to church like myself. It's like T in the fucking Park. Everyone's that loud, dangerous, hysterical sort of way, but the lassie behind me pushes me towards the one free seat, half-way up the aisle, right in the middle of the bastards. As I shuffle into it, I realise what all the hoo-hah's about. Sitting in front of me are a Mongol couple, I don't know what age, you can never tell. About a hundred kids are throbbing round – laughing, staring, screaming. At the next stop, even more kids squeeze on and join in. There's adults down the front, but they, like me, just stare out the window, pretending nothing's happening.

Two laddies from fourth-year Remedial are kneeling in front of the trembling Mongols, prodding at them.

'Fucking do it, do it again.'

The male Mongol looks back at us all with a sort of indescribable scared, help-me look. It just gets them in even more of a frenzy.

'Do it, do it, do it, do it . . .' each one louder than the last, till my head's swimming with it. The male Mongol, getting more and more agitated, suddenly smacks the female Mongol in the face. They keep chanting, wanting more, making him hit her again and again. It's obvious he's only doing it cause he's shit-scared, but his girlfriend's greeting cause she doesnae understand. Her arms are stretching out to him for a cuddle but the mob won't let him stop. There's red blotches all over her face where she's been skelped. It's a fucking shame. Even a couple of sixth-year lassies are sitting up on their seats, scranning chips, screaming,

'Hit her, hit her, hit her, hit her . . .'

They're like they wild chimps you see in documentaries. When he clouts her, it hardly makes any noise at all, not like in films, but somehow it sounds much sorer. It's sort of sick-making. Then Diabetic Elaine from English starts smacking the guy round the back of the head, not hard, just to annoy him. I cannae take much more of this. Watching it and no doing anything makes me as bad as the rest of them.

My legs are jellified when I stand up. As I make for the stairs, a podgy hand reaches from the rabble, the chippolata fingers grabbing for help. I'm so scared, I just nash down the stairs and ring, ring, ring on the bell. I'd tell the driver what was going on, but what could he do? They'd probably just turn on him instead.

The bus is still pulsating with screams and floor-stomping as it pulls away. Why did I not make the driver do something? I can't get the vision of these desperate, fat little fingers out my head. If I'd just waited for Sean, I'd have missed the whole thing. Running away like that just seems so pathetic now.

When I get to the stair, I hesitate outside his door, trying to work up the guts to knock. It feels like hours since I saw him with these two cunts, but it's only been about 15 minutes. Maybe they're in there with him, waiting for me. Maybe they're taking turns at Eva in the meantime.

Horrified by all the possibilities, I go upstairs and try to lose myself in *FIFA*. I play crap though, 'cause the stuff on the bus keeps coming into my head. Stress-relief wanking's no good either, as I keep getting images of that Mongol lassie's bashed face. I cannae wank about that. This is ridiculous. It's the Easter holidays, for fuck's sake.

I go through to the kitchen for a glass of Ribena. Dad's pills are lying out on the bunker. They're supposed to make him happy but, if that's him happy, he's an even sadder bastard than I thought. Popping one out the metal packet, I pull the grey and green sections apart. Powder spills onto the bunker. Inspired, I carry the fullest end through to the living room and get the framed photo of Joni and me when we were wee, from the mantelpiece. Emptying the remaining powder onto the glass, I chop at it with the edge of mum's video card. I've no idea why they do this in films, but it feels dead cool and it's dead easy to work it into three lines. Rolling a minging old pound note from my pocket into a tube, I stick it up my nose and snort. The pain is shocking. Like I've been shot between my eyes. There's a revolting half-swallowed paracetamol taste in my mouth and the pain, oh my God, just keeps spreading – behind my eyes, up my forehead, in my temples, like it's burning into my skull. I'd blow my nose to try and get some of it out, but I'm scared I'll end up with a hankie full of brains. I ease myself back on the settee – blinded. It feels like my head's melting. Mum's going to come home and find me lying here like Sean Connery at the end of *Highlander*.

I sit for over an hour, waiting for my life to flash before me, waiting to see the light that folk that've died talk about but there's still just this incredible soreness. When I do open my eyes again, it's just a blur, like trying to see through rippling water. Once I manage to focus, I think it's a miracle. My head's still nipping, but it's not even in the same solar system of pain as before. These pills must be really fucking strong. Next time, I'll maybe just try smoking them.

As I clean up the evidence, I start to feel a different kind of odd. Maybe this is the happy part taking effect. On the other hand, maybe you just feel naturally happy after a near-death experience.

The doorbell goes as I'm hiding the dismembered pill in an old crisp bag. I'm so completely overjoyed to see Sean's reflection through the frosted glass I forget about the possibility of Shug and Daniel being behind him with baseball bats.

'You must be smoking better weed than me, man.' He laughs at my Dracula eyes as he trots in with his joystick.

Too embarrassed to admit what I've done, I blame it on hay fever. The bogging stuff I'm sneezing up by this time helps convince him. There's blood in my snot and everything.

I tell him about Muirie collaring me and my new all-teachers-are-poofs conspiracy theory. He's dead impressed I didn't grass Danny up, but only because Eva gets her blow from him. He'd been scoring for her when I ran away. They both think he's a wanker too, but he only charges £25 a quarter. I'm so relieved, I could swear allegiance to the Pope . . . well, perhaps not quite that relieved. I don't bother mentioning the Mongols now as I don't want to spoil my moment of born-again happiness by thinking about it again.

Since nobody's due back for hours, we spend the afternoon round mine, making dirty phone calls. It's brilliant. You just hang up if men answer. The majority of women put the phone down as soon as you start, but there's plenty that get really into it, to keep you going. I tell them I'm a fireman with a ten-inch cock. Sean's a young black boy that wants to get his hole before his arranged marriage.

It goes down a storm until the wifie in the hairdresser's round the corner says, 'I know who you are and I'm calling the police,' after I've told her I've been watching her house as I choke the chicken. I sort of go off it after that. Thank fuck we were doing 141.

We have two full-length games of *FIFA*, the first really boring, Germany versus Italy, as Klinsmann gets sent off in the first half. The second isn't so bad, an Old Firm match which goes to penalty kicks after a 30-all draw. By this time, though, we're so bored with it we probably feel like real footballers do at the end of extra time.

We go down to Sean's about eight, as Mum's due back and I don't want him subjected to her. Eva's working on the computer, so we play *Tomb Raider* on the PlayStation, through the lounge. Lara Croft's nothing on the babe in the next room, though, and I get killed all over the place.

It's half-nine before Eva comes through and, even then, it's to ask us to keep the noise down. For a terrible moment I think she means the nyaffish *peow peow* sound effects I've been doing. When we shut up, though, she says it's coming from the stair. It takes me a while to make out, as my ears are still ringing from explosions and gunfire. But gradually I hear a steady, regular, banging and groaning, like someone hammering a nail and hitting their finger every time.

'It's that Irish nurse next door getting screwed,' whispers Eva. I get an instant willie twitch. God, it is, and it sounds like they're really going at it. Faster and faster, then, with a wolf-like howl, it suddenly stops.

Sean and Eva go into hysterics. I pretend I find it funny as well, but I'm too desperate for a wank now to be very convincing. It's been building up since we done the phone calls this afternoon. Maybe Dad's pills have got rhino horn in them.

Too conscious of my stiffie to act normally any more, I tell them my hay fever's playing up again. I'll just end up saying something stupid to Eva when I'm like this. She's four years older than me as it is. I have to try and act at least a wee bit mature.

As I limp up to our floor, a drunk guy suddenly appears from nowhere and almost knocks me flying as he staggers down the stairs. He snarls something at me as he steadies himself on the rail and takes tiny, careful steps down to the next landing. Who the fuck is that? He must have come out of Mrs Anderson's, but I can't imagine an old sweetie wifie like her knowing someone like that. Then I mind hearing about her embarrassing son that's not allowed to go round there any more. He supposedly went to America to join the Ku Klux Klan, so he's probably an alkie as well. I wonder what he's come back for? It'd be barrie if he'd just murdered her.

Chapter Twenty

ANGIE

FUCK, WE WERE back here last night. I've no idea if anyone was in, or came in, or what, but Raymond was definitely here. Scared to go through to the living room for fear he's lying unconscious with his cock out, I hide under the shower for 15 minutes, trying to wash the sweats away.

Towelling my tender body dry, I squeak condensation from the mirror and check the damage. My eyes, like my skin, are completely bloodshot. The right side of my face is covered in a corned-beef rash. Scrubbing my teeth and the roof of my mouth with bicarbonate-of-soda toothpaste, it's more ow than wow. My skin drinks up moisturiser like a plant left to starve over the holidays. By the time I dress and get my make-up on, I'm sweating like a bastard again.

The living room looks fairly innocuous. There's a lump of duvet on the settee, but the protruding raw, picked feet are proof enough that this is only my husband. Retrieving my crumpled coat from the kitchen floor, I try to make the door without waking him. Just as I click down the snib, though, he comes coughing through in all his turquoise Y-fronted, milky-skinned glory. There's a purple bruise above his left eye. Has there been a punch-up in my honour?

'All right, love?' he mumbles, cagily.

'I've got a fucker of a migraine.'

As this isn't taken as a cue to make some drink-related crack, I assume I'm still in the clear.

'Take a sickie. It's no your fault they don't employ enough staff.'

I grab my bag, hastily pulling the zip over the empty vodka bottle. Shit, if we polished that off, Raymond must have been here for hours.

'If it doesn't go away, I'll come home. It's the Head Office do tonight, though. I promised I'd show face.'

He gives me a scary, we-need-to-talk kind of look.

'Ange, about the other night . . .'

'What other night?'

'Thursday, y'know. I don't want us to fight all the time. It's no good for anyone.'

What the fuck did I do on Thursday? What day is this? Saturday? Is that the night he went fishing? I didn't give a shit he was late. Raymond left early for a management meeting, I was just pissed off.

'Aye, Vic. See you later.'

There's a bus at the stop. As soon as I get on and the doors close, I start over-heating something awful. I feel a damp patch blossoming on the back of my dress. What am I wearing a fucking coat for? Oh Christ. Someone's crunch, crunch, crunching on a bag of cheese and onion crisps, behind me. Fucking what? Who eats crisps at this time of the morning? Believing I can actually taste the smell provokes a hastily swallowed rush of vomit. I have to go downstairs and stand. It's even hotter down there. My mascara's probably streaming down my cheeks. Giving up, I get off.

The joint spur of seeing Raymond and having a large vodka encourages me to run the rest of the way. The fucking pub's closed. It opens an hour later at weekends. There's nobody at the shop yet, either. I don't believe this. We're not due to start work for another half-hour. The pub along the road, the one that opens earlier for shift workers, beckons. Just as I start to walk towards it, though,

Raymond's car squeals round the corner. He notices the dormant pub before he notices me.

'Fuck, I forgot they opened late on Saturdays. Ach, well, there's always this,' he says, producing a half-bottle of Grant's from his hold-all. We decide to go to the shop.

I go through to the kitchen and pour us a couple of large ones as he pins up the *Racing Post*. I'm taking it over to him when someone knocks at the door. As it's probably just some over-ardent punter wanting early prices, we ignore it. Going back behind the counter, Raymond puts his arms round me, and nibbles the back of my neck. I rub myself against him, desperate for a quick, sticky shag to start the day off. But still the knocking. It's so fucking distracting. Raymond lets go of me and starts marking a sample bet up on the board. I light a fag.

'We were back at my place last night, eh? Nobody came in, did they?'

The phone rings before he has a chance to reply. Answering it, he immediately starts arguing with someone on the other end. I pour us both another drink.

'. . . look, we're fine as we are . . . nothing we can't deal with . . .' The knocking starts again. '. . . all right then, awright, I don't seem to have an option . . . fine,' and he slams it down.

'They've sent us a fucking relief cashier. I've got to take her. Fucksake.'

Knocking back the fresh drink, he throws a mint in his mouth and goes to open the door. I don't believe this. I can't believe we've wasted the only time we're going to have alone at work today, working.

Then suddenly he's walking back towards me with this tanned, blonde piece of white trash. Her name is Debbie. She isn't wearing a bra and immediately proceeds to tell us she's really a model and is only working in bookies' at the moment to make a bit extra cash for her wedding. Model my arse. She has tiny, rat-like eyes; in fact, with a different hair-do she could pass for Frank Skinner. It's probably not her face they photograph though.

'So where do you model?' asks Raymond, seemingly fascinated.

'Oh, magazines mainly. Glamour shots. Tasteful, though. I've not been doing it long. I was in my 20s before I accepted how attractive I was.'

Raymond goes to make coffee before he falls down her cleavage.

'Just a cup of boiling water for me, please. I don't touch caffeine, it's really bad for the skin.'

So's boiling water, if you throw it in someone's face. Desperate for a distraction, I open the shop ten minutes early. Old Harry's up immediately with his dog bets. He writes them out the night before as he comes off the night-shift at six, so is usually blotto by opening. I go up to serve him but he gestures to Debbie.

'I'd like her to take it.'

Cheers, Harry. I gesture to the till. Debbie stays where she is, chewing her lip.

'Actually, I've not been doing this very long. I'm a bit uncomfortable taking bets. Can I do the pay-out? I'm fine w'that. D'you mind?'

Inspired, Harry starts pulling ancient betting slips out his pockets, studying them, searching for that elusive key to the kingdom of Debbie. Debbie, taking my silence as some kind of agreement, sits down at the pay-out and starts thumbing through a *Brides* magazine. I feel ashamed to be female.

The whole point of the gambling business is that we take money, not give it out, subsequently she's glued to her seat for most of the morning. At eleven, one of the Chinamen wins two grand on a dog forecast. Raymond has to go out to get money from another shop to pay him. He asks if we want bacon rolls brought back. Debbie almost chokes on her hot water.

'Oh, I couldn't. How can you eat things like that? You'd be as well eating pure fat, the damage it'll do to your thighs.'

I suggest that people usually eat such things for the taste, rather than the desire to have lumpy legs. However, not wanting her looking down her nose at me if I so indulge, I decline Raymond's offer, despite being fucking starving.

As he's leaving, half the Ming Dynasty dash in and start scribbling out screeds of bets. There's already a queue of about five people. Harry insists on early prices for all his horses, so I have to flick them up on the screen. Debbie slowly peels a nectarine.

'Is it usually this quiet?'

I'm taking bets for a solid 20 minutes before there's a lull. Escaping briefly to the toilet, I scream as I piss. It's near impossible to work up the incentive to get off the pan and go back through. When I do, another huge queue has formed. Debbie is showing Harry her engagement ring.

'I said it was daft to spend so much, but that's what Daryl's like. He always has to get the very best for his princess.' Harry's just standing gawping. I used to like him as well.

Fumbling for my fags, I light one up. She starts coughing, but I ignore her, since I only lit up to annoy her in the first place.

'Hack, hack . . . oh sorry, I'm asthmatic . . . hack. Cigarette smoke's one of the worst things for it.' I continue puffing. '. . . I thought the shops had a no-smoking policy behind the counter these days.'

'No this one.'

She goes on until I finally stub out.

'Oh, I don't know how you can do that. It really makes people stink, euch. I couldn't stand smelling like that.'

I look at the clock. Five fucking hours to go. By the time Raymond comes back, I'm ready to hand in my notice.

'Any problems? No pissed-off Irish psychopaths?' he asks, devouring his roll.

'It's been dead, hasn't it?' Debbie says, inexplicably.

The saucy bacon smell soon saturates the tiny space we're working in. As this is due to Raymond, however, Debbie says nothing. Peeling another nectarine, I'm convinced she's rubbing the segments on her lips as she speaks to him. She has the sort of face that usually has come running down it.

We're chock-a-block in the run up to the first race from Aintree. Still, Debbie ploughs her way through the complex text of her *Brides* magazine. Even the Chinese guys, who usually don't give us the time of day, hang round the pay-out, leering at her. One of the ridiculous bastards knocks on the glass partition.

'I'm not being funny, but are you Baby Spice?'

Rolling her eyes, she howls with laughter.

'Ooh, I don't look that old, do I?'

Jesus, the whole shop's in fits. It's like *An Audience with Debbie*. By two-thirty I can stand it no longer, and escape to the pub on a makeshift late lunch. It's heaven to be away from her but, pretty quickly, the paranoia sets in. Twenty minutes is as long as I can stand before visions of Raymond pawing her drive me back there. It's like fucking Hillsborough by then.

The National starts. Three horses look like they've had it immediately.

'I hate when you see them twitching like that. You know they're fucked,' confides a new, sensitive Raymond.

Debbie, having had her attention drawn to the spectacle, gets very emotional, and runs off to the bog, in tears. It's the first time she's left Raymond and me alone all day. We're too busy to even look at each other. The race is run and replayed, the injured horses destroyed, the bets settled and paid out, before she reappears. Not that it really matters as she's fucking useless anyway. She says she's been sick and feels terrible. She doesn't feel right paying money out to people who are partly responsible for the deaths of horses.

Raymond tells her if she wants to go home, he'll still pay her till the end of the day. She's so overcome with gratitude, she seems to forget she was ill in the first place. Still, being rushed off our feet till closing time is a small price to pay for the beautiful image of her walking out that fucking door. The shop's still packed for the last race, the 5.25 at Hereford. But at least she's fucking gone. We finally herd them all out at ten to six.

We agree unanimously that the shop we borrowed the two grand from earlier can wait till Monday to get it back. Raymond insists on cashing up, so I can get my face on for the do. Miraculously, it's spot-on first time. He throws the till roll at me to countersign and phone through to Head Office, as he splits the money between the two safes. I long for him to come back through and fuck me on the carpet. Instead, he comes back through, with his hold-all.

'I forgot to do my fucking washing. Our machine's fucked. She'll make me do it when the match's on tomorrow, now.'

I don't like when he mentions 'her'. I almost feel like crying because he has a washing machine with another woman. For God's sake.

As we walk towards the door, the alarm behind the counter goes off. Raymond runs back and fiddles desperately with the digit display. Christ, it's such an awful noise. It reminds me of Debbie's laugh. Both are still ringing in my head as we make for the pub.

'I don't know if I can be arsed with this Head Office thing. I'm no in the mood for hobnobbing with a bunch of wanky Area Managers. I saw them aw the other night.'

'Have a few drinks and think about it.'

We do have a few drinks, but it doesn't get mentioned. After my third double, I'm feeling less compelled about the whole thing anyway. Raymond makes up for not fucking me in the shop, by fucking me verbally, whispering obscenities as the two bitchy barmaids sneer at us. By eight-thirty, half an hour after the do was due to start, we're desperately trying to think of somewhere we can go to have sex. We can't go back to the shop or the alarm'll go off again.

'What about your place? I can fuck you up the arse in Mr Scott's bed again.'

'We did that?'

'You can't remember? You were crying out for it last night, you dirty bitch.'

I don't doubt him but if I forgot that, I could forget anything.

'Have you any idea when it was you left? My mind's blank from the pub onwards.'

'I'm no sure. *Sportscene* was on when I got in, so it must've been before ten.' His recollection of events seeming more assured than my own, I take it as gospel and assume nobody saw him. We have another double each, then leave.

'It's getting dark. Fancy a bit of a Lady Chatterley up Colinton Dell?'

I agree. Rather spookily, however, the traffic's been diverted, and we end up in a tailback right next to the pub where the function's taking place. Convinced that fate has brought us here, we decide to go in for a few swifties.

When we get inside and I'm suddenly surrounded by high heid yins and faces I'd forgotten existed, I suddenly feel rat-arsed. I'm scared to talk to anyone in case they notice. This senseless feeling soon passes, though, so I position myself strategically against the free bar. There's no spirits left but gallons of wine, so I get stuck into the Chardonnay. Raymond gets accosted by a group of management knobs. I have to resist the temptation to hang round him limpet-like. Everyone else is mingling. As I get fired into my third glass of wine, Katy, a cashier I used to work with up Tollcross, throws her arms round me. We never got on that well, so she must be half-cut. We do the usual dull small talk. She's working down Portobello now. I tell her I'm working with Raymond.

'Oh God, Ray Ramage? I once worked relief with him. It wusnae the kind of relief he had in mind, though. He's awfie slimy, d'you no think?'

'I find him all right. Can't say I'd noticed.'

'Oh, come off it. I tell you, if Ray's no made a pass at you, I'd take it as a knockback. You must be the first.'

How dare she refer to him as Ray. He doesn't even let me call him that. I go quiet. The conversation somehow turns to her husband's gall bladder. Knocking back another glass of wine, I look for an escape route. Unfortunately, I have to endure a full forty minutes of her family woes and frantic bitching before Raymond finally rescues me. He's taken his jacket off and can't remember where he put it. His shirt is sodden with perspiration. His eyelids are droopy and inebriated. Grabbing me, he plants a soggy kiss on my cheek and waits to be invited into the conversation. His appearance seems to unnerve Katy, and after a derisory glance at our embrace, she feels a sudden need to circulate.

Struggling, with Raymond's full weight on my shoulder, I drag him over to a seat in the corner. He seems to collide with every table we pass, cursing as he goes. When I finally get him seated, he tries to pull me onto his knee.

'Aw, babes, sorry I got lumbered w'these bastards. Are you throwing a moody on me?'

Struggling free, I sit opposite.

'They're probably taking notes. I bet they just have these things so they can spot the staff that look like they're screwing each other.'

He stares across at me with a big glaikit grin on his face. His pupils seem to be moving independently of each other.

'Ah'm gonna fuck you, Mrs Scott.'

'Ssh.'

'Ssh, what? What are you shushing me for? I'm just saying, ah'm gonna fuck you.'

I gesture to the District Manager, who is standing not ten feet away from us.

'What? I dinnae want t'fuck him. I want t'fuck you.' He starts shouting. 'HOI EVERYONE, I'M GONNA FUCK ANGIE SCOTT. See, so what, nobody gives a shit.'

Hopefully, the boom-boom-boom of the makeshift disco will have drowned him out but, really, if anyone heard him, we'll both be fucked. Draining my wine, I suggest going back to our pub. Raymond's just starting to warm up, though. Not wanting to seem like a wife, I let him drag me up for a slow dance. The only other couple up are Ian Dawson and his Filipino bride. I give them a what's-a-girl-supposed-to-do smile as I try to avoid Raymond's tongue.

As soon as the record ends, something fast, boomy and tuneless comes on and my desire to leave returns. Raymond keeps a grip of me, jostling me about to the thump of the music, jigging around in that embarrassing way people over 35 call letting their hair down. Then he starts grabbing at my arse, trying to grind against me. I see a group of managers, standing by the buffet, smirking at us. I see Katy giving us a knowing smile. I suggest we get another drink before it runs out and we stagger back to our seats with another two overflowing glasses of wine each. Raymond immediately drains half of one. I look at the rest in trepidation, knowing that if we consume them, all hell will break loose.

'Maybe we should just go. We're being dead obvious. Ian Dawson saw us th'now.'

Raymond scans the room for Ian.

'Fuck 'em. Fuck 'em all. Fuck him and his mail-order fanny. I dinnae care what the fuckers think any more.' Stress forces the glass to my lips. '. . . ah mean t'say, have you any idea how much fucking dosh we make these bastards?' He tries to stand up to address the gathering. I grip onto the back of his shirt. He's too drunk to work out why he can't get to his feet.

'Look at them, fucking celebrating. What about poor fucking Pashto? What 'bout the poor bastard that's been training Do Rightly for the last nine months? For what? Fucking dog meat.'

'Well maybe we should . . .'

'. . . aye, maybe that fucking bimbo was right this afternoon. Do they fucking care? Do they fuck.'

Shit, Ian Dawson's approaching, with a concerned, official look.

'You all right there? A bit worse for the wear?'

Raymond grins at me.

'I'll show you what I mean. Right, Ian, tell uz, how much d'you earn, y'know, all perks included, in a month, eh? Ow much?'

'It's how little I've got left that's the problem,' Ian smiles, trying to make light of it.

'Naw, seriously though . . . no bullshit . . . I'm trying to prove a point here. I'm no trynabe funny . . . just . . . roughly, how much? C'moan.'

An Area Manager comes over with Raymond's neglected jacket. I take it, thank him, apologise to Ian and start pushing Raymond towards the exit.

'I'll see him into a taxi.'

A band start tuning up on the other side of the room. Raymond lunges, out of my grasp, towards them. I'm left standing with Ian, the Area Manager, and the jacket. By the time I get over, Raymond's trying to wrestle the guitarist's instrument off him.

'C'mon, I was in a band. I'll show you fuckers a thing or two. ERIG CLABTON EEDYAR FACKING HARD AHT!'

The band try to humour him but Raymond's adamant he's going to have a shot. People are gathering round to watch the proceedings, like it's a cabaret. Eventually, Ian has to intervene, but not before Raymond's given the singer his phone number and insisted he call him for an audition. The band help escort us to the door. By Monday, this will be a piece of bookie legend.

We wait till everyone goes back in before collapsing into the car. Someone's probably already phoned the registration number in to the nearest police station, but fuck it. I'm damned if I'll let these back-stabbing bastards deprive me of a shag.

Pulling hesitantly away from the pub, we revert to Plan A — Colinton Dell. We pass a police car on Slateford Road, but luckily they're too engrossed in their chips to notice our rather wavy progress. Unnerved, none-the-less, I suggest we take a sharp left and drive up the back of Meggetland. A perfect dark little spot behind the hut.

'Howji know about this place, you dirdy bitch?'

I pretend it was just a lucky guess, but really I was fingered here in my youth more times than I care to remember.

Raymond stares at his crotch, disconsolately.

'I donno if I'm up t'much, to tell the truth. Wine fucks me.'

Cupping his trousered balls in my hand, I kiss his chest.

'. . . honest, id'll just be embarr'sing. Lemme suck on your cunt or something.'

Although it's the first time he's offered such a thing, I'm aching to be fucked. Unbuttoning his trousers, I slide down the zip. He feels semi-hard through the material. Gently liberating his cock from his blue, shapeless Y-fronts, I begin licking the tip. It's faintly stiff but floppy. He stops protesting. Pulling back his foreskin, I suck, lick, try to kiss some life into it, as his middle finger strains for his arsehole. The racket he's making encourages me to keep going, to take it right down my throat.

'Oh, you fucker, you fucker . . .'

He grabs my hair and forces in as far as it'll go. I let him fuck my windpipe till I've no breath left, then start bobbing and sucking again. My jaw is starting to ache and my glands are throbbing. Seeming to sense this, he puts his hand over mine and starts wanking pneumatically. As he screams, I hold my tongue out, for him to splash onto, but it merely dribbles, pus-like, down the shaft.

'Yer zome woman, know that? Ah love you.'

I don't say it back, although I think I do. I'll scare him off if I respond too quickly. The moment passes and he starts to drive me home. I hate this. It's really intense and wonderful, but I just miss him so much in between times.

We stop at the lights at the top of Robertson Avenue. He seems to read my mind.

'We can't fucking go on like this, Ange. Lez jus' do it, eh?'

'What?'

The lights change.

'You know, lez just fuck off zomewhere.'

If only life were that simple. Perhaps it is and I just don't realise any more.

'Where'd we go?'

'Fucking anywhere, anywhere y'like. Zomewhere hot were the booze's cheap. Zomewhere we can lie and fuck in a wee shack aw day then get slaughtered it night for the price ova Mars bar. Any-vucking-were.'

Pulling into my street, he parks a few doors down from the stair.

'. . . j'no think? Go get yer pazzport. Tell'm you're goin for chips.'

'Stop it, Raymond. You'd get a shock if I said yes.'

'Try me. Go on, juz fuckin try me.'

A tear disappears down his cheek. I can't help myself.

'I love you too, Raymond. I didnae say before 'cause I thought it was ridiculous, but I do.'

I open the car door. He grabs my hand.

'Come on, zweedheart. Lez continue this conversation in Mexico.'

I kiss him goodnight and get out, hoping he'll suggest meeting up on our day off tomorrow. He doesn't.

'Kizz the kids for me,' he says, sarcastically.

I unlock the stair door as he does a clumsy U-turn and beeps goodnight. Kiss them? Kick them more like.

Chapter Twenty-One

JONI

EVERYONE'S OUT, SO Rosie and me have the flat to ourselves. We were going to go to the Venue, but we're both too hung-over. She's been going on about her and John for hours. It suddenly seems like nothing else is worth talking about any more. Even when we were listening to CDs earlier, I realised for the first time that every song ever written's about being in love with your best pal's lover.

She's telling me how sexually frustrated she is for about the twentieth time, when Mum comes crashing in. Jesus, it looks like her hair's exploded. It's sort of pulled up in two straggly peaks on top of her head. God knows who she's trying to look like – Björk? The Prodigy? The Devil? – but it's fucking priceless. Noticing her runny make-up, I decide it is definitely the Prodigy.

'Are you doing that for charity, Mum?'

Looking bewildered, she checks the mirror. I think even she gets a fright.

'Oh, Christ.'

'So is it Children in Need or what? Careful you dinnae scare the dog.'

I'm only having a laugh. After all, it's not every day your mum comes in looking like Ken Dodd's stalker, but she throws herself onto the settee and bursts into tears. Rosie doesn't know where to look.

'Mum, what are you playing at?'

'I don't know . . . that's the problem, I don't fucking know.'

It seems like a good time to go to my room. Rosie escapes, but I get grabbed on the way out.

'Why do you hate me so much, eh? You don't even want me here, do you?'

'What you on about? Stop it, you're hurting me.'

She tightens her grip on my wrist.

'Just admit it. You can't wait to see the back of me, can you?'

Oh fuck, she's stinking of booze. Oh, no.

'. . . CAN YOU?' she yells, shaking my arm like it's a tin of hair mousse. Her drinky breath's making me boak.

As I manage to wrench myself free, she throws herself onto the carpet in a performance worthy of Gillian Anderson.

'Just fuck off, Mum. Dinnae make a fool of me, just 'cause you're pissed.'

Springing back to life, she wallops me across the jaw. I get a rush of adrenaline but I'm too stunned to move. Turning her attention to the lamp-shade, she starts sobbing at it, 'Why am I here? What am I doing here?'

It's like she's been possessed by spirits. It certainly smells like she has. I make for the door again, while she chats to the light, but she lunges at me. As I duck, she falls, arse over tit, onto the settee and starts bubbling again. What a fucking mess.

Rosie's holding a hairbrush in front of her like a dagger when I go through.

'She fucking belted me a beauty.'

Standing up, she scans my face for wounds.

'I better go. Is she having a breakdown or something?'

It'd be better if she was. Less embarrassing. They could just take her away and give us her back when she was better, or not. My breathing's going like the clappers.

'She's fucking pissed. It's like something out of *Alien* when she's on the vodka.'

Rosie pulls her jacket on.

'Aw, please, dinnae leave me with her. Dad'll give you a lift. He winnae be long, please.'

She reluctantly agrees but keeps her jacket on.

'I came here to get away from my mum, as well.'

Right on cue, there's a faint knocking at the door.

'Joni, Joni, I'm sorry, love. I'm so sorry. Don't tell Dad, please . . .'

'Just go to your fucking bed, eh?'

There's a whimper, then I hear her staggering back through to the living room.

'My mum's a cow, but she'd never do that to me. That's terrible, that. You should tell someone.'

Why is life so unfair? People you want to see, you can't see. People you don't like you have to live with. John's maybe going to jail for doing nothing, yet Mum can act like that and it's perfectly OK. The world's fucked up.

'So is she an alkie, or what? I've never seen her like that,' whispers Rosie.

'She supposedly stopped when we moved here. That's how we had to move in the first place. She turned the whole fucking street against us.'

I'm dying for a pee but I'm scared to unlock the door. If Rosie wasn't here, I'd just do it in the milk jug I keep behind the telly for emergencies. Sitting on the hard chair, I squeeze my legs together but it just makes it worse. I'm going to piss myself.

Quietly unlocking the door, I look up the hall. The house is burring with the awful sound of Mum's snoring. She's still in a heap, lying in her coat with her gob wide open and that fucking awful noise pouring out of it. How could Dad have ever have shagged something so grotesque?

The joint relief of the pee and her being out for the count is good while it lasts. When I dry myself though, I realise I'm bleeding. My last period only stopped three days ago. How am I going to lose my virginity by Friday if I've got constant fucking periods? It says in the magazines you can still do it, but I don't want to be smelling like an abattoir the first time. It's not very romantic.

Rosie looks dead concerned when I go back through.

'Fuck, Jo, you were ages. I couldnae hear any noise. I thought she'd killed you and I was next.'

'Nah, she's unconscious. Listen to the snoring. Did you think it was a chainsaw?'

She starts thumbing through last week's *Radio Times*, bored now the excitement's over.

'Where's Jake? Is he coming back tonight? I think he's quite nice, actually.'

She's pulling my pisser.

'Don't be revolting, he's my brother.'

'So, I wusnae suggesting *you* should shag him,' she says in all seriousness. God, she's so thick sometimes.

'He's a wee poof. I think he's shagging the guy downstairs, he's never away from the place. I dunno though, he might be desperate.'

She thumps my sore arm.

'Piss off. You can talk. What about that speccy guy in Fibber McGee's last night? I thought his tongue was going to get lodged down your throat.'

'He was OK. I thought he was a bit of a Jarvis Cocker.'

'Cocker Spaniel, more like. Honestly, Jo, you'll neck anyone.'

He was actually quite a good kisser, a bit snobby but a good kisser. I was just pretending it was John, but he seemed to like me. I'd never go out with someone posh like that, though. It wouldn't bother me, but I'd just get slagged.

Rosie's looking thoughtful.

'Jo, see when we're pissed. You don't think we're as bad as your mum, d'you?'

'I'm trying to block it out of my mind.'

The front door slams. Rosie and I jump off the bed. Hopefully, it's Mum gone up the canal to try and drown herself, like she used to. Dad used to have to go and rescue her. They'd both come back soaking.

Nervously tiptoeing into the hall, I nearly give Jake a heart attack.

'Fuck, Jo, what's wi the creeping about?'

Yanking him into my room, I shut the door. Rosie and him get matching beamers. It's so touching . . . not. He's a bit deflated when I tell him about Mum. He was probably expecting a threesome.

'Sure it wasnae your own breath you could smell? You were pretty steaming last night.'

'Fuck off, Jake. I'm no joking. She fucking punched me . . . and look, I'm getting a bruise on my arm where she grabbed me. Rosie'll tell you.'

He glances at Rosie, then at his lap.

'. . . go and look if you dinnae believe me.'

But he's starting to look so upset I know he already does.

'She better no start spoiling everything for us. I couldnae go through all that again. Where did she hit you?'

'Right in the face. I had to push her over or she'd probably've killed me.'

He shakes his head and gets up.

'Fuck it, I'm going to bed, I'm knackered. I've been playing five-a-side all day.' He glances at Rosie, then looks anxious. '. . . dinnae mention it to Dad.'

'But we have to.'

'No that, about the five-a-side. He'll want to play with us. He's too old.'

As I lock the door, Rosie lets out a little purr.

'He is definitely cute. How old is he again?'

'Fourteen, ya dirty paedophile.'

'You're joking. I thought he was older than you. He seems dead mature.'

She quizzes me about Jake for the next hour. Revolting as the whole idea of someone fancying my brat of a brother is, it at least keeps my mind off Mum. How can Rosie possibly like that wee nyaff when she's got John, though? Mind you, it would be better for me if she did.

Dad comes in at quarter to one. Replaying the whole story again, I show him the bruise on my arm. It's starting to go yellow. He seems to erupt. I've never seen him like this before. He goes all angry and protective. It's sort of nice.

'Where is she? I'll bloody kill her if she lays a finger on you.'

I grab his hand.

'No, Dad, please. Leave it till morning. She'll just start up again if you wake her. You've got to take Rosie home.'

'Is Jake in? You pair come with me.'

'I'll lock the door.'

He sucks on his knuckles, trying to calm down. His eyes look all heart-broken.

'Chuck her out. It's your house. You won't let them put us into care, will you?'

'Dinnae be so daft. I'll be with you no matter what.'

He looks like he's reading the air in front of him for an immediate solution.

'Will you, though?'

'What?'

'Give Rosie a lift home? She stayed with me and everything . . .'

'Oh, aye, of course. Are you ready to go now, Rosie?'

As soon as they leave, I want him to come back. He should be with me, not Rosie. I suddenly don't feel safe any more when he's not here. Not that he stands up to Mum or anything. She's just less likely to hit us when she's got him to batter.

Chapter Twenty-Two

VIC

DRIVING ROSIE HOME, I blether some rubbish about exams, ask if she's going away for the holidays, then dry up. I know what's on both our minds and it's not Easter. She probably views me as some sort of ogre who's driven his poor wife to drink. It's always the same when a woman's an alkie. People assume her man must be responsible.

Rosie's also at that dangerous age. She's younger than Joni, but she has a worldly air that makes her seem much older. Added to which, she's jaw-droppingly stunning. I'd be scared to let her out the house if she was mine. I keep my eyes on the road till we get to her street.

'Ta for staying on tonight. Jo's lucky to have you. Sorry about all the . . . y'know . . . with . . .' God man, spit it out. Rosie flashes her very white teeth at me.

'No sweat, Victor. My mum's mad as well. My uncle says all women are.'

Opening the door, she wriggles out. I get a flash of red knickers as her micro-skirt rides up her thighs. The door slams and she blows me a kiss through the open window. I'd generally wait to check she got in her stair, but I take off, feeling uncomfortably old.

Angie's snoring is audible before I even reach our landing. I go straight through to Joni's room. She won't unlock the door till I say who it is. Her face is the same greyish-white shade as her night-shirt.

'What did Rosie say? Aw, dad, it was so embarrassing. I dinnae want everyone knowing Mum's an old lush. Talk to her, tell her she'll have to leave.'

'Telling your mother something, and getting her to do it are two very different things, Jo, you know that.'

'But you have to. If she doesn't go, I will.'

Christ, a nine-hour shift and then this. I'm too knackered for ultimatums. Besides, it's not a criminal offence to be pissed in your own living room, unfortunately.

'I'll sort it, promise. Maybe it was just a one-off. She was at some work do.'

Maybe that's it – someone slipped her a Mickey, or she couldn't not drink without admitting why.

'Aw, Dad, you always take her side. Why d'you make excuses for her?'

'I'm not taking anyone's side. I just don't understand what would have set her off again. It could have been acciden-tal.'

'Oh, fuck off, Dad. This is exactly what happened last time. It ended up getting really bad 'cause you wouldn't admit it was happening away at the start.'

'I was just trying to keep the family together.'

Jumping into bed, she yanks the duvet round herself.

'You shouldn't have bothered. Families are stupid. There's always one person drags everyone else down.'

I can't really argue, although in the case of Angie's lot, they were all like that.

'Maybe the four of us should sit down together in the morning and talk about it.'

The suggestion doesn't seem to impress her.

'It's not our problem. You're the one who married her.'

With that vote of support, I leave her to it.

The living room's reeking of drink. Surely I'd have smelt

it, if she'd been at it before tonight. The thing is, I never see her. She could roll in cow shit for kicks and I'd be none the wiser.

As I rifle her bag for fags, I find an empty half-bottle of vodka. God knows how many more might be deposited round the flat. I look down at the gaping-mouthed snorting bitch, as I smoke. No wonder I can't get it up any more. Generally, I'd turn her onto her side in case she vomits in her sleep but I don't bother. At least I get the bed tonight.

My head hits the pillow, ashtray eyebrow first. The pain seems to give me clarity. Was she pissed when she threw that at me? Has she been lying through here bevvying when I've been squashed on the settee? Maybe Joni's right. I do go into denial. That's how it managed to get so bad last time. We had a lovely cheap housing-association flat up the back of Fountainbridge – no repair bills, nice big garden. Then Angie got reported for abusing neighbours, smashing the place up, threatening to jump out our third-floor window in the middle of the night. Why didn't I just let her?

Twisting my industrial ear plugs in until they nip, I can still hear snoring, and the counteractive boom of Joni's music. Hiding under the duvet, I try to get lost in my breathing, but my head's still fizzing with it all hours later. She was sober enough when I took her for lunch the other day. Maybe the anniversary of her dad's death set her off.

I'm still mulling it over when it starts to get light. There's probably accompanying birdsong, but by now the plugs have inflated in my ears. Apart from what's going on in my own head, I can hear nothing. Oh to be deaf and dumb.

I wake at half-ten, with a strange presence in the bed beside me. Staring under the quilt, I'm confronted by my first erection in over a year. I have to touch it to check it's really mine. Talk about bizarre timing. Then I remember my dream about an impending tidal wave that involved Rosie squirming around on my lap, with her little red panties stuffed in my mouth. Jesus, is that what I'm really like? Is it not the Prozac after all? Am I really just a dirty old bastard? If I thought someone my age was having thoughts about Joni like that, I'd bloody kill them. I can't even wank now, I feel so off.

When I go through, the settee's been vacated but the shower's on. Making two strong black coffees, I sit on the armchair and wait. As soon as I hear the water being switched off, though, I start trying to talk myself out of confronting her. I'm an A1 coward. I admit it. I've never won an argument in my life. What's it going to resolve anyway? I'll just get a load of abuse. I'm lighting another of her pilfered cigarettes when she comes through, towelling her hair. The cloud of smoke in the darkened room seems to startle her.

'Jesus, what is this? *The Third Man*?'

'I took one of your fags.'

Putting on the light, she looks in her bag to confirm this.

'So you've been raking through my handbag. Bored, were we?'

Launching into my rehearsed line about finding the bottle, she drowns me out with the hair-drier. I toy with pulling it off her and choking her with the flex, but I keep calm, keep dragging on the cigarette, waiting, trying not to lose my nerve.

When she eventually switches the sodding thing off, I retrieve the bottle from the bin and wave it in front of her. She blanks me and goes to the bathroom. I follow.

'Anything you want to tell me?'

'Not particularly.'

She pulls a grotesque face as she applies her lipstick.

'Like what that bottle was doing in your bag?'

My voice is breaking up. I'm not used to this assertive shit.

'No idea what you're talking about.'

'Oh, come off it, eh?'

'No, Vic, you come off it. If you've got something to say, then fucking say it. Otherwise, I'd like to piss in peace.'

Say it, just say it, you mouse.

'You were drunk last night, weren't you?'

'I wouldn't say that.'

'What would you say, then? Were you or weren't you?'

'You tell me. You're the one making the accusations. I don't even remember seeing you last night.'

'You were sleeping when I got in.'

There's a growl from the back of her throat as she tries to push me into the hall.

'Oh, right, so was I slurring my zeds or what?'

She tries to shut me out but I jam the door with my gorilla feet.

'Why don't you ask your precious daughter how the bottle got in my bag, 'cause I don't fucking know.'

'Or can't remember . . .'

'Oh, spare me the Endeavour Morse, Vic, please. You always have to take their word against mine, eh? That's what's fucking wrong with us.'

Giving up trying to keep me out, she pulls down her knickers and starts peeing. Difficult as it is to engage in serious conversation with someone while they're on the pan, I'm determined not to let her phase me.

'I know you were pissed. Just admit it.'

She wipes herself and pulls up her knickers.

'What's the point? Vic says I was pissed, so I must have been pissed.'

'But I want you to hear yourself say it.'

She darts through for her coat and bag. I wait in the hall.

'Tell you what, Vic. So you don't need to keep repeating yourself, I'm going out. So you and Joni and your fucking son can have a good old fucking talk about me. Dream up what you're going to accuse me of next.'

She opens the front door. I soften my tone to spare the neighbours.

'Where are you going? The pub?'

She looks at me with utter loathing.

'Actually, I'm going to see my poor, sick, mentally disturbed friend, Caroline, for some intelligent conversation.'

'Angie, we need to talk.'

'What have we just been doing? Sorry, Vic, time's up. You're just irritating me now.'

Trundling down the stairs, she hesitates on the landing below.

'D'you think she doesn't do the same thing with me? Make up stories about you to turn us against each other. It wasnae me she was threatening to phone Childline about, eh, but I stuck up for you. That's the difference, I know when someone's just being vindictive.'

'She didn't make it up,' I croak, inaudibly.

I wait till the stair door slams before going back in. The bitch has taken her fags. She's definitely bullshitting me. Joni wouldn't make that up. I wish she had, but no, surely not. Rosie didn't exactly back up her story, but I still find it hard to believe. I take a sip of tepid coffee. The only thing I know for sure any more is that one of them's a bloody convincing liar.

Chapter Twenty-Three

JAKE

I REFUSE TO let the Mum thing put me on a downer. It's the holidays. I'll just spend the next fortnight down Sean's and avoid her. I'm going down there to watch the Old Firm match this afternoon. I've got more to worry about than my stupid family.

As Eva's going to be there, I force myself under the shower. I hate showers as I never seem to dry myself properly, so my clothes go on all sticky and squint. Plus, dirt protects you. The more bacteria there is on your skin, the harder it is for germs to get into you. Without my layer of filth, I feel like Samson with a baldy.

Once I'm back through in my bedroom, it's not quite so bad. Despite constant nagging from Mum, I refuse to tidy in here. Why make it easier for the rest of them to find my stuff? That's if the combined smell of minging socks, shitey trainers and a thousand farts clinging to the wallpaper doesn't put them off coming in here in the first place. It's a protective seal, just like my dirt.

I don't know what top to wear – Rangers or Bayern Munich. Never having watched an Old Firm match with Celtic supporters before, I don't want to seem like I'm taking the piss. My Klinsmann top's probably the safest bet. I used to love old Jürgen, till Dad took me to see Bayern play a friendly against some shitey Fife team and the bastard sat on the bench for the entire match. Everyone'd paid double to see him as well. Fucking Kraut, he's past it now anyway.

I go through to make a sandwich. Joni and dad are sitting at the special-occasion table, deep in thought. Jan's staring up at them as if she maybe wants to have her say as well. My appetite vanishes.

'S'down, Jake. We need to talk about Mum.'

I don't want to talk about Mum, I want to get psyched up for the match.

'Da-ad. I'm in a hurry. I dinnae have anything to say.'

He lights a fag off the one he's already smoking. It pisses me off when he goes all serious like this, so I go back to my room. Joni comes barging in behind me.

'What's the problem, scab? We need to sort this out.'

Sometimes I prefer when she's not talking to me. She's been ignoring me for months. Why drag me into this?

'Aw, get a life, Jo. I'm no ganging up on Mum. She's no even done anything.'

'Fuck off. What about her hitting me last night?'

'So what? She hits you, you hit me, I hit you. What's the fucking difference?'

'Aye, but we dinnae do it 'cause we're pissed.'

'So. You get pissed an aw.'

'That's different.'

'How?'

'I dunno . . . like . . . y'know, it's no like I've got a family to look after. I dinnae do it every day.'

'Not yet, you dinnae.'

I'm sick of this. So my family's a disaster. Who cares? I've got a decent family downstairs I can spend time with.

As I make for the hall, her face takes on its more familiar sarky expression.

'Rosie's got the hots for you.'

'Don't talk shite.'

'Honest, she said last night. She wouldnae shut up about you, actually. Fuck knows why.' She blocks the doorway. '. . . I'm telling you, she's just become single again. You could get her on the rebound, no problem.'

Does she really think I'll fall for this? I push past her into the stair.

'Going to Sean's?' she whines.

'Yeah, so?' I expect some sarcastic poofy comment, but she keeps smiling.

'He seems nice. I should come down with you some time.'

'Oh aye. You, me, Sean and Rosie can double-date. Sure, Jo.'

Escaping down the stairs, I don't ring Sean's bell till I hear the slagging bitch go back in the flat. I'm unprepared when Eva answers.

'It's the little orange man,' she shouts, patting my bum as I walk up the hall. Wow. Wise move wearing these baggy shorts.

Sean comes out his room and pulls me back into the stair.

'I've got to take soup up my fucking auntie's. Goan chum eis. I want to get it done, so's I can settle down for the football.'

Still in an Eva-fondled daze, I stumble after him. We walk behind Burger King, up the old railway. Stopping to smoke a few fags, we smash a bin bag full of beer bottles someone's dumped. There must be about 40. It's like the dance floor in a Paki musical by the time we've finished. Then an old dear comes towards us with her dog, so we nash before its paws turn to mince.

I wait outside Sean's auntie's stair so he has an excuse not to stay. She lives on her own, so she's probably just lonely like Granda, but it's Old Firm Day, for fuck's sake. Luckily, a neighbour answers, so we manage a quick getaway before his auntie gets out the cludge.

We pass the Catholic Church on the way back down. Sean says the priest in there's an old paedophile, and shags all the bairns from the Sunday School. I think he's just winding me up, so he takes me in to see for myself. It's disgusting, the guy's absolutely ancient, y'know, about 90. He does boys and girls apparently. Gets them to confess they've been wanking, then makes them show him what they mean. The old spunk-face is straight over as soon as we're in the door.

'Oh, it's you, Sean. Don't tell me, you're going to arrange a sponsored walk for the Church Roof Fund?'

''Fraid no, Father. I've just come to light a candle. My pal here wants to light one too.' He squirms away from the old bugger, towards this big wedding-cake-type thing with candles on it. Dropping 20 pence into a little box, he hands me a candle from the floor. For a horrible moment, I think I'm going to have to stick it up the priest's arse or something. The old cunt just gives us a horrid, pervy grin, squeezes my shoulder and fucks off. I get the giggles.

'Ssh, he'll hear you. Just light it and say this, "Hail Mary Full of Grace . . ."'

'Fuck off.'

'Dinnae, Jake. He'll come and shag you.'

We both start giggling. The priest comes back up the aisle, looking pissed off, so Sean starts saying the Hail Mary thing, the whole thing. It's weird stuff about sinners.

'Wish for something,' he whispers, after repeating it so often even I know the fucking thing off by heart, '. . . anything you like. I got the Internet with it. And I asked for Dad to come and see us the other week and we bumped into him two days later. It definitely works.'

I don't exactly feel comfortable about this but, since having your wishes granted isn't exactly an everyday occurrence, I give it a bash. Shutting my eyes, I wish with all my heart that Rangers'll go top of the League, it'll be an Old Firm Cup Final and Rangers do the double.

'How many wishes do I get?'

'One for each candle.'

Oh, well, if I just say Rangers for the double, then that's just one. Excellent. Why don't Proddies have stuff like this? Ten pence for Rangers to win the double, amazing.

When we get back to Sean's, Eva and me have a *FIFA* preview of the match to get us in the mood. She's so hopeless at it, it's embarrassing. I give her a chance at first, but it makes me look shite. Just sitting next to her for half an hour is fucking ace, though.

At three o'clock, we go through to the living room and drape ourselves about the floor cushions for the game. As soon as it starts, I suddenly feel like a Nazi storm trooper at a bar mitzvah. It's not Sean or Eva's fault, they're just getting into it, shouting for fouls and penalty kicks, calling the ref a Mason, normal stuff. It's the fact that what they're saying's so inoffensive in comparison to what I'm used to coming out with on such occasions. I can't exactly sing anti-IRA songs, so I just have to sit, quiet apart from the odd grunt, or 'you bastard'. Celtic are all over us in the first half as well. If it wasn't for Randy Goram, they'd probably be about eight-nil up by half time. I'm fucking seething.

The second half's not quite so bad. Without opening my mouth, I watch Rangers win two-one. Sean's still going on about the Stewart McCall handball when the highlights come on. I've never felt so unenthusiastic about an Old Firm match in my life. Thank fuck we're only playing Hearts in the final.

Sean's mum calls us through to the kitchen and produces a massive lasagne. It feels odd to eat at a table. It's like we're in a sitcom. All the different cutlery's set out but I just use a fork, or I'll get it everywhere. It's so gorgeous and cheesy, it makes my mouth really slavery. Sean's mum tells me to call her by her first name, Terry. We talk about the football as we eat. She's dead nice about Rangers winning, even though she's a Celtic supporter.

'It would be good if Rangers got the Cup and Celtic won the League.'

What did I just say? I don't know where the words came from. Granda'll be spinning in his grave. It's like *American Werewolf.* I'm turning from a Hun into a Tim in front of their very eyes. Why did I let Sean take me in that fucking church?

By the time we go back through to watch Sky Sport, I'm getting dead paranoid. Is this how Catholics convert people? Sort of like Mormons, except they invite you round their place? I'm sure I'm getting subliminal messages from that picture of the Pope on the mantelpiece. Leaning back on a cushion, I fall into a dream, watching Eva watching telly. The fear goes.

I lie in this gorgeous little dwam until half-seven. Eva suddenly gets up and turns the volume down.

'Listen, it's the nurse again, listen . . .'

All I can hear is Sean sniggering, Butthead-like. When he calms down, though, the banging and voices are really clear. It sounds more like they're fighting tonight. You can almost make out what they're saying. Fuck, they sound awfie familiar.

'. . . boring fucking bastard . . . bottleless fucking cunt.'

Tell me I'm dreaming, please. Mum can't burst her way into my safe little world like this. I pretend there's something fascinating on the telly. I start gibbering away a load of cheesy old jokes from the Chubby Brown video. Eva looks totally unimpressed but I'm just desperate to drown them out upstairs. They'll realise who it is, any minute. They probably already know but are too embarrassed to say. Then it suddenly hits me like a train. The most revolting thought I've ever had. If the shouting's coming from my house, who the fuck was getting shagged up there the other night?

Chapter Twenty-Four

ANGIE

I CAN'T LIVE like this. I've not left for work yet and already I'm dreading coming home. Home – the place where Raymond fucked me the other night, that's all it is to me now. I have more affection for the bed he buggered me in than I do for my family. He was right on Saturday. We need to get away from here, away from fucking Britain. There must be bookies all over the world crying out for people like us.

I shower and dress in the bathroom. Vague recollections of an apocalyptic barney about my drinking last night render the rest of the house a no-go-without-aggro zone. Whatever might have been said, though, I know my boring, fucking husband will still be through there on the settee. A bulldozer couldn't get that cunt out of here. My emergency vodka's in the kitchen, but I don't want a confrontation before work or my face'll run. If I leave now, I can have a little settler in the pub before Raymond arrives. I love drinking but it feels like I've got cancer in between times. The subsequent incentive of alcohol gets me to the pub 15 minutes early. The blonde barmaid from hell gives the manageress an is-she-barred look as I walk in. As if, the fucking fortune they make out us. Subduing fantasies of glassing the bitch, I smile and ask for a double. It galls me, but as long as this place is the unfortunate centre of our universe, I have to kiss ass.

I go over to our usual seat. It seems busy for nine-thirty – four young postmen playing pool, a simple guy who seems to live here, getting a heat by the fire, the usual sprinkling of old men with nowhere else to go. Every time the door opens, my head swings round *Exorcist*-like. The bitchy barmaid notices and sniggers something to the postmen, after which a roar of laughter goes up every time someone comes in. When I go up for a another drink, she sneers at me,

'Husband not joining you this morning?'

Accomplished grin-and-bearer that I am, I ignore her. Fuck, it's ten to ten. We'll have to go straight to work if he doesn't hurry. What if he's had an accident? Why did I let him drive home so pissed the other night? He could be dead for all I know, nobody would bother to tell me. It makes me feel worthless.

Why didn't I buy a paper? I keep drifting off and coming to, with old men leering at me. They'll think I'm on the game. Even watching *The Big Breakfast* would be better than this.

By ten I'm too tense for another drink. Sweetening my breath with chewing gum, I try the shop but there's nobody there. Alternately pacing and standing aimlessly, I wait for his mucky silver Astra to appear. It doesn't. Maybe he got stopped on Saturday. I check the faces of people getting off a bus. The next one drives straight past, overstuffed with Riccarton-bound foreign students. Hearing the purring crescendo of an approaching taxi, I get a rush like a pishy-panted teenager at a boy-band concert till it drives past too.

We should have opened 15 minutes ago. I'd phone and see if he's slept in but I don't know his number. There's no note of it in the shop, so they can't bother him on his days off. I'll top myself if he's sick. Waiting another ten minutes, I reluctantly call Base Office. Raymond'll think I'm a grass, but I have to at least let them know I'm here. They put me through to Ian Dawson, of all people.

'Sure you didn't swallow him on Saturday?'

Brilliant. Stage II warning here I come. He tells me to give him five minutes to call Raymond, then phone back. I take another hopeful walk up the street in the meantime.

Bollocks, if they send someone from Base Office to open up, they'll notice the two grand we've not returned to the other shop. Raymond'll go spare at me for dropping him in it. When I call back, the phone's swallowed 23 pence credit before they put me through. There's no reply from Raymond's, so Ian's coming over to sort out a relief manager. That bastard could sniff out truffles in a field of shite, he'll notice the extra money immediately. I get enough grief about cash differences as it is. They'll sack me and get Raymond a new cashier. He'll dump me and start shagging the replacement. What if they give him Debbie? Maybe I should just go back to the pub.

Instead, I just stand there sucking mints, getting in a right state. It doesn't help when Ian turns up and opens the shop without even acknowledging me. We're behind the counter before he speaks.

'I needed to come down and have a talk with you today, anyway.'

Without elaborating, he pulls a sheet of staff phone numbers out his pocket and tells me to try Raymond again. I'll vomit if his wife answers but, God, there it is, his fucking number. Weh hey. I memorise as I dial. It rings five times, there's the whir of an answering machine and Raymond's tinny voice saying something incomprehensible. Not wanting to alarm him by leaving a message, I hang up.

'Still no joy,' I smile, but the humourless bastard just scowls and demands the pay-in book. Digging it out, I escape to put up the *Racing Post*. I'm still trying to open my box of pins when he comes storming through on the verge of cardiac arrest.

'Who's responsible for the banking here?'

Oh, Christ, he's found the two grand. Here we go.

'Me . . . usually.'

He squints through the pay-in book.

'What about last week?'

I have to think about it. I've been on autopilot at work for the last fortnight.

'Erm ... hang on ... no, actually, Raymond did it last week.'

I'm so amazed I've managed to remember, I start grinning.

'Why?'

'Just to give me a bit of a break, y'know?'

To sneak to the pub between the dogs and the horses, angel that he is.

'So you can explain why no banking's been done since last Monday?'

'Yes, there has. We banked money every day last week, twice on Friday.'

It was Aintree, we were going like a fair. Ian slaps the pay-in book on the counter. I check the stubs. The last recorded pay-in was on 30th March. It's in my handwriting.

'I don't understand. Maybe he filled in slips at the bank.'

'And where would they be, if he'd done that?'

'In the safe.'

My whole body starts shaking as he goes through to the kitchen. I hear the keys jangling, the metal door squeaking open, then Ian roars my name. Staring into the very empty safe, my first impulse is to search his pockets. I drop to my knees, and pull up the square of lino that covers the floor safe.

'Maybe he's put it in here, since it was the weekend.'

He watches me tremble and fuck about trying to unlock it before pushing me out the way and doing it himself. Sticking his hand into the hole, he fumbles about. Pulling the secret side panels off, he fumbles some more.

'How unexpected.'

As I gawp at the second empty space, I think about Debbie sloping off early. But the money we made after she left is missing as well. Even the bags of change are away. Ian taps his mobile.

'Houston, we have a problem.'

Wanker, I bet he's waited his entire career for this. Isn't he jumping the gun a bit, anyway? Raymond's maybe come in early to take the money to the other shop and do the banking. I keep checking the two safes, thinking it's some kind of illusion.

Ian bleeps his phone off.

'Did you leave here together on Saturday?'

There's not enough time to contemplate lying.

'Aye, the relief went sick. We didn't get away till about half-six.'

Inexplicably, this makes him go King Kong ape-shit – cursing, banging his fists, ears purple, really going for his little moment of uncorroboratable power. If my employment wasn't already teetering on the brink, I'd have him done for bullying.

'So what the fuck were the pair of you doing at the function? Gloating? Trying to rub our fucking noses in it?'

'Look, Ian, I know nothing about this.'

'Save your breath,' he spits, 'Base Office are phoning down south for last week's figures. We're probably talking about 15 grand here, though. I hope your boyfriend told you what to tell the police before he fucked off.'

'Police!'

A smile at last.

'I can only go by what I saw the other night, Angela, but for your sake, I hope it wasn't what it looked like.'

I say nothing, scared to open my mouth till I know what's going on. Claustrophobic from him towering over me like Moses, I go and lean on the counter.

'D'you want to open up?' I ask, for the sake of saying something.

'Are you blind or just fucking stupid? We don't even have a

float. The fucking till rolls are gone. He's probably taken the fucking tea bags as well. I've been back my holidays three days and I have to fucking deal with this.'

I go back to the kitchen, to hide.

'Fancy a coffee?'

'If I do, I'll make it myself.'

What? Does the ridiculous wanker think I'm going to poison him and make a run for it? His mobile parps. Making a point of standing in the doorway so I can see him, he turns his back to me before speaking. Area Managers live for moments like this. It's the nearest they ever get to 15 minutes of fame.

'. . . there's nothing left to tamper with . . . she's still here. All right . . . see you shortly.'

Leading me through the shop floor, he locks the counter behind us.

'I'm going to get these figures for the police. Stay here,' he says, rather gratuitously, since he's holding me captive anyway.

As soon as he leaves, the phone behind the counter starts ringing. I convince myself it's Raymond. He's waiting for me in the pub with a double Stoli and two plane tickets. I want to kick the door down, answer it, warn him off. He can't do a runner till he speaks to me. Staring at the pay phone opposite, I repeat his number to myself. The one behind the counter stops ringing. I dig two ten-pence pieces out my pocket.

His garbled message comes on before I realise they could trace the call, and chicken out. So fucking what, though? I try again but it's engaged. He must be doing a 1471. He's fucking there. I try again. Five rings, voice, click . . .

'Raymond, please answer. It's me.'

This'll end up as evidence if he doesn't pick up.

'Hello, who is this?'

It's a woman's voice. I'd hang up, but how else can I get in touch with him?

'It's Angie from the shop. Is Raymond there?' There's a silence,
'. . . hello . . . please.'
'He's not here.' Her voice is empty, like she's reading it
off a page.
'Please, I've no more money. Where can I contact him. It's
very important.'
There's a muffled noise, like she's put her hand over the
receiver.
'Please . . . hello, is he there? Please . . .'
'Can I give him a message?'
The display's flashing and I've no more change. Mumbling
something about missing money and police, she seems to get the
gist and hangs up. Fucking bitch. I hate her for answering his
phone. I hate her for breathing.

It starts to sink in, how bad things are looking for me, but
I still can't believe he'd implicate me like this. Surely he wasn't
that confident I'd bugger off with him on Saturday night that he
didn't even consider it. Did he do this all for us, only to have
me knock him back?

The shop door opens. Ian comes in with two policemen. They
all look at me like I'm a child molester, then lock themselves
behind the counter. One of them's the Irish cop that came
round when the guy threw the wobbly. He'll have told Ian
we were stinking of drink. As I cherish my last few moments
of employment, I think about all the lassies who've topped
themselves in Cornton Vale over the past few years.

They talk, they laugh, they stare at me, they go through and
look at the safes. Ian shows them the pay-in book. They all look
at me again. Their walkie-talkies keep squawking, though, so I
can't make out what they're saying. I'm left stewing for half an
hour before the two cops finally emerge and lead me to the far
side of the shop. 'Angela Scott, isn't it? We met the other day.
No more trouble there?'

He didn't think it was trouble then. His tone's so chummy, it's disconcerting. I only manage a nod.

'. . . well, we have to take a statement off you about this. Your boss is closing the shop to get some figures for us, so if you'd like to come down the station.'

'But I don't know what happened either. I'm sorry.'

'So you won't mind answering a few questions?'

How can I? I can't grass Raymond up, I'm in love with him.

'But I told you, I've nothing to say.'

The younger copper pulls out his notebook. The Irish one looks irritated. His tone confirms this.

'Let me put it this way. You usually do the banking for this shop. Don't you?'

This being common knowledge, I figure I can't implicate anyone by admitting it.

'. . . so last week, completely out the blue, your manager decides he's going to do it. And now both him and that money have disappeared. I'll ask you again. Will you voluntarily come down the station to clarify a few things for us?'

'Sorry, but I'd really rather not, not if I have an option.'

'Well, I'm afraid I'll have to caution you. We have enough to detain you under Section 14(95) of the Criminal Justice Scotland Act.'

What happened to the fifth amendment? This is blackmail.

'If you take me in forcibly . . . y'know, do I have to say anything?'

He laughs. The other policeman laughs. I despise the police.

'That's entirely up to you but, if you're not involved, it might be a good idea.'

'I've done nothing wrong,' I squeak.

'That's a new one,' smirks the younger cop, springing into action. 'You're being cautioned with regards to the offence of theft. You are not obliged to say anything . . .' It's like a thousand cheesy crime dramas I've seen on the telly. Please let there be a commercial break soon. When he finishes his recitation, they let me get my bag from behind the counter.

'We'll be in touch with your P45,' whispers Ian through his little brown teeth.

As we drive past our pub in the panda car, I half expect the barmaids to come out and give me the finger. Please make Raymond already be at the station. Will they put us in the same cell if he is?

Two hours alone in a bleak, tiny room without so much as a cup of tea helps reality to sink in. Where the fuck are you, Raymond? Will I ever see you again, outside the Sheriff Court? I hear the loud clunk of the door being unlocked and a ten-year-old boy in a uniform leads me to a room down the hall. A grey-haired mean-looking bitch in a two-piece suit comes in and introduces herself as DS Duffy. Typical, I get the only cop in Scotland that isn't a Mason. She switches on the tape recorder (tape recorder? Who do they think I am? Rosemary West?).

The first few questions aren't too bad – formalities, like, name, address, work history and responsibilities – so I answer them. Then it starts to get a bit hairy and I wish I'd kept my gob shut.

'Did you go anywhere with Mr Ramage after the function on Saturday night?'

'No comment.'

She raises her eyebrows at the ten-year-old.

'Was Mr Ramage carrying anything when you left the shop that evening?'

Fuck, the hold-all.

'No comment.'

'Are you having a relationship with Mr Ramage?'

'No comment.'

Squeaking her chair back, she stares at the ceiling. In her head she's Helen Mirren, except her chin's not as hairy.

'Look Angela, I don't know what you've been watching on telly but, if you continue being evasive, you're going to end up in a lot of trouble. Personally, I think it's unlikely you'd have turned up for work this morning if you knew your boyfriend had taken the money. I'd say he'd done a runner and left you in the shit. You know what I'm saying? If you want to keep answering no comment to defend someone who'd do that to you, go ahead. Just bear in mind he's not in the next room trying to defend you.'

We have a break to give me time to mull this over whilst weeping uncontrollably. What does he expect me to do? Why didn't he tell me? I'll do or say whatever means I'll see him soonest. At least if they put him in jail, I'd know where he was, he wouldn't be with his wife. I could visit him, sort my life out for him being released. If they lock me up, though, I'll never see him. He could be trying to get in touch with me at this very moment. Just talk, get out, find him. Let him explain, then fuck me senseless, or fuck me senseless, then explain. I decide to co-operate.

Chapter Twenty-Five

JONI

FIRST DAY OF the holidays and I'm bored already. Rosie's at the doctor's with her mum, getting referred to a shrink, so she'll talk about John. I wasn't aware she had any other topic of conversation. It's stupid, anyway. Royalty shag their uncles. Is it just wrong when poor folk do it? And the Asian lassies I know have arranged marriages at 14, but they're supposed to be religious fanatics.

I've decided to leave school, rather than waste the next fortnight worrying about exams. I got an application form from the video shop yesterday. Exams are pointless. The only subject I failed last year was business studies but still the careers officer thought office work was my only option. He suggested I start as a filing clerk, then work my way up to the typing pool, through night classes. Aye, right, I'd sooner get meningitis.

To reward myself for filling the form in, I decide to try John again. Besides, my period's stopped for five minutes so I want to make the most of it. I'm wearing the black platform ankle boots I stole from Clark's last week. I was going to pay, but the assistant took so long I got pissed off. I've also got on these fab purple bell-bottoms I pinched out a posh shop in Stockbridge. They were supposed to be £65. The black ribbed top I bought myself but, naturally, with money stolen from Mum. I'm ready as I'll ever be.

There's a 33 at the stop. I jump on before noticing Dad's driving.

'What y'up to, love?'

Racking my brain for reasons I might be going to Haymarket in the middle of the afternoon, I say I'm meeting Rosie from the doctor's.

'What's wrong with her?'

He's not supposed to talk when he's driving, it's dangerous. I sling him a deefie, in the hope the other passengers think he's talking to himself.

'I'll give you a few quid if the pair of you want to go out on Friday.'

Or maybe I'd just like to stay in and shag her uncle. We pull in to the stop and I escape.

'Aye, Dad, we'll see.'

Crossing the road, I walk past the butcher's and down John's street. There's a man in a car outside the stair, reading a paper. He's probably an undercover cop, but I just stride straight past, praying the door's still knackered. It is, thank fuck. As soon as it shuts behind me, I suddenly don't know what I'm doing here. Should I pretend Rosie sent me again, or see if he wants anything from the shops? As I feel my way down to the basement, the voice in my head's saying *he likes you, he likes you.*

Knocking four times, I peer through the letterbox. There's a football-on-telly noise. I whisper through, 'It's me, Joni. Can I come in a minute?' Before I even stand up, he's pulled me into the flat and slammed the door. The look of terror on his face is not really the reaction I was anticipating, it has to be said.

'What're you fucking playing at, eh? Are you trying to get me hung?'

His bedroom door's open. There's a purple duvet scrunched at the bottom of the bed. I've no idea what to say, I just want to look at him. He's angry but his eyes are all over me.

'Is this a fucking set-up? Rosie cannae keep sending you round like this . . . fuck.'

'She didnae . . . it's just . . .' What do I say? Do I just come out with it? I'm going to get thrown out in about five seconds.

'Just what?' He's looking straight into my eyes, like a hypnotist.

'I . . . I . . . I want to do it with you.'

At least it makes him smile.

'You . . . you . . . you want to do it with me?' he giggles. He has a lovely giggle. 'Do you say that to all your pal's uncles?'

'It's no like that. I'm no a slag. I've never even done it before.'

He leans against the door, amused.

'And you want to do it with me, in particular?'

'Aye, it has to be you . . . no some stupid wee laddie . . . before I'm sixteen.'

He lets out another gorgeous snigger.

'Have I got that much of a reputation? Really, you shouldnae believe all you read on bus stops.'

I've not noticed anything on bus stops. This is embarrassing. I didn't expect to have to do so much talking.

'Look, hen. It's one of the nicest offers I've ever had, truly, but you really better go. I'm in the shit as it is, and I have to say, I'm a wee bit suspicious of your motives.'

The rejection gives me second wind.

'I don't have motives. Look . . .' and I pull five tenners I nicked earlier, out my back pocket, 'I can pay you, then nobody can say you forced me.'

He inspects the notes and hands them back.

'I wish I had a camcorder. This would be great for my defence.'

He has to do it. I've gone this far. I'll never be able to show my face in public again if he knocks me back.

'John, please. D'you no like me?'

Taking my hand, he squeezes it round the cucumber in his

trousers. Oh my God, I think I'm going to faint. I didn't realise they had bones in them. When he lets go, my hand stays glued there, but he pulls away.

'You better go.'

It's all-or-nothing time.

'Please, John, I winnae say anything about you and Rosie to anyone.'

He smacks his fist off the wall.

'I don't fucking believe this.'

It's not going to happen. I feel every bit of confidence I ever had slipping away.

'We could meet somewhere else. It doesnae need to be here . . .'

I'm just saying anything now. The blood's going round my body in tidal waves.

'You'd do that? Meet me tonight?'

Fuck, he's into it.

'Anywhere, just say.'

He looks deep in thought. I wish I could read his mind.

'I could pick you up at a bus stop. Would you like that? Take you into the woods and fuck you over the bonnet of my car?'

'Oh yes, when? Tonight? Definitely,' I pant.

'And you wouldn't tell another living soul? No even Rosie?'

'Promise, specially not Rosie. Can we?'

He kisses the top of my head. I'm so fired up I'm surprised he doesn't get an electric shock. He says he'll pick me up at the bus stop next to St Thomas's Church on Glasgow Road at eight. I've never heard of these places, but he makes me write down directions and tells me to ask the driver to let me off at the church. It better not be Dad or any of his mates. On second thoughts, Dad doesn't have any mates.

As I walk back to Dalry Road, my hand seems stuck to my mouth. I can't believe I just came out with it. It was dead brave.

Maybe that's the secret. If you want something, you just need the guts to ask.

I rush home to X^2. I'm so horny, rubbing's not enough and I end up using my roll-on deodorant as a John substitute. I'm so wet, I pretend he's already done it and this is the second time. If doing it's half as good as this, I'll have a breakdown. I'm still peching, when the door bell goes. It's Rosie.

'They're sending me to a counsellor, to make me grass. Sick bastards.'

It gives me a kick, listening to her go on about her and John, not realising they're already history.

She's arranged to meet Twiggy at the graveyard to get a sixteenth. I'm still avoiding Daniel, but the thought of doing it for the first time stoned is too much to resist. I say I'm going to my auntie's at half-seven, so I can't stay long. We haven't talked to auntie for years but Rosie's none the wiser.

They're all pissed by the time we get up the crypt. Daniel looks pleased to see me and is straight over with the White Lightning. What was I worried about? He's just a daft wee boy.

Twiggy hands over the teenth. It's the biggest bit dope I've ever seen. I think of getting some for later but end up paying for Rosie's as she's forgotten her money. As I'm about to steal her man, though, I don't make a fuss. I thought a teenth was about seven-fifty, but I get no change from a tenner. Not wanting to look stupid, I say nothing.

They're dead impressed by my wad. Daniel keeps offering me cider and Twiggy gives me the joint to light. They sit round, smiling at me as I toke – nice, friendly smiles. It's like I touched John's cock and suddenly everyone wants to be my friend.

'If you've money to throw around, I know a guy could get you an ounce for 90 quid. You'd sell it dead quick. Fifteen, ten pound bits, no problem.'

Who'd buy it, like? All the folk I know who smoke it get it off Twiggy.

'I dinnae think so. I've only got 40 quid left.'

'Get another tenner, I'll get you half an ounce.'

'Naw, really, thanks, but I've got to hold onto it.'

Fact is, she could offer me a room full of ecstasy and I wouldn't part with the rest of my cash. It's got John's DNA on it. I could have him cloned.

'Honest, Jo, the guy's desperate for folk to sell it.'

'Why doesn't he sell it?'

'I dunno . . . he wants to give other people the chance to make a bit money.'

It's making me the centre of attention. I'm getting offered more booze and spliff than any of them. Plus, the idea is starting to grow on me. I could support John if I was dealing drugs. It's a pretty cool thing to do anyway.

'I'll need to know by the weekend if you want to do it. He needs folk quickly.'

I have to pledge my birthday money on Friday before she changes the subject.

'Like your trousers, by the way. What are they? Velvet?' she says, fingering my bell-bottoms.

'I nicked them.'

They seem even more impressed.

'Get eys a pair in an eight and I'll give you a bit toot.'

Slugging back cider, I feel more villainous by the second. Why have I been avoiding these people? They really like me. Rosie's being practically ignored. In the course of one afternoon we've swapped places. I'm now the popular one, the one that's going to get shagged by John in . . . oh fuck, it's seven o'clock. Giving the auntie excuse again, I say I'll have to go. Rosie looks confused.

'I thought you didnae speak to your auntie?'

God, she picks her moments to exercise that huge brain of hers.

'Naw . . . no a real auntie, just some friend of Mum's they don't think I'm mature enough to call by her first name. She's in hospital. They think she'll die any minute.'

Rosie's face falls. 'Aw, that's terrible. You shoulda said.'

I'm in no mood to discuss imaginary sick people. I need to leave now, in case I can't find this church. Wishing them goodbye, I nash down to the bus stop before she says anything else.

After a quarter-of-an-hour wait, I change at Haymarket then it's another 20 minutes before a 26 comes. It's five to eight by the time I get to the church. Could he possibly have picked a more public place to meet? There's posh houses on both sides with a fucking motorway running down the middle. An old dear's already waiting. Surely he wouldn't have arranged to meet here though, if there was a chance we'd get caught. If we do, please make us have done it first.

I stand for ages. The old dear buggers off on the Airport Bus. A car slows down and I get all trembly, but it's just some guy getting dropped off who waits at the stop till another 26 comes along.

It's five to nine before it starts to dawn on me that John maybe only arranged to meet me so I'd go away. A hitch-hiker walks past and disappears into a car at the junction. Another 20 minutes pass. Thoughts of shagging are slowly getting eaten up by thoughts of seeing my fucking mother, not having one up on Rosie after all, spending next week (and probably the rest of my life) X^{2}ing.

Twenty past nine and I'm still standing like an arse. I walk up towards the junction, heading anywhere but home. I should stick my fucking thumb out and see where I end up. Whatever happened, it would be better than this. I'm at the crossroads before I work up the nerve. Almost instantly, there's a mighty screech and a massive, fuck-off juggernaut stops at my side. The door opens and Sinbad from *Brookside*'s double smiles down.

'Where you headed, love?'

I'm in shock. It happened so quickly. I repeat his question, over the roar of the engine.

'Paisley tonight, then up Aberdeen th'morn. Any good?'

Where the fuck is Paisley? Wherever, it sounds better than standing at the side of a motorway, trying to work up the nerve to walk into the traffic. Prince has a recording studio in the park there so it must be quite cool.

As it turns out, Rory, my chauffeur, is a real sweetie. I'm dead shy at first, but he's really chatty and gives me a half-bottle of Bell's to slug as we drive along. The Rolling Stones are blaring. I used to think they were shite, but the stuff he's playing's just like the Verve. Once I get over the feeling of wanting to gag at the whisky, I start to like it and feel very rock-and-roll.

Rory has a lovely smiley face and twinkly eyes. The more I drink, the nicer-looking I realise he is. He's so completely into everything I say I'm soon inventing all sorts of nonsense to impress him. Having noticed a Red Hand of Ulster tattoo on the back of his hand, I tell him my parents were killed in the Enniskillen bombing when I was five. He looks confused so I change this to seven. I was brought up by my auntie Terry, an artist, who's just died of AIDS, so I've moved in with my boyfriend, John, a care assistant. Rory seems fascinated, which encourages me to spin wilder and wilder tales as we speed through the darkness towards God knows what.

When we get to Paisley, it's not the Cincinnati of Scotland I was expecting. The buildings are so old and dirty-looking it's like being in a black and white film about the war. It's raining as well, which doesn't do it any favours. Rory says I'm welcome to sleep in his cabin, but it'll be a bit of a tight squeeze. He's not joking, the bed space is so wee I'll probably have to sleep on top of him. He's fucking sexy, actually.

We go for a drink in a very seedy bar near the lorry park.

Rory's the second youngest person in there by about 20 years. I feel proud to be seen with him. He drinks whisky and Guinness and I have a Hooch and a nip. He won't let me buy drink, even though he knows about my £40. Leaning against his shoulder, feeling beautifully giddy, I start on about my imaginary life again. About the farm where I grew up in Donegal having bullet-proof windows, meeting Princess Di at my parents' funeral, the celebs that buy my auntie's paintings, my weekend with Liam and Patsy . . .

Unfortunately, they call last orders when we're only on our third round. Rory gets us a nightcap. I watch him come back over with his lovely, lop-sided little smile. Maybe it would be better if John wasn't my first, so I'd know what I was doing. He doesn't even deserve me after what he's done tonight. Besides, if we're both sleeping in that wee bed, I may not have an option. Rory's pretty tipsy as we leave the pub and squeezes my hand as we walk back to the lorry. My hyper-horniness from earlier returns.

When we get back, he pulls a big curtain round the windows and we drink more whisky. It's dead cosy, like a wee Wendy house. Flashing me his smile, he leans over and kisses me. 'Time for bed, d'you think?' Here we go, here we go, here we go.

We get undressed in the front. I'm so pissed and turned on I'm not embarrassed stripping in front of him; in fact, I do it as sexily as the space will allow. Rory's got a freckly back and tattoos up both arms, dead masculine. Once he struggles out of his underpants, his willie's a bit disappointing, but it's maybe better to be broken in gently. Leaning down, he starts sucking my nipples. I'm worried they're too sticky-out but he moans his head off, really into them. It feels immense. I've not had a shower for two days, so my fanny smell's really obvious but it's like a magnet to him. He vibrates his hand against it, as he sucks my tits. He's almost as good as me at it. Then he tells me to crawl through to bed and climbs on top, kissing and licking my ears, neck, face. It's the best thing ever. Just me and this big, sexy man, alone in the middle of nowhere.

'Do it now,' I moan, unable to wait another second. He gently spreads my thighs with his knees. It's cramped, but I manage to get my legs round him, till my feet rest on his arse. His willie's right against me, prodding, trying to get in, then he suddenly thrusts forward and I feel a pain, the most gorgeous pain. It goes right into me and makes me yell. I feel his balls on my arse. He pulls out, in, out, in, out, in, and wails as his whole body starts quivering. He's just so good. Rolling off, he lets out a groan.

'You're some girl.'

Why's he stopped? It was wonderful. Was I rubbish? Was I hurting him by doing it wrong?

'You got me too excited,' he whispers, cuddling up.

What, is that it? Reaching between my legs, I feel his stuff running out. I can't believe that was it. Do they just lie about how long it lasts in films? I'd ask him to explain, but I don't want him to think I didn't enjoy it because I really, really did. I just expected there to be a lot more of it.

'You're some girl,' he whispers again. Five minutes later he's snoring.

When I wake up, it's light and we're completely entwined in a hot, sticky, gorgeous way. I study Rory's face, arms, chest, every detail, as he sleeps. I've never watched someone wake up before, especially not a big, sexy man that's fucked me the night before. I'm hoping we'll do it again, but we just have a bit of a kiss then he takes me for a bacon roll in a greasy caff. As I sip on a mug of hot, sweet tea, he tells me how sexy I am. I just gaze at him, thinking *we've done it, we've done it*. It feels like we belong to each other. There's no way I can leave now, so I decide to chum him up to Aberdeen. I expect him to be pleased, but he can't take me 'cause he lives there with his family. He says it so matter-of-factly I think he means his mum, but he explains.

I'm stunned. How could he do that to me if he was married? He seems so decent.

As he walks me to the station, I go quiet. He'll think I'm some silly, wee, huffy lassie, but I can't help it. He holds my hand again. It feels lovely but I don't know why he's doing it, if he's just going to dump me. The Edinburgh train's arriving as he buys my ticket so I don't have time to give him my number or arrange to meet him again, or even find out what his second name is.

We say goodbye as the guards bang the train doors shut. He gives me a long, warm kiss and a big squeeze and tells me I'm some girl again. I'm crying when I get on the train, so I run in the toilet so he can't see me. I don't believe it. He won't even be able to come looking for me when he's in Edinburgh, 'cause I told him complete lies about myself. Why did I say that stuff? He would have liked the real me. How can I possibly never see him again after all that? If I even had a wee photo or something to remember him. He didn't even know I was a virgin, for God's sake.

Chapter Twenty-Six

VIC

WHERE'S MY BABY? I've phoned Accident and Emergency, on the hour, since four this morning. The same woman keeps answering and she's really starting to sound pissed off. I woke Rosie's entire household to try there, but Joni supposedly left at seven last night to visit a dying auntie. What's she on about? We haven't seen Jean for over a year but the last I heard she was, regrettably, alive and well. Oh, and I woke Jake up as well. He's not seen her since Sunday.

I'm desperate to go out and start searching. However, Angie barricaded herself, pissed, in the bedroom when she got in last night, so is probably incapable of answering the phone, or remembering who called if she did. Besides, if Jo walks in to another confrontation with that bitch, she'll be off again by the time I get back.

I'm supposed to be early shift but phoned in sick. Jake surfaces at ten. He senses from my edgy, wide-eyed, chain-smoking demeanour that Jo's still not back. Getting his Ribena fix, he sits down.

'Surely if she pretended to Rosie she was going somewhere, she must have had somewhere to go, y'know? It's less likely she's been raped and dismembered.'

I feel sick.

'Dinnae even say that, Jake, please. She must have told you something. D'you know if she's got a boyfriend?'

He guffaws.

'Hardly, she's been trying to get an invite down to Sean's with me. I think she fancies him.'

God, if she's resorting to forcing herself on her brother and his pals, she must be really desperate. Turning up the telly for the Scottish news, I feel terrified. It's the same old shit they've been broadcasting all night though – the fresh inquiry into the World's End murders has come up blank, the serial rapist who escaped from a work placement in George Street on Monday's still on the loose. I put the volume down again. Jan starts whining in an unnerving psychic-pet sort of way.

'Have you tried the police?' asks Jake, as she affectionately toys with his leg.

'They won't class her as missing till she's been gone 24 hours. It's bloody ridiculous. What if she's been abducted? They should be looking now.'

'I was thinking more that they'd maybe locked her up.'

The phone rings. As I dive for it, it feels like there's a riot going on in my chest.

'Joni, sweetheart, is that you?'

'Can I speak to Victor, please?' says a crabbit female voice I immediately recognise as being my father's neighbour.

'Mrs Moodie. This is Vic. Look, I'm waiting on a call. Can I ring you back?'

'No, Victor, I wouldn't want you to put yourself out. I just thought you might like to know, your dad's in hospital. Sorry I disturbed you,' she says in a tone that could freeze the Forth.

I ask her what's happened, but my mind's still in orbit around my existing crisis. She takes it as a cue to give me a detailed analysis of the ins and outs of her turgid life.

'. . . so I went round to tell him my daughter was running me up to Safeway's if he needed anything, but you know your dad. He's so proud sometimes. He . . .'

'Please, Mrs Moodie. Could you just tell me what's happened?'

'. . . and you know how he hates being stuck in that house. The loneliness just eats away at you. I'm the same since I lost my Jimmy. Of course, my family have been good, which always . . .'

'Mrs Moodie. Is Dad OK?'

She huffs. 'That depends what you class as OK.'

'Please, Mrs Moodie . . .'

Dad's had a fall in the street. He's been in the Infirmary since half-eight this morning. Thanking her for letting me know, I tell her I'll go up as soon as possible, but will she get off the phone?

'Actually, I wondered, if you're going anyway, could you possibly run me up? I'm awfully close to your dad. I check on him every day, so I feel awful I wasn't there.'

Buggeration!

'To tell the truth, we're having a bit of a red alert as it is at the moment. Can I ring you when it's sorted? I'll call the hospital now.'

'I've phoned twice. He's supposedly stable but I don't trust hospitals. My Jimmy went in with varicose veins and never came out again. I need to see him for myself.'

Do I really need a guilt trip from this old bag?

'Look, I can assure you, I'd be up there right away if I wasn't in the middle of something. I'll get back to you.'

'Of course, Victor, I know how busy you are, your dad's told me all about it.'

Thanking her again, I slam the phone down. Jake's been listening in, concerned. When he finds out it's just his granda though, he goes to his room.

For the eighth time this morning, I phone the Infirmary. Luckily, the torn-faced cow I've been bothering all night has finished her shift. They put me through to the nurse. She says it's only superficial bruising, but dad got a bit of a fright so they're keeping him in for observation. It's almost a relief to have something new to worry about. Christ, what a way to think.

I go through to Jake's room to update him. He says, uh huh a few times but isn't listening to a word I'm saying. As soon as I hesitate, he changes the subject.

'Da-ad, see when I'm at Sean's, we can hear Mum shouting. It's dead embarrassing. Can you speak to her?'

'But it's me trying to speak to her makes her shout in the first place.'

Grabbing his jacket, he tells me he has to hurry before America wakes up. I don't ask.

Without Jake to distract me, the fear returns with a vengeance. Turning the telly back up to ground myself, I discover Tammy Wynette's popped her clogs. Things aren't all bad then, I muse, immediately feeling guilty for thinking such a thing. Tammy was someone's daughter too. Jesus, what must her mother look like?

The discovery that I've smoked the last of my fags brings on acute nicotine withdrawal and forces me through the bedroom, into Angie's bag. The smell and sound of her snoring are torturous but I have to dig through last night's chips, a half-bottle of vodka with a mouthful left, and other womanly shite, before I locate her Silk Cuts. By then, the urge to rub the chip paper in her face is almost irresistible.

Nicotine fix in hand, I go through to Joni's. I hate invading her privacy, but there must be some sort of clue around here. I've only just opened the bedside-table drawer when the front door goes and she's suddenly there, in front of me, breathing.

'What the fuck are you doing in my room?'

I almost fall at her feet in relief.

'Where have you been, love? I've been phoning bloody hospitals all night.'

'What for? I was watching the *Friends* videos at Rosie's. We crashed out.'

'Come on, Jo. I phoned Rosie at four this morning. What's going on? Have you been crying?'

'Aw, Dad, stop hassling me. Stop stinking out my room with your fucking fags.'

She looks on in disgust, as I stub out on the side of her bin.

'Just tell me where you've been.'

'Walking, right . . . just walking.'

'All night?'

'Yeah. So? It's safer than staying here, getting smacked about by Mum.'

Her chin starts trembling on the last three words but she fights back the tears. I try to cuddle her but she jumps away.

'I'll speak to her, love, honestly.'

'And other famous last words.'

As she lurches into bed, fully clothed, I notice her top's on inside-out but I can't bring myself to mention it. I'm already on the cusp of losing the place, and figure that one unhinged parent at a time is enough. She starts sobbing into the duvet as I open the door.

'D'you want anything?'

'To fall asleep and not wake up.'

Join the club. When I go through to make a coffee, the news is still on. By now, though, I'm too busy contemplating my daughter's inside-out top to give a shit about anyone else's problems. Walking all night, bollocks! Who is he? Why would she not even tell her best pal about him? Is it a teacher? Someone Rosie fancies? Whoever he is, he's dead.

I sit, raging, with images of my daughter getting screwed flashing through my head until *it* skulks into the room at half-eleven. There's no point even mentioning Joni, since the selfish drunken bitch slept through the whole thing, anyway. I try to tell her about Dad but she's obviously too preoccupied with where her next drink's coming from and blanks me.

When I go through to warn Joni of the hellish awakening, there's a sheet of paper stuck to her door with 'No Smoking' scrawled in black marker. I persevere and stick my head into her room.

'That's the She-Devil surfaced. I'm popping up the hospital. Granda's been taken in.'

'Shut the door, Dad, eh?'

I decide not to phone Mrs Moodie. There's only so many nippy bastards I can take in one day. Right on cue, Angie stomps past with the chips and half-bottle.

'Working today?'

'Fuck off, Vic.'

I'm used to it. This is just the way people speak to me.

'Well, if you start on that stuff before I get back, keep the bloody noise down, eh? They can hear you downstairs.'

Snarling, she unscrews the vodka and defiantly swigs the last few drops.

'So fucking what? They're just a bunch of Catholics, aren't they? How dare a single parent judge me.'

She needs strangling. I leave before I decide to do the honours.

My pulse is racing on the way up to the hospital. I have to breathe into a bag in the car park for a few minutes before I'm ready to go in. By then, I'm feeling like a complete bastard for not giving Mrs Moodie a lift. As I walk up the ward of sad, neglected old men, I wonder how many of their ailments are woman-related.

Dad's bed's in the middle, next to the nurses' station. The right side of his face is black with bruising. His hands and arms are the same colour. There's a stitched gash at the side of his jaw. I only recognise him when I see his big grin, shining out from the prune of a head.

'God, Dad, what were you doing?'

'Just getting a bit fresh air, son, honestly. I tell you, the potholes up that street are worse than bloody land-mines.' He tries to hide the stitches with his hand, like I might give him a row otherwise. 'Really, it's not as bad as it looks. I'm just such an old git, my skin's like tissue paper.'

I look down to spare him his embarrassment. His legs are horrifically bruised as well, and so skinny. They seemed so massive and sturdy when I was a wee boy. Now they're like a sparrow's. Taking my hand, he brushes it with his thumb.

'You're shaking, son. Is everything all right?'

Why can't I just tell him? He's the one person on earth that actually seems to like me . . . to love me. It would be too like a confession of my own inadequacy, though. I don't want him hurt by it as well.

'How're my two favourite grandchildren?'

His only grandchildren, poor sod. I assume a facial expression of long-suffering contentment. 'Fine, really. I'll bring them both round to see you when you get out,'

. . . then eradicate world poverty!

'And Angela?'

'Working hard.'

It makes me sick to say it but I just want to protect him. Still, he seems to sense that something is rotten in the state of Gorgie, but he doesn't pry, he just keeps squeezing my hand.

'See him two beds down . . .' he whispers. There's a boy out for the count, can't be much older than 20. '. . . went off his head this morning. He's been sectioned but there's no room for him at the Royal Ed. They had to take the tranquilliser gun to him. He kept battering the nurses and trying to escape. I'd have been safer if they'd left me on the pavement.'

The image of him lying, helpless in the street, makes me nauseous with shame.

'How about the rest of them, are they OK?'

Shuddering, he gestures to the empty bed on his left.

'That old bugger's away for a colonic irrigation at the moment. Serves him right. He's been bending my ear all morning. Wee Frees and all that rubbish.'

A nurse comes over to take his blood pressure. It's not the visiting hour, but she doesn't say anything. Mind you, I think they only specify hours to give visitors an excuse to leave. Dad introduces us. I'm unsure if he's showing me off, or trying to fix me up. Her pale little Irish face flushes when I smile at her but this is probably more to do with sleep deprivation than desire.

When they start bringing round the lunches, I use it as an excuse to go. I'm enjoying Dad's company but I don't want to give a false impression of how much time I'm prepared to spend with him. He asks me if I could possibly give Mrs Moodie a run up tonight. Please say I imagined that disconcerting twinkle in his eye. All I need is that old atrocity for a stepmother, that'd really be the icing on the shitty cake. He's asked me three more times, before I escape.

By the time I leave the ward, I'm starting to resent him. Am I destined to spend the entire day with twisted bitchy women? I'm so put upon, I feel like a character out the Bible. On the way out, I pass the Intensive Care Unit, where Mum died. There's coronary problems on both sides of the family so no doubt the rest of us will end up there in the end. We've always been the same. Our hearts get us every time.

Chapter Twenty-Seven

JAKE

SEAN'S GOT THE dentist, so they turf me out at lunch time. He'll only be an hour, but rather than face a second helping of Dad bleating on about his beloved Joni, I wander round the shops. Fucking fascinating they are too – hideous jumper shop, the place that sells horrible old ladies' knickers, a florist – no wonder they're all closing down. There's just so much for people my age to do round here. I try ringing a few buzzers to cheer myself up but it's no fun on your own. It's like being homeless.

As I walk along Dalry, my thoughts turn to my missing sister. Will we get to do a TV appeal if she's been murdered? Eva'd definitely fancy me if she saw me on TV. You know what women are like, even the Yorkshire Ripper gets marriage proposals. Thing is, though, the folk that do these appeals always seem to end up being the actual killers. That's a point, I wonder if Dad's checked the freezer yet.

A fast black blur suddenly flashes past on the other side of the road. At first I think it's a weasel or a runaway dachshund, it's such an odd size. Then I notice the long, snaky tail sweeping behind as it scurries along like it owns the place. A fucking rat. I've never even seen one in real life before, y'know, not in a cage. I run across the road, like the Pied Piper on rewind. It takes off into the grave-yard like it's going for the land-speed record. What if there's a lair of them? I read about it in a book once. They'll get in the Mecca and chew the old dears' innards out while they're playing bingo.

It's dead quiet in here ... haw, haw ... dead quiet, no, really but, you wouldnae guess it was next to a main road. Mr Rodent's long gone, but I walk up the path, on the off-chance I find a half-eaten dosser. I could be anywhere, if it wasnae for the gravestones. When we first moved, I used to play here, but it's no seemed right since Granda died. They wanted to cremate him but I pretended to Mum he had an incinerator phobia, so I'd have somewhere to visit. I've no been up since. As far as I mind, he's up the top, but I was in a hearse the last time, so I cannae be sure. All I mind is he was next to someone called Thomas Mason. I thought he'd be chuffed about that.

They've tidied the place since then — cut the grass, pulled up they Triffid-like bushes that used to block out the sun — but it's still grotty. Lots of stones have been kicked over and there's spunky condoms, bloody tampons, discarded knickers, gluey crisp bags, syringes everywhere — like Liam Gallagher's hotel room. Maybe junkies come here so they dinnae have as far to go when they OD. Shagging here's just desperate, though. Plus, it cannae be nice, finding a leaky Durex on your nearest and dearest, when you bring flowers up. I'm no getting buried anyway. My ashes are getting fireworked over Ibrox.

The silence is barrie compared to the screaming round our house recently. It's completely deserted. Mind you, most of the gravestones are ancient so the relatives are probably long dead. It's all wee kids, folk killed in the war or really old cunts. Nobody else seemed to die back then. It must've been before cigarettes were invented.

It takes 20 minutes to find Thomas Mason. I recognise the spot immediately. I mind hiding under the tree in the corner after the funeral, embarrassed by Mum's loud crying. Granda's stone's been knocked over, face down. The grass is starting to grab it into the ground. Even worse though, some bastard's sprayed 'Robbo' across it in red. Laudrup, McCoist, but fucking Robbo?

Digging my fingers under, I try to lift but a million beasties start scrambling round my feet. Beasties give me the willies, specially slaters, the world population of which seem to live under here. Wiping out a few generations, Godzilla-like, with my trainers, I kick them off the stone, and sit down. It would take a fucking crane to lift it anyway.

It's weird knowing someone you used to be close to is lying under you, rotting. I wonder if Granda's still recognisable, or if there's just a suit and shirt stuffed with awfie fat worms. His DNA's probably in the flowers by now. I bet these bluebells were snowdrops before they buried him.

I sit for ages, watching the birds. There's millions of them once you start looking. They live off the DNA-eating beasties, so I wonder if they've got Granda in them too, if that's what reincarnation is. I'm just starting to think how philosophical the peace and quiet's making me, when I hear voices approaching. No wanting to get cornered by some grief-stricken old dear, I walk back to the path. Then I hear the words, 'Hey, cunt!' being yelled, so loud a cloud of starlings get frightened off a bush. Call me psychic, but I immediately sense that I'm the cunt in question. The sight of Daniel, Shug and a manly lassie I recognise from fourth year tanking up the path towards me, confirms this. How the fuck did they find me here?

Nashing down the back way, I hit the edge of a grass-covered stone and snap over on my ankle. When I try to put weight on it, the pain throws me onto the grass.

'Uyay, uyah!'

Daniel and Shug land on top of me, punching.

'If it's no the dirty Hun himself.'

Rolling into a ball, I yell at them to stop, but even the lassie gets stuck in. A kicking's bad enough, but by a woman? Trying to get up again, I get an electric shock of pain, right up my leg. Shug takes a step back and starts unfastening his jeans.

Oh, my God, he's going to shag me. He cannae shag me. Please dinnae let him shag me. It's almost a relief when he smacks his belt round my face. My teeth rattle, I see my eyeballs from inside but at least my arsehole's intact. When I cover my head with my hands, he smacks them as well. Fucksake! They're going to kill me, in a fucking graveyard. I'm going to die because Sean went for new trainers. On and on he beats me, round the arms, neck, across the back. I'm too stunned to cry.

Then I feel someone straddle me. I open my nippy eyes to see a Stanley knife being waved in my face.

'Please, dinnae, Shug. I'll get your magazines. You'll get the jail if you kill ies.'

The blade's so close I can smell the rust.

'Shut it, fuckhead! The drugs are better in jail anyway. My brother says.'

Making Daniel and the lassie grab my arms, he yanks up my jumper and pricks the knife into my chest. Daniel puts his hand over my mouth to stop me screaming. Shug draws the knife down and across in a crucifix. It's no deep but it's fucking agony. I almost pass out when I see little bubbles of blood oozing from the gash.

'Will I do yer bollocks, now? Have they dropped yet?' he growls, so insane-looking, even Daniel seems scared.

'C'mon Shug, that's enough . . .'

Shug just ignores him and presses the knife against my Adam's apple.

'How about a nice wee string of rosary beads round your throat, eh?'

'Dinnae, man,' says Daniel, grabbing him from behind and pulling him off me. My ankle's so sore I can almost hear it, but the threat of castration gives me enough of a rush to get up. My chest's nipping like fuck as well. It grates against my top as I limp away like a crab on speed. Luckily, they dinnae chase me, they're too busy laughing.

The pain and shock dinnae really hit me till I'm onto the street. My legs buckle but I keep going, gulping back tears as I hobble towards my stair, towards safety, I hope.

Mum's drinking when I get in, staring at herself in the hall mirror. It's like she's been waiting there to finish me off.

'For fuck's sake, Jake!'

When I try to get to my room, she grabs one of my bad arms.

'Ow, dinnae, I fell down the steps at Wardlaw. Please, Mum, I just want to lie down.'

'Don't give me that. I'm not an idiot. It was these bastards downstairs, eh?'

Only Mum could think that.

'I told you, I fell.'

She still winnae let go my arm.

'Dinnae lie to me. Tell me, really, Jake, they're not getting away with it.'

Swallowing her drink, she starts pulling me into the stair. I scream and struggle, but I feel like I'm going to die from the pain in my ankle. When we get to Sean's, I start lashing out with my fists but I can barely lift my arms. She cannae, she just cannae. The buzzer rasps. As I pray they're no back yet, I hear someone padding down the hall.

'Dinnae answer, please, my mum's having an eppy, dinnae answer,' I scream, but the door's already open. Terry looks at Mum, then me. Her eyes seem to bulge. Mum thumps me towards her like a volleyball.

'D'you want to explain this . . . the fucking state of this?'

I try to pull her back up the stair, but she's like a big lump of lead.

'Please, Terry, shut the door, she's pissed. Just ignore her.'

'Will I get the police?'

Mum throws a punch. My life flashes before me as I squeeze myself between them. Somehow, I manage to get her to the other side of the landing, straining like a muzzled pit-bull.

'Go on, then, get the fucking police. Explain to them how my son looks like he's been in a road accident.'

Oh, Jesus, Sean's at the door now as well, gawping at me like I'm Stevie Fulton. I didnae make it to the bathroom mirror, I must look fucking terrible.

'Please, Sean, jist shut the door. Please, pal, it's awright.'

But he stands there frozen. In desperation, I grab the handle myself and slam it behind us. Mum throws herself onto it, and does the breast stroke with her fists.

'KEEP AWAY FROM MY FAMILY, YOU FENIAN BAS-TARDS!'

I've never felt such hate for someone, no even Shug. How could I have stuck up for her the other day? I wish she was dead. Leaving her pummelling the door, I struggle back upstairs and collapse onto the settee, too sore to make it to my room. Where the fuck's Dad and Joni? Jan puts her head on my lap and tries to look as miserable as me. It's the final straw. I start bawling my eyes out. I can still hear her creating downstairs.

When she finally comes back up, she acts like nothing's happened.

'Poor baby, will I phone the doctor? What've they done to you? What have they done to my baby?'

'Fuck off, Mum, just fuck off.'

I dinnae want a doctor, I just want to fucking die, I just want *her* to fucking die.

'I only did it 'cause I love you,' she wails, trying to cry, trying to pretend she's human.

Staring straight ahead at the telly, I cannae see through the tears. I'm too rubbery to stand up. It's fucking torture. I try to pretend Mum's no there, but someone starts singing 'Stand By Your Man' on the news and she lobs her empty glass at the screen. The TV survives but the glass isnae so lucky. I crunch on it as I use my last bit strength to go to my room to die.

Someone knocking on the door wakes me at nine. The look on Dad's face says it all.

'Oh, my God, was it her? What's she done to you, for Christ's sake?'

His expression's so pained you'd think it was him had been battered to fuck. He strokes my head. Even my hair hurts.

'She did this, eh? C'mon, Jake, you've got to tell me.'

'Naw, Dad, honest, but she attacked Sean's mum. She was calling them Catholic bastards and everything. I hate her, Dad, I really do.'

Still, he seems to think if he stares at me long enough, I'll say what he wants.

'Jake, just say, it was Mum, eh? Just tell me.'

Maybe I should agree to get my own back on the old bag. She'd only kill me. I repeat my story about falling down the steps but he's having none of it. He wants to call the police. If he does that I'll end up with Shug's brother after me as well. He's a fucking armed robber. It takes ages to talk him out of it, then even longer to talk him out of calling a doctor.

'Please, Dad, I need to rest.'

But still he sits, as if I might get hit by lightning if he lets me out his sight. I force him to tell me about Granda, no 'cause I'm interested, just to take his mind off me. He tells me Joni's back, but wouldnae say where she'd been. At least she's got somewhere else to go. I dinnae any more.

Should I mention the shagging noises? Surely he'd throw her out if he knew she was screwing other men. Maybe she'd fuck off and live with her alkie boyfriend. It's such a shitey thing to have to tell him, though, it takes ages to work up the nerve. It eventually comes out somewhere between a belch and a whisper.

'Dad, I think Mum's seeing someone else.'

He doesnae respond. I'm scared to look at first in case he's tanning his wrists. When I do, he's asleep in the chair, hardly surprising since he's been awake since yesterday morning. I think about waking him but he'll only end up on the settee. Maybe the time's come to start looking out for each other anyway. Besides, I'm too sore to wank now and I finally feel sort of safe.

Chapter Twenty-Eight

ANGIE

I WOKE UP crying the past three mornings. The hopeless, waiting days go downhill after that. Can you die from anticipation? Raymond's answering machine's switched off now, but I've been killing time listening to his phone ring out. Nobody's been in touch – the police, work, not even a solitary, gloating ex-colleague. My only consolation is that I told the police about our affair. Whatever happens now, we'll always be together in the annals of criminal history. Pity I didn't mention the Mexico thing, though. I'll probably just look like some woman who was once given a using.

There's no sign of Vic. I'll have to tell him about my job today. I refuse to turn into one of these radges that leaves at the same time every morning, years after they've been sacked.

On my way to the kettle, I nearly cripple myself on a puddle of shattered glass. Drops of blood trail across the carpet into the kitchen. I half expect to find Vic's tiny severed penis lying beside the fridge, but it's only the dog. Her paw's lying in a burgundy pool on the lino, stupid, fucking creature. I'm not paying vet's bills for something that was meant to be on its last legs when we got it, a decade ago. I only agreed to getting her in the first place because I thought she'd be dead within the month.

She offers me the damaged paw. A glass toe-nail clipping protrudes from the pad. Who am I, fucking Daniel? Her awful whimpering reminds me of Vic when he's having one of his holier-than-thou tirades. However, in a rare moment of compassion, I empty the only booze in the house, the Xmas Advocaat, in front of her. The snivelling mess, poorly as she is, laps it up in seconds. That should dull the pain.

Several minutes' searching establishes that the flat is a cigarette-free zone. I'd go to the shops but Raymond might call when I'm out. Vic appears as I'm taking the phone off the hook. Giving me a look of impending reprimand, he closes the living-room door behind us.

'D'you want to explain about last night?'

'Eh?'

He shakes his head.

'Your brawl with the neighbour? The laddie comes home looking like that, so you attack his best friend's mother? Nice one, Ange.'

Oh shit, now he comes to mention it.

'I was trying to protect him. Where were you, like? One minute he's down there, the next he's had the shit kicked out of him. What was I meant to think?'

He looks at me with such hatred I almost find him attractive.

'You didn't think to ask Jake what'd happened, like? Was that too easy? Or did you just feel like having a go at someone when I wasn't in?'

I make for the door but he won't let me go till he's said his little piece.

'Please, for our son, go down and apologise before work, eh? You'll be too pissed by the time you get home.'

Just tell him now. At least get that out the way.

'Actually, Vic, my employment's been terminated. They sacked me on Monday.'

'You're kidding me . . . naw, don't tell me . . . the drink.'

How dare he suggest I work at anything less than full efficiency when pissed.

'No, Vic, not the drink, sorry to disappoint you. The manager fucked off with the takings. I'm responsible for the banking, so they sacked me.'

'They cannae do that.'

'They just did.'

He eyes me suspiciously.

'So were you involved?'

'Give me some credit, eh? Think I'd still be here, if I had been?'

He slaps the side of the armchair. Ooh, temper, temper.

'Jesus Christ, they cannae do that. What're the union saying?'

'Piss off. You know as well as me what a fucking waste of space they are. I've been sacked, that's it. If I'd known he was going to bugger off with the takings, I'd have banked them before he had the chance. I'm not Uri fucking Geller.'

'I'll phone and have a word with them. Who actually sacked you?'

Can he not just keep his nose out?

'What does it matter? I wouldn't go back now if they begged me.'

He scowls at his signed photo of Dennis Skinner, for inspiration.

'Whose gonnae employ you if you've been sacked for dishonesty? You have to clear your name.'

'Look, Vic, I spent five hours in the cop shop on Monday, trying to clear my fucking name. I've had enough. They can think what the hell they like.'

'Cop shop?'

'A big building with bars on the windows where they put bad people like me.'

I finally get past him.

'Look, I'm sick of this. I'm going out. If anyone phones, take a message.'

'Who are you expecting, like?'

Leaving him to mull that one over, I'm suddenly on the street, with nowhere to go, and my only means of communicating with Raymond back inside. As always happens on sorry days like these, I try to think of people to annoy but only come up with Caroline. Raymond has to come back. I need more than my shitty family and a mental defective to keep me going.

The sad bitch answers on the first ring. The tortured way she says hello, as ever, makes me want to hang up. Lacking an alternative venue to drink myself silly and go on about Raymond, however, I invite myself round. It's my way of doing my bit for charity. God better be watching.

Visiting the Cashpoint en route, I discover I've only 50 quid left in my account. These bastards won't be in a hurry to pay me the two days I'm due, but I withdraw it all, regardless. I can always dig into the bill money till Raymond comes to the rescue with the 15 grand.

The bus appears as I wait to get my card back. My face is tight and hot, as I run after it, waving like an idiot. The driver mutters to himself as I fumble for change. I hate fucking bus drivers. They are the lowest form of life.

Crashing into the disabled seats, I immediately regret it.

'Will you look at that? I'm 76, and I still leave these seats free,' whispers the old sweetie wifie behind me to her friend.

'What d'you expect in an area like this?'

'I know, see all the To Let signs. It looks terrible.'

'No wonder, all the coloureds round here. I tell you, if they open another shop in Ashley, I'm moving to West Linton with my sister. It breaks my heart.'

If I'd had a drink, I'd get wellied into them, but I just sit with a fixed smirk. At the stop past Somerfield, another victim gets on – a teenage mum, struggling with two infants and a buggy. She sits behind them.

'Can't be a day over 16.'

'No wedding ring, naturally.'

'Mmh.'

One of the kids starts coughing – a painful, almost tubercular-sounding cough. I'm two seats in front but I can feel dots of saliva hitting me.

Heuck, heuck, heuck, goes the kid.

'Get a cold at our age, it can be enough to finish you off.'

Three cheers for viral infections.

'Should I give it a sweetie? I've some Tunes in my bag.'

'Oh yes, do, Ena, for goodness' sake.'

Heuck, heuck, heuck.

'Would she like a sweetie? They have menthol in them.'

'She doesnae eat sweets, ta.'

I laugh out loud.

'I've never met a child that didn't like sweets before.' Heuck, heuck, heuck. 'Oh good Lord, what sort of a cough is that?'

'Ah dinnae ken but she's given it tae me.'

That has them in convulsions. I'm so engrossed I almost miss my stop. Hopefully the emphysema will get them by morning.

I cross over to the grocer's for booze. The shuttered-down windows are plastered with 'Paki's Go Home' and BNP graffiti. It must be fresh, as I didn't notice it last week. It was probably those two old bags. I try to compensate by being over-friendly with the woman as serves me. She doesn't reciprocate. I can't really blame her.

Walking round to Caroline's, I push the farty buzzer.

'Who is it?' asks a pathetic, scared whimper from within.

'Death,' I say, in my finest Grim Reaper voice.

A rancid, cabbagey stench knocks me sideways when she opens the door.

'That's not funny, Ange. You can bring on things like that by saying them.'

I'm sure she used to have a sense of humour. Going through to the kitchen with the drink, I find the smelly culprit – a miasma-spewing bin bag. Pulling the collar of my dress over my nose, I wash something suspect from inside her only two glasses. The water's freezing.

In the living room, the stench is slightly less intense. However, Caroline's hair, and the back of her jumper, are covered in fish-food-sized flakes of dandruff, which is equally revolting.

I'm on my third drink before she takes a breather from regaling me with her tedious woes. I'm hoping if I let her get the shit out her system now, though, she won't interrupt when I start. When I get onto my fourth vodka and she's still banging on, I decide enough is enough. At my first mention of police, she's straight up at the window.

'What if they followed you? Did you check? They'll think I'm involved.'

Too irritated to indulge her paranoia with a response, I try the deserted-by-the-man-I-love angle. She of all people must be able to relate to that. No such luck. She seems more concerned about Vic. She's never even fucking met him.

'How could you could cheat on such a lovely, caring guy. I'd never cheat on someone like that. I wouldn't even cheat on a bastard.'

As if she'd get the chance of either.

'You're welcome to him, honest, have him with my blessing. Raymond's worth three of Vic.'

This makes her very annoyed.

'Who are you kidding? He sounds like a shit. How could you cheat on a nice man like Vic with a shit like that?'

'I just bent over, he did the rest.'

'Stop making a joke of it. You don't deserve love, if that's how you treat folk. I wouldn't treat anyone like that. How come you've got two men and I've got nobody?'

Because I don't think every news item carries subliminal messages about me and my ex-lovers. I don't line my window-sills with stewing steak as offerings to Pan. Change tack, quick.

'The police were bastards. It was like I was a prostitute, y'know, did he pay my mortgage, did he give me money, gifts? So fucking insulting. It was a woman, though, you know the type? Shag men and you're a traitor to your sex.'

I notice, with regret, that she's starting to knock back the voddie. Pouring myself another, I splash some in her glass before she has time to empty it. She's straight back onto cheating on my dull husband being a sin akin to genocide.

'I couldn't live with myself if I did something like that. Honest Angie, I've got so much love in me going to waste. If I had a man, I really feel I could get better. It's not drugs I need, it's someone to look after, to look after each other.'

The conversation always has to come back to Caroline. I make the mistake of asking how things are going with the hit man and her. She shushes me down, as if he's maybe through in the bedroom with a silencer.

'Please, don't mention Clive. He was just head-fucking me like the rest of them. Don't say his name again, please, pretend I never mentioned it.'

I didn't say his fucking name. Please, God, can I die before I get like that?

'Couldn't you get a job in a charity shop or something? You'd meet men there.'

It's patronising and pathetic but I'm just trying to be realistic.

'What about Vic? Doesn't he have any pals you could fix me up with? He must know nice people.'

Why doesn't she just get a taxi round there and suck his dick? Mind you, I wouldn't wish the smelly bitch on my worst enemy.

'Vic doesn't have any friends, Caroline. Vic is a boring tosser.'

She's mortified, fucking nerve, judging my relationships when she can't sustain one herself. Why are single people such arse-wipes? None of my married friends see fit to throw their oar in about my marriage. Glugging down her vodka, she demands a refill. There's hardly any left. I know I've drunk most of it but I expected a litre to last slightly longer than an hour and a half.

Her next swallow reduces her to tears. Bubbling over to the unit, fleeing, she knocks the fresh drink onto the carpet. It's so obviously deliberate, I feel like braining her. Instead, I pour her a spit-full and top it up with the last of the Diet Coke. Thankfully, she can't drink it straight. I can. A bottle of pills are rattled in my face.

'Diazepam, I'm saving them. The hospital think I'm on three a day but I've not taken any for a fortnight. Twenty's enough to kill you but I want to make sure I do it properly.'

What am I supposed to say? If her life's as horrendous as she makes out, it's hardly my place to deter her. Maybe I should suggest she does it somewhere more isolated, though. If nobody found her, I could move in and live off her Disability Living Allowance. Sadly, in my experience, people who threaten suicide, never actually do it. It's always the ones who grin and bear it that seem to blow their brains out.

'If Raymond doesn't get in touch, I might join you.' She looks ghoulishly excited. '. . . he better, I'm not spending the rest of my life with that cockless catatonic.' I smile into my drink, feeling pissed enough now to enjoy getting a rise out of her.

'You don't deserve 'im. You sold yer soul to Satan for a good shag.'

'When's the last time you had a good shag, like? I don't think you ever have or you'd understand what I was talking about. It was sooo good, Caroline, sooo fucking good. I just want to fuck him again, you know, just fuck him.'

She looks gobsmacked, for some reason.

'I cannae believe you, I cannae believe how selfish you are. I tell you I'm going to kill myself and all you care about is getting screwed. Haven't you any feelings?' She sits down, knackered from her little oration.

'Gie's a break, Caroline. How do we always have to talk about your problems? It gets monotonous after a while. And you wonder why I don't come round much. I'm the one with the problems today, so YOU have some fucking feelings.'

The waterworks start again. It gives me a little buzz of sadistic satisfaction.

'Is that true? You don't visit because I'm boring? I'm just good for a using when you need to escape? Well, to be honest with you, Ange, you got what you deserved.'

Emptying the last of the vodka into my glass, I swallow it and struggle to my feet.

'If that's your opinion, Caroline, then you can poke it. I come round here out of kindness, to listen to that shit? Naw, pal, I'm not wasting my life humouring you.'

Grabbing my coat, I leave her weeping on the settee. It takes so long to negotiate the intricately bolted door, though, she comes wailing through after me.

'I'm sorry, Ange. It's none of my business. Please don't leave. I can't stand to be alone any more. I'll take those pills.'

Locating the final lock, I open the door with a flourish.

'Sorry, Caroline, but it's hard enough keeping sane without spending time with you. It's best you don't phone me again. I hopefully won't be there much longer anyway.'

'You'll be punished for this, Ange, you will. Karma'll see to it,' she yells after me.

'Fuck off, you fucking witch,' I reply, as I stumble down the stairs onto the street.

It's fucking snowing, I don't believe it. Skittering towards the bus stop, clueless as to where to go next, I curse myself.

Brilliant move, girl, falling out with the only person in Scotland who was still talking to you. What an arsehole. No friends and 35 quid to last me the rest of my life. I should have stolen her fucking pills.

Chapter Twenty-Nine

JONI

AS JARVIS COCKER once sang, '. . . I feel as if my 'ole life 'as been leading to this woon mow-ment.' The stars are lining up over Dalry. Why? Because John's not going to jail, yee hah, the police have dropped all the charges. We found out this morning. Emma can't give evidence cause she's a spastic and Rosie didn't grass, so they've nothing on him. That's not it, though. It's the fucking timing. In two day's I'll be able to shag him legally. Tell me that's just a coincidence. Honest, it's all predestined, even him not turning up the other night.

Poor Rosie's not been so lucky. Her mum's forbidden her to see him . . . arf, arf . . . or go near his house . . . zip-a-de-doo-dah. Goes to show, not all parents are useless. Sadly, as a result of this, she's been hanging round me like a limpet all day. We babysat her wee brother in the morning, not that he's any bother. He has a disease makes him fall asleep all the time, so it's like looking after a teddy bear. Having to watch Richard Madeley and not X^2, though, was very frustrating. And see when Rosie mouths off about her and John now, I want to laugh in her face. Being such a good friend, however, I let her ramble on and have a quiet wee smile to myself.

We went up town with my birthday money in the afternoon. I choried these beautiful Rennie Macintosh ear-rings out Fraser's (I'm going posh), a waistcoat out Country Casuals and a pornographic red micro-dress from Monsoon. Now I have something to show for dad's money, I can spend it on drugs for John and me. I was going to pinch a pregnancy-testing kit from Superdrug too but I didn't want to have to explain to Rosie. I'm gimping to tell her about Rory, but I'd die if John found out. Virginity's far too good to lose just once.

She was dead nosy about Monday as well. I said I crashed at an old pal's up Fountainbridge. Mum had battered me again, so I had to get out. Unfortunately, this made Rosie all protective of me, dippit cow, which is why I've just managed to get rid of her. It's fucking tea time and I still need to have a wash. John probably went out celebrating yonks ago.

Wanting in and out the house as quick as possible, I try to sneak in unnoticed. Dad shouts me through before I even make it to my room. Ignoring his and-today's-catastrophe-is . . . face, I show him my plunder. He's so pre-occupied, he doesn't even pretend to think the dress is a top. It's worrying.

'Joni, love, Mum's lost her job.'

Why am I being bothered with this information?

'So? I thought you were chucking her out anyway.'

'Well, that's a bit difficult now, isn't it? If she's no earning, y'know . . .'

Oh, so that's it, is it? Dad craps out again. The rest of us have to suffer 'cause he's such a wuss. Trailing me through to the kitchen, he hovers as I slug Diet Coke and it fizzes over my face. As I blow juice down my nose, onto kitchen roll, he tells me Jake's been in an accident.

'He apparently fell down stairs, but I dinnae believe him. Your mother's got something to do with it. There's nothing surer.'

Aye, fucksake, so does she have to kill one of us before he chucks her out?

He wants me to got through and be nice to Jake but 1) that's impossible and 2) I'm already OD'ing on this fucking dump. He tries the do-it-for-daddy gaze that worked when I was five but now just makes me feel uncomfortable. Staring down at Jan to avoid it, I see her front paw's lying in a puddle of blood. It's so gross I let out a squeal.

'Christ, she must've stood in that glass your mother smashed. I left it for her to clean up. Poor Jan, it's all my fault.'

As I stroke her belly, she seems even more rug-like than usual.

'Is she breathing?' I ask, prodding, squeezing her bad paw, flicking her nose. Nothing. Dad lifts her eyelid, the pupil's glassy and fixed. He grabs his mouth, then his chest.

'Oh Jesus, no, not the bloody dog now.'

Running to the sink, I try to wash the deadness off my hands. Yuck, I've touched a minging corpse. When I turn back round, Dad's gone the colour of washing powder.

'It was probably suicide. I bet she deliberately tanned her paws,' he wails.

I give him a reassuring pat on the back.

'Dinnae worry, Dad. She's better out of it. None of us walked her anyway. She's probably been dead for weeks.'

'Cheers, pal.'

Leaving him to mourn, I'm tempted to go and see what sort of state Jake's in but I've been held up enough already. By the time I've washed my hair, put on make-up and convinced myself I'm not still stinking of lorry driver's spunk, it's seven o'clock. If Rosie's already sneaked round there, I'll fucking kill her. When I go back through, Dad's stroking the dead dog like a demented person. Definitely time to leave.

It was snowing earlier. The sunset's shining pink on the wet tenements, making them glisten in an amazing way. Tonight is the night, I can really sense it. Then when I'm half-way down John's street, suddenly, like I've made it happen by concentrating too much, the stair door opens and he's walking towards me. He clocks me and looks at the pavement. The fact that he's right here, in the open, makes me feel like I'm doing a silly walk. As he draws level, I start smiling, waiting for him to look up, but he walks past. I think he's trying to be funny, but he keeps going.

'John . . . John!'

This just makes him walk quicker. Catching up, I touch his arm. He yanks away.

'Fuck off, eh. It's broad daylight for fuck's sake.'

What's wrong with him? He seems all angry. Maybe he thinks I stood him up the other night. I run ahead and stand in front of him.

'Get out the fucking way, eh?'

'What's wrong? They've dropped the charges, is that no good? It's my birthday on Friday. You winnae even get into trouble.'

He looks around, terrified, as if there's maybe snipers between the double-parked cars.

'What the fuck are you on about? You're a stupid wee lassie. I'm no interested in you. Fuck off 'fore someone sees us.'

He tries to push me out the way.

'I turned up the other night. I waited an hour and a half, St Thomas's, that's where you said, is it no?'

Suddenly his face is next to mine. As I pucker my lips, he whispers,

'Look . . . whatever your name is, I've telt you, fuck off and dinnae come back. Or will I tell Rosie what a desperate little slag her pal is, eh?'

I'm in shock, as he nashes up the street. How's he gone like that? She's got round there first, I bet. Or does he think he doesn't need me any more, cause they've dropped the charges? I bet the dirty bastard did do it to Emma. I'll tell the police about him and Rosie. If I can't have him, why should she? I'd go round and try to suss her out but I made up one of my lies about visiting Granda. I'm sick of the smug bitch, anyway.

I'm far too depressed, as it is, to even think about going home yet. Besides, the flat's probably been hit by a Jumbo Jet by now, or Dad's announced he wants to be a woman. When I left, I was on fucking cloud nine as well.

I wonder when Rory's due through Edinburgh again. I'm so glad he was my first, and not that bastard, even if it was pretty rubbishy. If I went up the motorway, I might see him again. He's maybe been up there looking for me since Monday.

I've just got to Ryries when a 26 whizzes past. As I wait, shivering, for the next one, an old jaikie staggers into the shelter, beside me. He's got right schemie, junkie eyes and can't weigh more than six stone. He keeps fidgeting in the pocket of his combat jacket. I think he's going to pull a knife. There's nobody else in the street.

'Doin' business, sweetheart?'

Not waiting for a reply, he bangs across the other side of the bus stop, pishes like Niagara Falls, then shuffles off. I'm thinking it was quite horny, till he lets out a wet, thunderous fart, dirty bastard. It puts me right off the boil. As he disappears back into the pub, it starts snowing again. I'm not even wearing a jacket. Who'll pick me up hitch-hiking like this? They'll think I'm on the run from the Andrew Duncan.

Marble-sized hailstones batter my face and bare arms as I run back round to Dalry. By some miracle, the bus appears right away. I go upstairs. It's only five stops but I want to see if Twiggy and the rest of them are in the graveyard. By the time we go past it, though, there's such a blizzard blowing I can't even see the crypt. As if they'd be standing in weather like this. They're not fucking desperate like me.

My upper body's numb when I get in. Icy bits are melting down my back and cleavage. It feels like someone's thrown grit in my hair. Getting a towel from the airing cupboard, I go through for a drink. Mum's watching *ER* with an empty glass in her hand. Who's she going to gouge tonight, I wonder? There's an odd-shaped bin bag beside the fridge. Giving it a feel, I realise it's Jan's coffin and almost puke. I block it out with the fridge door. There's no fucking juice.

'Aw, Mum, where's my Diet Coke?'

An ugly head keeks into the kitchen, and slurs, 'Sorry, hen, ah didnae realise' in the Wester Hailes voice it puts on when it's pissed.

There's only tonic and fucking vodka. Banging around jars and prehistoric vegetables, I try and knock the bottle, accidentally, onto the floor. Gorgon-features leans over, stinky-breathed, and slides it to safety. Nursing it against her, she sways back through to the living room. I glug milk out the carton, then try to make my escape.

'Joni, sweetheart, has anyone phoned for me?'

'I dinnae ken, why?'

Her face goes all pleading and crumply-chinned.

'D'you hate me ashwell, Jo?'

'Och, shut up, eh?'

Really desperate by now, I knock on Jake's door. Fucking hell, it's like he's been experimented on by aliens. There's vicious-looking red streaks across his face, his lip's split, his left eyelid's the colour of theartistformerlyknownasPrince's bell-bottoms.

'Fucksake, Jake, where were you when the car bomb went off?'

'Dinnae wantie talk about it,' he mumbles through a mouth that can't open as well as it used to.

As I sit next to the bed, he shies away, like I'm going to attack him. I study his wounds. There's something strangely deliberate-looking about them. I'll have to sweet-talk him for a while before I get the truth out him, though.

'See Mum's job, eh? Has she said what happened?'

Being the bearer of great gossip perks him up. Mum's boss apparently nicked 50 grand, she got questioned by the police for five hours, then sacked. It's exactly the sort of far-fetched rubbish she used to come out with when she was drinking before, but I pretend to be interested nonetheless. It's a shame. Jake's face is a fucking mess.

'Think she'll get the jail? Ten years in Cornton Vale, that'd be cool, eh?'

He forces a sore smile. 'Is she pissed again?'

'Of course. And she's used all my Diet Coke for mixers, greedy bitch.'

Trying to lean towards me, he grabs his side and groans. He tries to speak, but it's so quiet I have to pull the chair in closer.

'She's got a boyfriend, Jo, I dinnae think Dad knows.'

'Who, Mum? Fuck off!'

The poor boy's obviously taken a bad blow to the head, he's speaking in tongues.

'Ssh, dinnae, really, Jo, we heard them shagging when I was down Sean's.'

Bollocks! No way is my lardy mother getting more sex than me. It's not possible.

'Naw, Jake, it was probably the telly you heard.'

'Honest Jo, I bumped into the guy. He was minging. He's like some dosser she's picked up when she was pissed. It'll be barrie if she runs off with him, though, eh?'

We get the giggles. Mum goes past the door, trying to sing. It makes us worse. I'm probably in shock.

'Shame about Jan, eh?' he sniggers, '. . . d'you think Mum murdered her?'

'Dad said it was probably suicide.'

We both must be in shock. Something Dad said's actually amused us. We bitch on about Mum's mystery man before eventually coming to the conclusion that someone's carried her home from the pub and she's raped them. It feels weird to be getting on for a change. You forget the people you live with must be going through all the same shit. At ten we watch *Wayne's World 2* on the portable. It's crap but it's good to lose myself in something stupid and block out real life, even for a wee while. Dad sticks his head round the door when he gets back from the hospital. He stayed two hours after visiting finished, probably for the same reason hitch-hiking in a blizzard seemed like a good idea earlier. I've a bizarre urge to ask him to join us, but that would just be sad. He doesn't bother us long anyway. Mum's crashed on the settee, so he's going to nab the bed while he has the chance. Poor bastard.

Remembering I've fags from the pub last night, I bring them through. Hailstones ping off the window as we smoke. I think about John shouting at me and imagine standing on a snowy Glasgow Road in a t-shirt. For once, it almost feels good to be home.

Jake, dizzy from two Marlboro in quick succession, suddenly comes clean about his injuries.

'No, Jake, you're mixing him up. My Daniel hangs about with Twiggy and that lot. He wouldnae do that.'

'It is him, Jo. Hairy guy, looks like Robbie Williams hit with a frying pan.'

This is a pretty accurate description, it must be said.

'. . . Shug was the one belted me, though. He slashed ies an aw.' He lifts his jumper; there's a cross-shaped scratch across his belly. It's not that deep but it's still a fucking sick thing for anyone to do. '. . . Daniel had to pull him off me. He was about to cut my throat.'

'Wait a minute, so Daniel actually saved you?'

'Nah, Joni, he was punching me an aw. And he's done it before. Mind the other week when my nose was mashed? He done that.'

I still can't quite believe we're talking about the same person. How many illusions can you have shattered in one day?

'But why? D'you owe them drug money?'

He gulps down a mouthful of saliva.

'Actually, I thought you'd got him to do it.'

'Eh?'

'Y'know, got him to batter me cause I piss you off. I dinnae ken.'

I'm stunned he could think such a thing.

'Honestly, pal, I ken I can be a cow and that, but, Jesus. He doesnae even know I'm your sister. Have you told Dad?'

'Aye right, he'd go radge. It'd make it worse.'

How could he think I hated him that much? Is that the impression I give to folk? I feel like such an awful bitch. We watch the rest of the film in silence. I'm feeling too ashamed to speak any more. I only realise it's over when the titles come up.

'Joni?'

I can't look at his battered face again. I'm starting to feel like it's my fault, somehow.

'. . . will you sleep in here tonight? I'm not being funny or that, but, like, will you?'

I'm feeling so guilty, it's almost a relief.

'If you want. D'you feel strange, like?'

'Nah . . . just sort of scared. I dinnae really want to be on my own, y'know?'

I force myself to look at him and smile.

'You're a sap? Is that what your telling me?'

'Naw, Jo, seriously, aren't you a bit scared, too, like?'

What, because everyone I know is either a bastard, a paedophile or a sadist?

'Aye, I suppose I am.'

Chapter Thirty

VIC

TWICE THIS WEEK I've woken up here, both times with a hard-on. Either God's trying to tell me to chuck her out and reclaim the bed or the settee's playing havoc with my dick. I attempt a wank but Angie's bleary-eyed face keeps intruding in my fantasy and puts me right off. Marriage, eh, you can't beat it.

Thank God I'm on special leave. It's usually reserved for deaths in the family, rather than the death of the family, but I'm definitely not up to taking 70 strangers for a drive. Plus, my hair's coming out in chunks. It's like I'm moulting for Jan. Whether this is linked to the numbness in my hands is anyone's guess. Smoking like a beagle can't help. I'll be in the Royal with Dad before you can say twenty Regal King Size.

First task of the day – burying Jan. The kitchen's buzzing with bluebottles as it is. Attempts to roister support for a small service round the weeds prove fruitless. In the end, the congregation consists of Jan, me and Matt Munro via the ghetto-blaster. Still convinced Angie was responsible for her death, I mark the grave with a customised cocktail stirrer. Clicking on the tape, the singingalonga 'Born Free' gives me such a sense of empathy with the deceased pet, I don't want to stop. Half-way through the first verse of 'From Russia With Love', though, the window opens and Joni yells out, 'Dad, please, that's horrendous!'

When I get back upstairs, the beast has surfaced and looks

sheepish. Offering me a coffee, she tells me she's going to see Sean's mother this morning before launching into a prolonged drone about work and what a devious shit her boss was.

'Should I try and contact him? It's doing my head in not knowing.'

'You've just called him every bastard under the sun. He got you sacked, for God's sake. You'd only end up battering someone.'

Still no reaction. In fact, if truth be told, she looks utterly bereft. Could it be remorse or is she running low on cash? As if in answer to my question, she asks me to take her to Somerfield. I've got the credit card, see. Trust it to be the guy who took her shopping did the runner. Remorse indeed.

I get my ear bent about him all the way to, round, and back from the supermarket. Every few sentences, she asks my advice, then immediately disregards it, despite the fact I'm trying to agree with her. I only let the credit card out my sight once, for her to get fags, but I notice she buys a sneaky bottle of vodka when she's at the kiosk. Stoli as well. Only the best for my dearest lady wife.

When we get back, I put the shopping away as she makes a home-made quiche. I intend hiding the bottle but it must be in her bag. A bunkerful of floury utensils are left for me to wash but I ignore them. When the quiche's ready, she tries to make us sit round the special-occasion table, like the Waltons. It's a farce. Jake's too sore to get up, Joni refuses to be in the same room as her, so it ends up just me watching her weep on her salad. Still, if it delays her first drink of the day. One minute at a time, sweet Jesus.

In the afternoon, I go up to the hospital to see Dad. He's not in bed when I arrive, but I assume he's just away for a dump. Pinching a few chunks of the Dairy Milk I brought up last night, I thumb through an ancient *People's Friend*. Shit, I meant to bring up *Killing for Company* for him. When he's not back by half-three, I check with the nurse to see if he's away for tests.

She has a perplexed whisper to the sister then tries the toilets. He's not there. The sister studies the case folder at the bottom of his bed.

'No, he's not down for anything today. The consultant'll be round to see him in the morning.'

The nurse looks in the side wards as I check his locker. Apart from a bottle of barley water and the half-eaten chocolate, it's empty. I don't believe this. How can they just lose a patient? A purple woman in the next bed, who look disconcertingly like Michael Winner, yanks off her oxygen mask.

'Are you . . . ach . . . Bobby's boy . . . ach?' She looks terrified to be breathing unaided.

'Bob Scott, aye, he was in this bed.'

A few more laboured gasps. I'm scared she's going to peg out.

'Ach, ach . . . he's away . . . ach, today . . . ach.'

The sister's face takes on a stony, Nurse Ratched scowl.

'You're wrong, Mrs Frazer, he's not been discharged.'

The old girl's dying to have a go at her, but only manages to splutter out that Dad's gone and she doesn't blame him before convulsing back into her mask. The sister looks relieved. I leave her to it. I'll report her once I find him.

Scanning bus stops on the way to his house, they're all ominously Dad-less. Every time an ambulance goes past, I shit myself. I spend my life doing mercy missions like this. I'd be better off in Rwanda. Having been flashed by a speed trap on Calder Road, I double-park outside the flat and let myself in with the spare key.

'Hello, son, there's a nice bit Wensleydale in the fridge, if you fancy.'

I collapse onto my knees.

'Jesus, Dad, you cannae walk out the hospital. You should've told someone.'

'I told the randy old bird in the next bed.'

'Y'know what I mean, a nurse or something.'

'No, no, no. They need the beds. That wee Irish lassie hadnae had a break for eighteen hours.'

Peeling melted cheese off a bit toast, he nibbles it.

'Come on, we're going back up.'

'Off you go, stop fussing.'

He's perky enough, despite the bruising, but you can never tell with Dad. He walked to Sighthill and did a day's work once, after he'd had a stroke – five minutes after. They didn't even realise till he went for his check-up three weeks later.

'I better phone. See what they think.'

'Please, son, I dinnae want to fall out but I'm no going back there. No to be treated like some half-witted old fart.'

I'm suddenly cuddling him, breathing in a mix of hospitals and Brylcreem.

'Godsake, Victor, what is it? Are you in trouble?'

I look at his discoloured face. 'Would you tell me if you were in trouble, like?'

'Of course not.'

When I phone the hospital, the mercenary bastards have already given the bed to someone else. They tell me to take him to out-patients tomorrow, instead. Dad's over the moon, even more so when the door goes and it's Mrs Moodie.

'I just can't manage the bus with my bladder . . . Did they say all the times I phoned . . . I'd have been up every day if I could've got a lift.'

Dad's glowing. Quite how that old baggage can make anyone glow is beyond me. Telling him I'll pop back with some shopping in the morning, I leave before she starts. Besides, they seem like they want to be alone. Yuck.

Only two hours have passed when I get in but Angie's already half-way to oblivion.

'Sit with me,' she wails, grey-faced from the cloud over her head. 'I'm lonely.'

'What d'you expect? That stuff puts you on a different planet.'

Stumbling over to the unit, she pours a huge vodka.

'Come onto my planet then. Please Vic, jus' once, drink with me. That's how we dinnae talk. You're always sober.'

Seeking refuge in the kitchen, she follows with the glass.

'Stop it, Ange. If you want to talk, just talk. What d'you want to talk about?'

'I don't know.'

'So what are you on about?'

'I don't know.'

I make a coffee. As two drinks are awaiting her attention, I don't ask if she wants one. When I go back through, she launches herself onto the settee beside me. A spring boings. The feel of her arm touching mine sickens me. Hiding behind the *Scotsman*, I long to be driving a bus full of screaming weans in a massive traffic jam.

'I've alienated myself from all my friends for a man who cannae fucking talk to me,' she mumbles.

As I'm incapable of speech, I merely rustle the paper.

'. . . say something, you big, dumb bastard.'

Crumpling the paper into a ball, I stand up and lob it at her. 'You want to talk? Really? OK, I've just been all over Edinburgh trying to find Dad. He did a runner from the hospital. He's 68 but he doesn't sit round pissing it up, whingeing cause he's isolated. It's the drink isolates you, girl. Can't you see that?'

She's smiling. The sick bitch is actually enjoying this. I slam the living-room door and stand with my hand against it, as if anyone would want to come in.

'Listen, Angie, I'm sorry I'm so boring. Sorry I'm no a thief, or an alkie, or the sort of guy'd land you in the shit, or batter his kids, or kill his dog . . .' Uh oh, she's gone crazy-eyed but I've started, so I'll finish. '. . . but if we're such a bloody chore to live with, why no just leave?'

'Think I've no had my chances? The kids need a mother. Don't flatter yourself I'm here for any other reason.'

'Nobody needs a mother like you.'

A jaw-rattling slap precedes a barrage of punches to my head and shoulders. As I try to defend myself, it stops as soon as it started and she grabs her coat.

'Give me money.'

'To get pissed?'

She shrugs. 'Or I could stay in and make everyone's life hell. You decide, oh masterful one.'

I pull out a 20 I've been hiding in my back pocket and chuck it across the room. With a catch worthy of Jonty Rhodes, she leaves. Collapsing onto the settee, dizzy with anger, I feel like there's a tourniquet round my chest. This is it, she's finally killed me. Joni appears, smiling and applauding. It's like some surreal near-death hallucination.

'Well done, that man, brilliant. Just like Tommy Lee and Pamela.'

All I can do is pech and clutch at myself. Instead of the usual, 'ocht, Dad', though, she sits beside me and takes my hand. Her hand seems twice the size it was the last time I held it, but just being near her's enough to make the pain subside.

'Dad, I've something to tell you about Mum but I don't know how you'll react.'

What could possibly shock me now? The phone rings and makes me jump. It's Angus, the grandfather, from work.

'Get over here pronto, Victor. This nutter's refusing to leave till she sees you.'

She? How the hell did she get up the Depot in five minutes? 'My wife?'

Angus guffaws, repeating what I've said to someone on the other end. They both have a good laugh.

'Sorry, Angus, she's rat-arsed. Can you get wee Melanie in the office to phone her a taxi?'

'Where to?'

'Here, Angus. She should remember the address, like.'

He goes momentarily silent. 'Jesus, Victor, you havenae told her where you stay, have you? She's a head-case.'

I'm not in the mood to have the piss knocked out of me.

'Look, can I just talk to my wife?'

'Fuck . . . no, it's no your wife, son. It's the gang-bang lassie. Last Bus Lil, ken.'

What the hell is this? That lassie doesn't even know me. I tell Angus this but he's adamant I go over, before the Depot Manager turns up and starts asking questions. Joni's waiting to be enlightened when I hang up. I don't know what to say without it sounding sordid.

'Is she at your work?'

'No, dinnae worry, just something I need to sort out.'

I try to get my shoes on before she has time to ask any more. My head's mince.

'Dad, about Mum . . .'

'Tell me when I get back, sweetheart. Winnae be long.'

By the time I get to the Depot, I'm convinced it's a wind-up. I'm the last person that lassie should have a problem with. As I walk past the office, though, I see her through the glass panel. Three younger guys over by the bothy, break into 'Annie I'm not your Daddy'. Gossipy Melanie gives me the wink, as I go in. The lassie stands up and offers me a clammy hand. I've done nothing wrong but I'm suddenly terrified of what she might say and don't want her saying it here. There's a full chorus going as I lead her out and down to the car. I've no intention of getting in but I don't know where else to take her.

'Look, hen, what's this about?'

Her voice is squeaky. All the dogs in the street can probably hear it, but I have to move reluctantly closer, to make her out.

'I'm Caroline . . . Angie's pal. She must've mentioned me.'

'Uhm . . . aye.'

Christ, Angie's mad pal's been shagging the drivers. What the hell? Have they been doing shifts? Has Angie made her do it, to get at me? I think I'm going to be sick.

'. . . you just sounded so nice. Oh, I wish I'd never come now.'

'Tell me what's going on, PLEASE!'

God, they're watching us out the office window and she's about to start greeting. What must this look like? After further prompting, she stammeringly tells me about Angie getting sacked. Is that it? Letting out a frustrated roar, I pull open the car door.

'Dinnae worry about it, I already know.'

As I try to get in, she throws herself against it, almost taking my fingers off.

'No, no, you don't understand. She was having an affair with the guy that stole the money. They're planning to run off to Mexico. I couldn't stand to hear her laughing behind your back, Vic, you sounded so kind. Are you angry with me?'

I'm not anything, I feel completely empty. My mind can't focus. I don't even know where I am.

'Oh, God, you're upset. That's not what I wanted.'

I'm crying my eyes out but it's relief more than anything – an impotent, black sort of relief. Giving me her number, she tells me to call if I need help with the kids. I shudder to think what she means, but take it anyway, to escape. As she slouches away, I feel clammy as her hand. My mind does a back flip to Angie's monologue about her boss in the supermarket. Laughing behind my back? In my bloody face, more like.

She had me feeling sorry for her but she was just twisting the knife.

When I get in, the drink from earlier lies untouched on the table. It's down my throat before I even think. Empowered by the warmth in my chest, I wonder if I should play her at her own game. Joni comes through as I'm pouring another.

'Fuck, Dad, not you as well.'

I'm so stressed I swally it down anyway.

'It's for courage, darlin'. She's out of here tonight, dinnae worry.'

I try to light a fag, but my hands are shaking wildly. Jake hobbles through in the clothes he was wearing when he had the accident. I'd forgotten all about that. I'm losing track of all the bashed faces. Jo jostles him to speak but, as he's as nervous a wreck as me, she does the honours. They know all about Angie's affair.

'Repulsive, eh? Like, no offence or anything, but . . .'

Jesus, am I the last person to find out about anything? How could she bring that bastard into our home? Do I sleep on the settee, so she can screw her boyfriend in our bed? Making them lock themselves in Jake's room, I go back through to drink, brood and rehearse my lines.

The door goes at half-seven. Behind it stand a male and female copper and my shoeless dishevelled wife. As she barges in, grizzling, the female tells me they picked her up in Morningside, causing a disturbance in a pub. She's been cautioned. They're leaving her in my custody till she's sobered up.

'Can't you just keep her?'

Neither seems amused. They leave her in my safe hands. She's arsed my drink and is pouring another by the time I get through.

'Just don't start, eh? You paid me to do it, remember?'

Lunging across the room, I pin her against the wall. The drink goes flying. Pushing me off effortlessly, she goes for a refill. It's completely wrong to hit women, I know it is, but I want to knock her fucking teeth out. She sneers at my trembling fists.

'Oh, are you going to punch me now? Go on then, go ahead. Convince me there's a man in there somewhere.'

Can't . . . stop it . . . can't . . . can't stoop to her level . . . calm, calm.

'Look, enough's enough. I want you out of here tomorrow, right?'

'Oh yeah, so what are you going to do? Beat me out the door?'

'Is that what that thieving bastard boyfriend of yours would do, like? Why don't you just piss off to Mexico with him? I'll give you a lift to the airport.'

This seems to hit her like a well-aimed punch.

'What d'you mean? Has he phoned? What did he say?'

She's not even got the decency to try and deny it.

'. . . please, have you spoken to him? Tell me, Vic, tell me, please,' she sobs.

Unbelievable. I'm terminating 17 years of marriage here and all she cares about is that bastard. It's tempting to make something up, string the cow along, but that's the sort of thing she'd do. She keeps pleading, drooling and desperate. I loathe her.

'For Christ's sake, shut up. I've not spoken to him, right? Your mad pal took time out from servicing my colleagues to tell me. And our son heard you, you slut.'

As she swipes the bottle off the unit, I cower beneath my hands but she disappears through to the bedroom and locks the door. Fired up with vodka, I want to let her have some more but if she goes on another rampage tonight, the police'll probably lock me up. I've no option but to leave the bitch stewing. Still, one last night on the settee. Tomorrow it comes to an end.

Chapter Thirty-One

JAKE

'IT'S GONE ALL quiet,' whispers Joni, seconds before Mum starts wailing in the next room. I hate when Mum cries. It's always about herself. Tonight, it doesn't even sound like real crying, just this loud, irritating whine, obviously designed to make us go insane. As we're all heading for Carstairs as it is, this isn't really necessary.

Holding my ears won't block it out. If we put on music, she'll just come through and kick the shit out of us. Plus, it reminds me of her getting-shagged noises which makes it ten times worse. It's starting to feel like the room's shrinking. Hobbling out of bed, I unlock the door. Luckily, I'm managing to put some weight on my ankle now, but it's still fucking sore. If I was a professional footballer, I'd be out for the season.

I want to go and check Dad's all right but Jo's in a mood about Mum not leaving and says she'll hit him if she sees him. In the end, rather than be left alone, she follows me through anyway. It's daft, being so scared in our own house. Dad's alive but looks completely fucked and much smaller than usual, somehow. Jo starts on at him.

'I'm getting sick of this, Dad, you promised. You cannae crap out again.'

Stubbing a half-smoked fag, he looks up. His eyes are red and shiny.

'I'm not, love. The police brought her home. I cannae let her go till she's sober.'

'When's she ever fucking sober, like?'

If I didn't know a couple of nice women personally, I'd think they were all like this.

'. . . well I'm having the settee. I'm no sleeping next door to that greetin radge.'

'Fine, love, whatever you want.'

Poor Dad, he tries to do what's best. He's just too much of a blouse to throw Mum onto the street. Where's her fucking bloke, anyway? If she's so into him, why don't they just fuck off together?

Joni, schizo that she is, is now sitting at Dad's feet, pulling grouchy faces, trying to make him smile. He leans forward and gives her a cuddle.

'I'm so sorry, sweetheart. It'll be OK, promise, I winnae let her hurt you again.'

Squeeze me, but when's Mum ever hurt Joni? I'm the one whose pal's been scared off. I'm the one with a face like Chris Eubank after one of his comebacks. This sort of thing really pisses me off. Do I give Dad a hard time? No, but I've hardly seen him since the night I got battered. Joni's as bad as Mum is to him but she just needs to sook up for five seconds and it's like I don't exist.

Knowing where I'm not wanted, I go to pour a bath. I've been too sore to wash, so I'm absolutely bogging. This wouldn't usually bother me but the blood's starting to smell like black pudding. I need to go downstairs and apologise tonight, so I don't want to be minging.

My top's stuck to the caked blood on my chest, so I end up pulling the scabs off as I try to get out of it. Even with the wound opened, the scar looks pretty crappy. It was agony at the time but now there's just two wee scratches. Never mind, I've probably caught AIDS off Shug's smelly Stanley knife.

The bubble bath nips like fuck. As I slowly relax, though, the pain floats off into the burny water. There's just the burring fan and ripple of water as I soap my soreness. You'd never guess they were filming *Evil Dead III* just on the other side of the door. Still, the cruel world keeps invading my feelings of calm. Even the football's fucked now. Celtic beat Kilmarnock last night and went three points ahead of Rangers. Is nothing sacred any more?

My thoughts turn sour again, and I decide to get out before I wrinkle. Just 'cause I'm the colour of a prune doesn't mean I want to be one. Checking the mirror, I realise it's already too late. Apart from the forehead and chin, my whole face is covered in a browny-purple rash. I was already pretty hackitt without this. Rubbing on some skin-coloured make-up I find in the cabinet, it makes me look like a pantomime poof. When I wash it off again, my face has gone the colour of a bell-end. I give up and go to get dressed.

I've already looked out the unworn, long-sleeved t-shirt Joni gave me last Xmas. It's bright green. Joni always gets me things she knows I'll hate but if ever there was a right time to wear it, this is it. Besides, what difference does wearing green make when there's a fucking crucifix carved across your tits?

Neither of them comments on my outfit, when I tell them I'm going downstairs. Joni takes five from grovelling at Dad's feet to try and force an invite. I say I'll come back up for her once I've explained about the other night. Aye, sure, I will. She's got Dad, Rosie, Daniel . . . millions of people. I'll be lucky if I've even got Sean.

When I ring his bell, I'm asked who it is before it's answered. Jesus, a nice, friendly family like that, scared to answer the door 'cause of me. My bottle's going but it's too late to make a run for it. Eva's already standing there, gawping at my face.

'It's Jake,' she shouts up the hall, like she now needs permission to let me in. It's too much. All the shit seems to hit me at once and I burst out crying. In front of Eva as well, but I just can't help it. Putting her arm round me, she leads me to the living room. I can feel her all warm against me. It's barrie but it just makes me sob even more. Sean comes through as I'm sitting down. I'm so pleased to see him, I get worse.

'I'm sorry . . . really sorry . . . 'bout mum. She's mentally ill . . . so sorry . . .'

'You don't have to apologise,' says Terry. 'We've just been worried. I wasn't really sure what to do. Would you like me to speak to someone about it?'

I don't care. I'm just so glad she's smiling. Eva kneels down and studies my face again. It's lovely. All the attention soon stops me greetin.

'Did your mum do this? You don't need to be scared. Just tell us.'

'Naw, honest. It was this guy from school . . . Shug . . . he's always doing it.'

What the fuck? It's about time I started telling folk about that mad bastard. Sean nods at Terry as if to say, 'Aye, that's probably true.' Eva starts stroking my hair. It hurts but I'm so pleased she's bothering I let her keep doing it.

I tell them about Mum and her bloke, not mentioning the fact we've all heard them shagging. They're too nice to know about something that gross.

'Dad says she's going in the morning. Go and put your telly up loud, I dinnae want you to hear them.'

'We're away early, anyway,' says Terry. 'We're going down the caravan for the last week of the holidays.'

Is this supposed to make me feel better? They cannae go away and leave me. How's Sean no mentioned it? I bet they're going 'cause of the other night. Oh God, I'm starting to sniffle again. They'll think I'm such a sap. Terry squeezes my shoulder.

'It's just a caravan park, nothing flash but you're welcome to join us, if you don't mind sharing a bed with Sean.'

Is she joking? The sudden unexpected possibility of something good happening, makes me go hyper.

'Really, you wouldnae mind? Honest, that'd be brilliant if I could. You're sure?'

She frowns and my heart sinks again.

'Oh, what about your mum? She won't think we're trying to abduct you, will she?'

'She's running off with her bloke, honest, she won't even notice. It'll be fine.'

They tell me to go and check it's all right but I ask if I can phone instead. I want Dad to say yes before Joni has time to put him off the idea. She won't be able to handle the fact that I'm escaping for a week and she isn't.

Dad's all for it, as long as Terry'll take something for my keep. For a moment, I completely forgive him for being in love with my sister. I'll be too sore to do much but who cares? I've never been away from my stinky family for more than a night. I once almost made it on a school trip to Melrose but got chickenpox three days before.

Sean's dead chuffed I'm allowed to go. As I'm waving my arms in the air and singing when I tell him, he probably senses I am as well. A caravan near the Holy Isle isn't exactly Alton Towers, but who cares? It's not home, that's the main thing.

I'm so excited, I decide to go and pack. Also, I'm concerned that Joni might have taken my phone call as the invite down she's been waiting on. She's really going to nip my head about leaving her but that's tough. Just 'cause she's been semi-decent to me for a couple of days, doesn't mean I owe her anything. I'm not dad.

Hobbling upstairs, I imagine Mum's bloke coming staggering down towards me. I can even remember what the jaikie bastard smelt like. But I don't give a fuck about him, or Mum, any more. I'm going to be living under the same roof as Eva for a whole week. She's being dead nice to me as well. Maybe that's why tomorrow's called Good Friday. Just a pity I look like shit.

Chapter Thirty-Two

ANGIE

I WAKE, FACE-DOWN, on a vomity pillow. Recoiling onto my side, I see another puddle by the dressing table, next to the empty Stoli bottle. Getting out of bed, I wipe up the worst of it with a pair of laddered tights. My mind starts replaying last night's highlights, in particular my professing undying love for Raymond to the two cops who brought me home. There's also a hazy memory of me threatening to glass some plummy English bitch, in the Canny Man's. Is that why I got picked up? Anti-smoking types really do my head in. I was only in Morningside to try Raymond's flat. There was no sign of him, of course, but just seeing the place he stayed gave me a sad sort of thrill.

I go for a shower, to remove my stomach contents from my hair. When I get out, I put on a fresh nightie. They can hardly throw me out if I refuse to get dressed. Christ, I'm going to end up a prisoner in my own dressing gown.

Stripping off the soiled bed-clothes, I take them through to the kitchen for a root about. Joni's on the settee under a duvet. Our eyes lock, momentarily, then she scarpers off to her room in silence. I'd have wished her happy birthday but what the hell, I wouldn't have meant it anyway. Vic's in the kitchen. Whether he's leaning his hand on the boiling kettle to try and intimidate me or he's finally lost the plot is anyone's guess. Either way, it's hard not to laugh in his face.

'Get lucky last night?' I smile, hoping he'll do the same.

'What?'

'Joni on the settee? I thought you'd maybe had company, so she'd let you use the bed.'

'I appreciate your sensitivity,' he spits.

As I'm not going to win the dour bastard round with humour, I revert to plan B – mock repentance. That usually does the trick.

'I'll apologise to her downstairs today. Is Jake up?'

'Forget it. They're away on holiday. Our son left with them 20 minutes ago.'

'News to me.'

His look of loathing fair has me shaking in my slippers . . . not.

'Why should he tell you? When have you ever been interested?'

On this I have to concede. It's just a pity the three of them didn't go. The kettle clicks off. He makes us a coffee. His shakes are almost as bad as mine.

'Mind, you're leaving today. I dinnae want trouble, I just want you out,' he says coldly, as he hands me my coffee in the 'mother' mug. Nice touch, Vic.

'Where am I meant to go, like? I don't even have a fucking job.'

He opens his mouth, probably to put the boot in about Raymond but no sound comes out.

'. . . go on, what am I supposed to do . . . enlighten me, please.'

Raging, he throws the teaspoon into the sink and goes to get his jacket.

'I'm taking Dad up the hospital. I want you out before I go.'

'For God's sake, Vic, at least let me stay till I find another job. You're not seriously going to put me on the street?'

He tells me to try my sister. We've not even had a Christmas card from them for the last two years. When I remind him of this, he suggests a hostel.

'. . . not a down-and-out place. There's women-only ones, are there no?'

'I'm your fucking wife. I don't recall anything in our vows about selling the *Big Issue*.'

'You can talk! You can bloody talk! Vows, Christ . . .'

'We can get help. I've stopped drinking, really. I'll see someone, whatever you want.'

It's lies, damned lies but, as he's already late for his Dad, is enough to secure a reprieve until he gets back. On his return he promises to will phone round a few dosshouses for me. I'm so touched.

'I'm warning you, though, if you're pissed, I winnae bother. Seriously, I've already made inquiries about restraining orders.'

Jesus Christ, no wonder he can't look at me. The conspiring bastards have got it all worked out. Eyes closed and thinking of England, I try to put my arms round him.

'Piss off, Angie. I know where you've been, remember.'

Going for a brief tête-à-tête with his beloved daughter, he leaves. I'm left gawping at myself in the hall mirror. This is beyond a fucking joke. What the fuck is happening here? I can't lose everything over a man who's already dumped me. And even if he hasn't, this is the only place he knows where to contact me. I'll handcuff myself to the fucking radiator till he gets in touch. I fucking will.

Shuffling through to the living room, I throw myself down at the special-occasion table. Surveying the wreckage, I dredge my brain for some possible distant happy memory of the place that might help me give a shit. Something must have kept me with that wet dish towel for the past 17 years. Every piece of furniture in here, aside from this 50s eyesore of a table we got when Vic's mum croaked, either is mine or we got from Dad's. Has Vic thought about that? Could they make do with his signed photo of Dennis Skinner, a few scratched singles and that ancient ten-a-penny darts trophy? Mind you, where could I put the fucking stuff? There's enough crap in here to furnish ten Greyfriars Hostels. If I end up in a bedsit, it'll probably be of the tiny damp boxroom variety. I can't live like that again. I'm not a fucking teenager any more. Images of the fifty-pound a week settee I shared in an Edmonton tower block when I was an au pair, bring on a sudden, bizarre affection for the cluttered midden I'm currently sitting in. It's like that temporary inability to see the shitty bits you get when someone you never really liked much dies.

Vic can't get this and leave me with nothing. If he divorces me, though, that's what'll fucking happen. I feel all possessive about my sofa and unit. If it was him, rather than me, who looked like the villain, it could all be so fucking different. Why can't he hit me? Just fucking once, just smack me in the gob? It would change everything.

My mind otherwise occupied, I find myself thumbing through the *Thomson's Directory* for Alcoholics Anonymous's number. My name is Angie and I'm not an alcoholic but it makes my husband feel better to hear me say I am. I can't find it. Not in the alphabetical index, not under Advice Centres or Helplines. There's just one number listed, in Hampshire. Great if you're Judy Finnigan, but not much fucking use to me. It's probably the Archery Association anyway. I wonder what happened to the two old guys from the AA who used to come head-hunting round the bookie shops, like the child-catcher in *Chitty Chitty Bang Bang*. What a pair of greasy-haired, purple-skinned, trembling old cunts they were. If that's what abstinence does to a person's face, pass me the fucking Smirnoff, quick! Sod it, I don't need some desperate weight-watchers-of-booze to get me on the wagon again. It's midday and I'm still sober. The day's half over already. I need to keep straight till this is sorted out. I need some of that sane rationale that drink tends to evaporate.

When I glance again at the still-open Heating Equipment/ Helpline page of the *Thomson's*, the words Lothian Marriage Counselling Service seem to jump out at me. A bit therapy couldn't possibly make the situation any worse. I need to be seen to be making some sort of effort. The number's ringing before I have time to talk myself out of it. I've not even thought about what I'm going to say.

'Eh ... um ... er ... I'm not quite sure whether you can, y'know, help me at all ... how quickly, y'know, see someone about, y'know ... problems ... !'

The telephonist, obviously used to such incoherent arseholes, gives me a spiel that sounds like it's being read off a bit paper – send you a leaflet, send it back with a tenner deposit, someone'll be in touch about an appointment. That's no fucking good. If I don't arrange something definite now, I'll crap out of it. I try to explain this to her in as quivering and desperate a voice as possible. Remarkably, it seems to work. The earliest appointment's a fortnight away, but there's two unconfirmed (i.e., not sent the dosh) later in the afternoon. She tells me to call back or come in and wait if I don't live too far away from Dundas Street, then starts hassling me for my name and address.

'No, please, do I need to give details just now? We'll be there, definitely. Thank you.'

I hang up, breathless at what I've just done. In a sad way I feel sort of excited about it. It's not as if I'll have to tell them the absolute truth. It's more like a damage-limitation exercise. Making Vic out to be a bastard can only put me in better stead if we do get divorced. What bullshit, though, really. As if talking to some lonely, old lesbian for an hour can make you miraculously fancy someone you can't stand. Surely they'd get stalkers taking their victims there if that was the case. Tell you what, if I ever see Raymond again, he's getting fucking dragged in by the hair.

Going through to switch the kettle on, I try not the think about the third drink, the one that always makes it better. His nibs won't go near the counselling if I'm pissed when he gets back.

Forcing myself to have another coffee instead, I lick my finger, and write an imaginary point to myself, in the air. One five-minute phone-call has put me back in control, you see, Vic won't be able to refuse. He wouldn't be able to live with himself if he knocked back the chance to give our relationship one last go. Christ, go on like this and I might even end up feeling better about myself, you know, I'm trying. At least I'm fucking trying.

Chapter Thirty-Three

JONI

TWO CARDS! TWO fucking cards! I know we're all pre-occupied with our lives going down the dumper at the moment but surely they could've stretched to a CD or some knickers. Even if they'd wrapped them in newspaper, like last year, when Dad was going through his Swampy-is-God eco-warrior phase. Jake got a computer for his 14th. It's not even a proper birthday. Plus, he gets to swan off to England for a week with his pal. Two cards! Thank you so much. When I got thrush off those bath salts, last Christmas, I didn't realise how lucky I was.

The first one's supposedly from Jake but I can spot Dad's baby writing a mile off. Dad's own card has another two tenners in it. Big deal. It's not even enough to get pissed up town with Rosie, if I could stand seeing her in the first place, which I can't.

The phone starts ringing. Please, let it be someone good. Mum tries to muscle past in the hall, but I beat her to it. The line goes dead before I've finished saying hello.

'Who was it? Was it a phone box?'

She's shaking like some old thing with Parkinson's, as she 1471s. What a state for a grown woman to get into. And I thought I was bad.

'0181 . . . 0181, that's London, eh?' she puffs, leaving it off the hook as she searches for something to write with. Finding a bookie's pen down the side of the settee, she runs back over. Slashing Nick Berry's face on the cover of *TV Quick*, she then starts clicking her fingers at me, to get her one that works. As if. Grabbing the phone off her, I slam it back down.

'Get your own fucking pen.'

As she scrambles over to the unit, it rings again. This time I let her get it. If it is her man, I don't want to hear his desperate alkie voice.

'Oh, Stewart, right. He just left . . . look, I have to go, I'm waiting on a call,' she snaps. That's right, take it out on Granda. As if it's his fault you're a drunken slapper. At least the waterworks have started. Watching her cry is one of the few pleasures I have left.

'Aw . . . why did you do that, Jo? How could you no just give me a pen like I asked . . . was it really too much to ask . . . waaah!'

What's she getting so Diana's funeral about? As if any man would get back in touch with that, once he'd already managed to leg it. It was probably just someone trying to sell double glazing anyway.

Going to make a sandwich, I put Chris Evans on loud to drown her out. The kitchen's like something out of one of these repossessed council houses you see in the papers. Dirty dishes from the quiche-that-nobody-would-eat are all over the bunker. Smelly eggy bits are floating on cold, oily water in the basin, beneath a tidemark of fat. Wiping a cheesy knife on a cheesier dish towel, I slice some corned beef from the opened tin in the fridge. Mum's standing behind me, watching in a cringey way.

'See when you fall in love, Jo, you'll understand. Dinnae hate me just for loving someone, for Christ's sake.'

What does she know about love? The mere idea of her getting shagged is the most horrendous thing imaginable. Someone give her a drink, quick.

'D'you no have packing to do?'

She does one of her amateur-dramatics hurt faces.

'Is that really what you want?'

Do we need to get t-shirts printed and petition the neighbours? I just do a Roger Moore with my eyebrows.

'. . . so why grab the phone? It might've been your big chance to get shot of me?'

Is it my fault her boyfriend's such a dickhead he didn't even speak? As she stalks me through with my sandwich, I know I should lock myself in Jake's room, like Dad said, but this might be my last chance ever to wind her up.

'So that's where you're running off to, is it? London?'

'Running off? You're the one hell-bent on making me homeless. My own daughter. I'd never do that to you, Jo, whatever you'd done, never. We can work this out, really. It's just a hiccup.'

Hiccup? More like the world's longest belch. Yeah, sure, it's doing us all the world of good – getting battered, having our pals threatened, dodging flying bottles. Don't wish me happy birthday, whatever you do.

Then, out of nowhere, she drops a fucking bombshell.

'If you're sure that's what you want, though, I'll go. I'll take the bill money from the bedroom and disappear. Will I do that?'

I know immediately that she knows. She's looking me right in the eye for some signal of guilt. Her face is daring me to say 'yes'. Oh fuck, she knows. She fucking knows. My cheeks are burning up. There's a sudden moustache of perspiration on my upper lip.

'What money?' I croak, the slight movement of my mouth causing my eyelids to go into nervous spasms.

'Ben the room. D'you want me to show you? Just let me stay, Jo, eh? Both try and start again?'

What is this? Is she offering me some sort of deal? Tell Dad not to chuck her out and she'll say nothing about the hundreds of pounds I've been chorying? Fuck, please don't let her come out with it. I'll crack up if she confronts me. She's still pleading away in the background but disbelief at the chance she's offering me has scrambled my brain. It feels like everything's going in slow motion till she suddenly lets out a wail and starts stomping towards the bedroom.

'No, Mum, dinnae, please,' I scream, pulling her back up the hall. 'You mean it? I winnae get into trouble if I tell Dad I want you to stay? Honestly?'

Back in the living room, she starts sobbing.

'Honest, no trouble. No more trouble. He'll listen to you, Jo. You're the reason he's throwing me out. We want to work it out. I've made an appointment for us to see someone. Please, Jo, one last chance.'

I can't believe this. Yesterday she thought we were all cunts from hell. Now she's willing to let me get away with all that 'cause she can't bear to live without us. What's changed? How long has she known? Just thinking about how much I must have nicked altogether makes me feel sick. I never even thought about what would happen if I got caught. If she tells them, though, they'll all hate me. Even Dad. I'd probably end up getting chucked out instead. I don't really have an option.

'OK, Mum. I'll tell him I want you to stay but that has to be it. We never mention it again.'

I half expect her to kiss my feet but instead she looks completely stunned, like she can't make sense of what she's just heard. I leave her to it. The moment of terror is lifting and I just want to go to my room and try to take it all in. I know it means we're probably going to be stuck with her now but I still can't believe my luck.

Locking my door, I get the old radio from under the bed and unscrew the back. There's eight tenners inside. If I can just get another 50 quid to keep me going, then that'll be it. It has to be. If I'm being offered a way out, I have to take it. I'm gutted and elated at the same time. It's like the end of an era. Oh well, Blockbuster Video here I come.

Chapter Thirty-Four

VIC

IT'S FIVE TO three on a Friday afternoon. I'm standing in the reception of the Marriage Counselling Service with a woman, who, two hours ago, I hoped I'd never see again. I left the house this morning, a single-parent-to-be. When I returned, Joni and Angie were fawning over each other like a pair of luvvies and the pair of us were going to see a head-shrinker. I'm not being sexist or anything but all women are insane. As I'd chickened out of evicting her again on the way up to the hospital, though, I'm just playing along with it. Besides, if those two have joined forces, I don't stand a chance.

We're standing opposite a cabinet of books with titles like, *Domestic Violence*, *Jealousy*, *Arguing*, *Alcohol*, *Sexual Abuse* and other staples of modern marriage. I wonder which one they'll start us on. We were meant to be taking over an unconfirmed appointment at three but the real couple turn up at a minute to. He's gaunt and fidgety, like he's just stepped off a big dipper. She's a little red ball of anger with painful-looking, tightly permed hair. She snarls something at the receptionist and we get turfed out and told to come back at five.

It's starting to piss with rain. Fear of being dragged round shops leads me to reluctantly suggest sheltering in the nearest P-U-B. This, aptly, turns out to be the Jekyll and Hyde. I'm suspicious when Angie submits without her customary gnashing of teeth and expect her to demand double vodkas as a reward. Instead, she asks for Diet Coke and goes to sit by the TV.

For the next two hours, aside from a brief interlude where she promises that her man and her are history, says it was the biggest mistake of her life and begs me not to bring it up in front of the counsellor, we barely speak. Up until her plea, I'd not even contemplated mentioning it. I'd be far too embarrassed. In fact, I wasn't anticipating having to say anything. I'd just sort of assumed Angie would spin them some yarn and they'd either offer a solution or laugh in our faces. I get so anxious about it, I start popping Rennie's like Maltesers.

Some joker keeps putting 'Je t'aime' on the jukebox. The fourth time it comes on, I have to take to the Gents', I'm finding listening to it and looking at her, so excruciating. At four o'clock, I use *Fifteen to One* as an excuse to get them to turn the telly up, but still the insatiable Ms Birkin puffs and grunts away in the background. It's the same when *Countdown* comes on. In fact, it's worse because, Jesus, are the letters cruel today. Two sevens – 'TRICKED' and 'USELESS', one eight – 'IMPOTENT'. But it's the conundrum that really takes the biscuit – 'ULTIMATUM', I ask you. By the end, Mrs Helen Marsh of Lichfield may be glowing from her 12-point victory, but I'm in bits. Shuffling back to the toilet, I have explosive diarrhoea. Christ, I'm not a well man. I'm not up to being cross-examined.

As we make our wordless way back down there, I pray that the next couple have appeared and we can go home. I'm on the verge of telling Angie she can stay, just so we don't have to go back in there. I spend so long trying to work out how to say this, though, that we're back at the reception desk and my chance is lost. Even worse, the other couple have already phoned to cancel and the counsellor's waiting when we get in. It feels like some horrific skeleton is about to be yanked from my closet. I can't remember leaving one there but you know what these folk are like. They subliminally plant stuff in your subconscious then charge you a fortune to get rid of it.

A plummy-voiced, red-haired woman with unfeasibly large hips introduces herself and leads us up the staircase. I've forgotten her name by the time we reach the first landing. There are five doors with engaged/free signs on them, which seems a little inappropriate. Two rooms lie open. One has toys and children's books strewn all over the carpet. The other is lined with chairs, like a village dance is about to take place. They must do polygamous marriages as well.

The venue for our inquisition is rather more sedate. An astronomically high ceiling makes the already stark room about as welcoming as a condemned cell. The dingy windows, looking out at a dreich, drizzly garden, don't exactly ooze hope, either. A lavish, cast-iron fireplace, straddling a puny electric fire with only one bar on, help to make the place look even more out of perspective. Aside from that, there's only three upright chairs and a small teak table with a box of tissues on it. Still, the less there is to throw around the better, I suppose.

From behind her clipboard, the woman explains in a tiny, petrified voice, that the counselling won't actually start today. This session's just to decide what sort of help would be best for us. As I weigh up the odds between a cyanide capsule and a hired assassin, Angie trembles and stammers her way through a jumbled synopsis of the past 17 years. Rather her than me. I know our marriage hasn't exactly bubbled with incident, but summarising the plot of *Coronation Street* since it started would probably be easier. There wouldn't be so many blank spots. The characters would be more consistent. Dr Ruth tries to stare me into adding something but a few affirmative grunts is all I'm capable of.

Sadly, silence does not remain an option for long. Soon, she's quizzing us about previous relationships. It's horrible being forced to resurrect my broken engagement with Jan. It immediately starts me pining for her. She got accepted to do music at St Andrews the same time as me. After our break-up, though, she had a bit of a breakdown and ended up working in Asda. The last I heard, she'd moved to Livingston with a Jordanian cabbie. I have a sudden urge to seek her out and rescue her. We could rescue each other. It could only do me more good than this hog's pish.

Oh Christ, she's got Angie started on that squaddie arsehole, Rab, now. They were only together for about five minutes, two decades ago, but in her head it's taken on *Wuthering Heights* proportions. I've had my ear bent about it so much over the years I feel like I've shagged him myself. Thankfully, snake-hips seems to notice my sucking-lemons expression and changes the subject. Oh God, here we go. What do we both see as being the problem? Is she not supposed to tell us that?

As my mind's now being bombarded with pornographic images of Jan and me up the canal, in the spare room at her granny's, up Arthur's Seat in the back of Dad's old Cavalier, I let Angie do the honours again. Anticipating confessions and repentance, I nearly choke when the beans start spilling.

'He just doesn't fancy me. There's no other way to put it. I feel like some big, useless ugh!' Clocking my stunned expression, she starts on me. 'Ocht, but y'know, Vic. We dinnae have sex. You can't bear to share a bed with me. You're so bloody critical all the time, I've no confidence left.'

The tissues are offered round. Angie sniffles into one, then blows her nose flamboyantly.

'But . . . the drink. What about the drink . . .' I whisper, cringeing at having to discuss such things in front of this complete stranger.

'Aye, Vic, I drink, or I did drink, but I was just trying to block out the fact that you'd stopped loving me. Why d'you think I drank? I thought it was obvious. I didn't mean for it to get like this. Honestly, love.'

What is this? Isn't this the woman who finds me so physically repulsive she wouldn't shag me if I had a gun at her head? Did she screw someone in our bed in the hope the stray pheromones might turn me on? Thing is, though, she really is crying. It's not like her usual hammy acting. She actually seems genuinely upset. The counsellor's after my response but my mind's seized up on Angie's revelations.

'I didn't know . . . I didn't think, y'know . . . I didn't know . . .'

Jesus Christ. Other than her snoring, I suddenly can't think why we don't sleep together. It's making me feel like I'm somehow to blame for everything. Is that possible? Have I pushed her off the wagon into the arms of some alkie because I can't bear to listen to her sleep? Because I can't get it up, or I'm too lazy to try? My paranoia isn't helped when the counsellor suggests referring us to a sex therapist once we've ironed out our other difficulties. I feel like some kind of eunuch ogre.

'Really? You honestly think we can get this sorted?' I ask, sounding more surprised than I'd intended. She's already thumbing through her diary for suitable dates for our next appointment.

'I'm not saying we can perform miracles, Victor, but you both seem committed to making it work. We're just here to help you decide the best way to do that.'

I give Angie a hopeful smile but she's too busy gouching out at the rain to notice me. Tracing her gaze to a window opposite, we watch a grey-haired man in a suit mauling a young lassie as she tries to fill a kettle. When we come to again, the counsellor's coughing and touching her watch. She wants to arrange a date for our next appointment before the clock strikes six and her Mondeo turns back into a pumpkin. I wonder if she's in a relationship herself and, if so, how long she's managed to slog it for. Does working here put her right off sex or give her a permanent wide-on? To be honest, she looks like a dyke.

We arrange to come back a week on Wednesday, my early-shift week. Hoping the promise of the £25 fee will be enough to secure our liberation, I put my jacket on. No such luck. There's a minute left and she wants to know what we're hoping to get out of counselling before she's letting us go anywhere. Since Angie's done most of the talking, anyway, I let her have the last word.

'Just to try and get on like we used to. Remind Vic I'm his wife, not some ghost, y'know? I have needs. Is that so bad?'

OK, so it's left with me looking like the bastard. To be honest, though, I don't really care. If that's what it takes to have a quiet life, then fine. I'm getting too old to enjoy being on the front line every day. Besides, Joni's all for it. I have to do it for her. Moved by my own decency, I get a huge lump in my throat as I shake the woman's hand and thank her profusely.

The rain's stopped when we get back outside. The shock of the clear air, compared to the stuffiness in there, gives me the weirdest sensation that we've just had sex in public. It's kind of erotic. We look at each other awkwardly. Angie's blushing.

'So how was it for you?'

I gulp back about a hundred comments on the sex thing and just say, 'I'll try and talk more next time.'

'I thought she was going to tell us to fuck off and stop being so silly,' she laughs. We both laugh. It's nice.

By the time we get home, at quarter to seven, Angie's been sober for nearly a full day. Joni's out. It feels like so long since we've come into the empty flat together, I somehow expect there to be piles of mail behind the door. When I go to hang my jacket up, two suitcases are still lying on the bed from earlier. I feel like a complete shit. To salve my conscience slightly, I volunteer to go to the chippie. In our early days, Angie always appreciated a white pudding supper more than flowers. As she's already started knocking together some loaves-and-fishes-type pasta creation, I put the telly on instead and have a fag and a fart.

We watch *Channel 4 News* as we eat. Apparently, they signed the Northern Ireland Peace Agreement when we were out.

'D'you think Jake's converted to Fenianism yet?' comments Angie. When I turn to tell her off, though, she pulls a 'gotcha' face and we manage to laugh together again. Christ, twice in one day. What's the world coming to?

I make a point of complimenting her several times on the dinner. It's fairly bland, but it seems to please her. The conversation remains stuck on spaghetti junction, even after the dishes are done, but I'm quite relieved, to be honest. I'm maybe buzzing with ideas about earlier but, as they're all potentially volatile, it's safer just to talk about food. I sip my tea and smoke another fag. The room is warm. I just want it to stay like this for as long as possible.

Joni appears at ten, looking anxious and wanting to know if everything's all right. God, is the sight of us not fighting really that unusual? Her mother tries to tell her about the counselling but her eyes glaze over and she scurries off to her room to watch a film on ITV. I'm quietly pleased that their touchy-feeliness of earlier has died down a bit. It made me feel uncomfortable.

Left alone together again, a different kind of silence takes over. It's as if, just by uttering the word 'counselling', Angie's thrown everything that was said earlier into the air again. It's like the 'don't mention the war' episode of *Fawlty Towers*. I try to relax to the lulling burr of the television. Angie goes to make us a coffee. Soon, the comforting dullness of it all settles the atmosphere down again. This is all I want. Please make her have been telling the truth about her man and the drink earlier. I'm big enough to feel partially responsible. It makes it easier to forgive her. If we could just pretend the last month never happened. I'm sure it was all right before.

At midnight, Angie wakes me up and says it's time for bed. Still half in a dream, it almost sounds like an invitation. Rubbing my sticky eyes into focus, I look up to see if her expression matches my impression. She's already gone through. Gulping back a mouthful of tepid coffee, I try to recall the exact tone she used. 'Time for bed.' It was the emphasis on the last word. It made it sound like a question rather than a statement of intention. And why wake me up and tell me? Why not just chuck the duvet over me? I don't know. After what she said this afternoon, I really don't know.

I sit to-ing and fro-ing about it until excited curiosity eventually gets the better of me. She's already in bed when I go through. The suitcases are back on top of the wardrobe. Glancing at her as I self-consciously undress, I see her expression is more one of puzzlement than longing. Still, she lets me under the duvet without screaming or punching me, which has to be a good sign. Braving my arm around her, she rolls onto her side, facing the wall, but doesn't pull away. I savour the feeling of flesh on flesh, just wanting to be snug and warm.

Only when I start to stroke her belly does she tense up but surely that's to be expected. It's so long since we've done this I feel like some fumbling virgin myself. She'd be back in the living room like a shot if she wasn't enjoying it, surely.

As I lean over to switch off the bedside lamp, I go hard against the warmth of her hip. Determination starts to grow. Burying my hand in her hair, I free her neck and shoulders for my kisses. God, I'd forgotten what skin tasted like. Still she remains motionless. Only when I reach up to gently brush her nipples does she start to respond. Her breathing becomes erratic. She begins quivering at my touch. It feels so unfamiliar. Almost like being with a complete stranger. I like it.

Buoyed by the effect I seem to be having, I pull her onto her back and ease myself on top. Her body starts to heave. Thinking she's really going for it, I crush my lips against hers and try to force my tongue between them. It's not until she turns her head, to avoid me, that I taste the tears. Their briny tang just makes me worse. I breathlessly inquire if she's all right. Her lack of response, other than the sub-sexual pant of her sobbing and her hands on my arse, is all I need.

As I push into her, she lets out a wail. Her arms drop to her sides but still she makes no sign that she wants me to stop. As I lean down to kiss away the fresh tears, the only resistance is in her eyes. I pretend not to notice. This isn't going to take long anyway.

REBEL inc. Started in 1992 by **Kevin Williamson**, Rebel Inc magazine set out with the intention of promoting and publishing young, urban writers. The book imprint is a development of the magazine ethos, publishing accessible as well as challenging texts aimed at extending the domain of counter-culture literature.

REBEL INC FICTION

The Golden Calf Henry Baum
ISBN 0 86241 984 0 £8.00 pbk
"Fast-paced, funny, intense, insane!" **John S. Hall**

An Unfortunate Woman Richard Brautigan
ISBN 1 84195 023 8 £12.00 hbk
"Still the best cantankerous writer I know of my generation" **Dennis Hopper**

Ham on Rye Charles Bukowski
ISBN 0 86241993 X £10.00 pbk
"The Poet Laureate of Skid Row" **The Herald**

Scar Culture Toni Davidson
ISBN 1 84195 000 9 £6.99 pbk
"What a novel! ... spellbinding" **Uncut**

Fup Jim Dodge
ISBN 0 86241 734 1 £7.99 hbk
"an extraordinary little book ... as good as writing gets"
Literary Review

Chump Change Dan Fante
ISBN 0 86241 958 1 £9.99 pbk
"Bruised, corrosive and utterly compelling ... This is soul fiction"
Kevin Sampson

The Sinaloa Story Barry Gifford
ISBN 0 86241 891 7 £6.99 pbk
"[a] rather beautifully weird and laconic tale" **The Guardian**

Southern Nights Barry Gifford
ISBN 0 86241 891 7 £8.99 pbk
"Hip, hot, hard-ass prose with the coolest of culty credentials"
The Herald

The Wild Life of Sailor and Lulu Barry Gifford
ISBN 0 86241 804 6 £8.99 pbk
"Gifford is all the proof you need that a writer who listens with his heart is capable of telling anyone's story" **Armistead Maupin**

Beam Me Up, Scotty Michael Guinzburg
ISBN 0 86241 845 3 £6.99 pbk
"Riveting to the last page ... Violent, funny and furious"
The Observer

Born Free Laura Hird
ISBN 0 86241 908 5 £9.99 pbk
"Deeply unsettling, deathly comic and peculiarly tender"
The Sunday Times

Nail and Other Stories Laura Hird
ISBN 0 8641 850 X £6.99 pbk
"confirms the flowering of a wonderfully versatile imagination on the literary horizon" **Independent on Sunday**

Stone Cowboy Mark Jacobs
ISBN 0 86241 889 5 £6.99 pbk
"A fantastical rollercoaster adventure yarn" **The Times**

My Brother's Gun Ray Loriga
ISBN 0 86241 806 2 £6.99 pbk
"A fascinating cross between Marguerite Duras and Jim Thompson"
Pedro Almodovar

The Museum of Doubt James Meek
ISBN 0 86241 945 X £10.00 pbk
"Meek has a gift for the surreal ... as though David Lynch had been let loose on the set of a drawing-room comedy" **The Times**

Kill Kill Faster Faster Joel Rose
ISBN 0 86241 697 3 £6.99 pbk
"A modern urban masterpiece" **Irvine Welsh**

The Cocaine Trilogy Sabbag/Jacobs/Guinzburg
ISBN 8 86241 977 8 £15.00 pbk
cased set of 3 novels

Rovers Return Kevin Williamson (Ed.)
ISBN 0 86241 803 8 £8.99 pbk
"Pacy, punchy, state of the era" **iD**

Children of Albion Rovers Kevin Williamson (Ed.)
ISBN 0 86241 731 7 £5.99 pbk
"a fistful of Caledonian classics" **Loaded**

You can order direct from:

Canongate Books Ltd
14 High Street
Edinburgh EH1 1TE
Tel (0131) 557 5111
Fax (0131) 557 5211

www.canongate.net
www.rebelinc.net